Ron Bush

———————

Is there life after Rock 'n Roll?

Other titles by Ron Bush.

Cordelia.   ISBN 978-1-461-9486-7

Heil, Heil, Rock 'n Roll! : ISBN 978-1-4092-2387-0

Chapter 1

As he stepped off the bus Michael winced. Reaching inside his shirt he stood checking that the medical dressing was still in place. His fingers touched stickiness. *Bloody hell, it's still weeping. That nurse said it would be OK.* He flicked a cigarette end into the air. *Well I'm not going back, I've had enough of hospitals to last me a lifetime. That Paul's dad certainly gave me a good going over. But it was almost worth it. You can't beat a woman with experience.'* Lighting another cigarette he walked carefully down the road toward the house where he lived.

'That you, son?' a voice called from the kitchen. 'Didn't know they was letting you out today, I'd have come and met you.'

'Don't bother to lie, dad. You don't give a toss about me, do you. All you're interested in is the money I bring home on payday.' Michael used two fingers to emphasise the contempt he was feeling. 'One day I'm going to bugger off and leave you to it. See how you get on then.'

Michael's father shuffled into the hall, holes in worn slippers allowing a pair of odd of socks to show through. 'I can manage, don't you worry about that,' he sniffed. 'You think you're god's gift you do, but you ain't.' Dragging a cardigan sleeve across his nose he sniffed again.

Michael grinned. *And you still think you're my dad! But the day I get to move out you're in for a shock or two.*

'So why *did* they let you out early? Trying your luck with the nurses now I suppose, randy little bleeder.'

'At least I'm a man, that's more than you can say, according to me mum.'

'She can talk! The only time she's interested in sex is when it gets her a bottle of gin or something. How he ever fell for you has always been a mystery to me.'

Yeah, I was surprised when I found out too! 'They let me out the hospital because they needed the bed, that's why. Bet if they'd known what it was I was coming home to they would have kept me in. Mind you there ain't much difference in the food here or back there, although their plates were clean, I gotta admit that.'

'What do you mean? I always wash up every couple of days or so. Nothing wrong with the plates in this house.'

'Well let's put it this way, *Dad!* If we run out of eggs it won't matter, just scrap what you want off the edge, that's if it's not gone too hard. Our plates are like bleedin' china menus; you can see what we've had all week.'

'OK, Mr Lah-di-dah, why don't you sling your hook? You're eighteen now, old enough to go and live with one of your precious mates.'

'I will! But when I'm good and ready. Now, piss off back to your racing paper and leave me in peace. I've got enough trouble as it is, without you starting.'

Michael retreated up to the one room in the house kept relatively tidy, his bedroom. Lifting the lid of his Dansette record player he placed his copy of Jerry Lee Lewis playing *"Great balls of fire"* on the turntable. As the rock 'n' roll maestro got into his stride Michael nodded in agreement and said, 'And that just about sums it up!' Easing his trousers off he lay back on his bed and watched cigarette smoke coiling up to add to the nicotine stained ceiling. *What a state to get in. All the fights I've been in and I end up getting clobbered by Paul's dad of all people. But things could be worse I suppose, at least I've escaped the hangman. That bloody Deiter wasn't worth dying for.*

Not far away another household was at war.

'Not again, Paul!' A woman, her hair tied up in a headscarf, stood with both hands on her hips glaring at her son. 'That's the fourth job you've lost in three weeks! What happened this time? *No, don't tell me, let me* guess. The clocking-in machine was fast, you weren't late. Or was it, "Nobody said to turn it off, so how was I to know?" I give up. When are you going to find a job you can do *and* keep it for more than a few days?'

'It wasn't like that at all. The foreman didn't like me. I did everything right just like he told me to but nothing could please the old fart!'

'Mind your language! You're not with your mates now! You know the rules in this house.'

Paul sighed. 'Yes, Mum. Sorry, Mum. But it's not fair, everyone picks on me, must be because I'm always the new bloke. I end up being the tea wallah, and then they all moan about how I make it. I wish I was dead sometimes.'

'Don't say that! That's an awful thing to wish. There's plenty of people worse off than you.'

'How? Have they got mums that have it off with people young enough to be their son? Have they got dads that are on the run from the police? How *can* they be worse off than me?'

His mother's cheeks flushed as Paul's words hit home.

'How dare you!' she retaliated. 'I'm only human after all! And we all make mistakes!'

You're right there, mum. But some mistakes are bigger than others. You cheated on me dad, but I cheated my old teacher out of the rest of his life, and just for money!

Paul stepped towards his mother, put his arms around her and gently squeezed. 'I'm sorry, Mum. I shouldn't have said that. Come on, let's put the kettle on and have a cup of tea. I'll get another job soon, I promise.'

She kissed the top of his head. 'I'm sorry too. Life's hard enough without us arguing all the time. I'll make the tea, you get the biscuits. They're in the tin, jammy dodgers, your favourite.'

Chapter 2

chael and Paul entered the graveyard as the church clock chimed the hour, roosting pigeons scattered in
nic. The friends walked slowly along the gravel path until they reached the burial plots.
'You put 'em on, Paul. It still hurts when I bend down, even in these baggy trousers.'
Paul stooped and placed the flowers on the fresh grave, their vibrant colours in stark contrast to the wilting
butes that lay on the stone chippings.
'OK, Mike. I'm not sure he would appreciate them though. He was funny about things like that.'
They stared down at the black marble headstone with its simple incised inscription, gold leaf letters
tching the last of the late evening sun.

✠

Deiter Adler
* 1935
+ 1958

'Don't exactly say much, does it.' Michael said, sliding the silver skull up and down his boot lace tie.
Checking his Brylcreemed quiff with both hands, he added. 'Still, it must be what his dad wanted for him.'
'Yeah, I suppose so. Strange though, he lives all through the war fighting for that 'itler
loke; then gets dragged over here and killed. Don't seem like it was only, what, a month since he
was buried? I mean, just think, he was only five years older than you.' Paul looked at his friend and they
exchanged glances. *It's alright for you, Mike. But I hate going to sleep now, all those bloody nightmares.
But it don't seem to bother you.*
Michael shifted his weight from one foot to the other. *I don't know what's worse? Thinking about it during
the daytime or having it visit me in the night.*
Tall shadows from headstones, statues and a family mausoleum reached out toward the ivy covered flint
wall surrounding the graveyard. Trees rustled, birds took to the air. Michael gave an involuntary shiver then
shrugged his shoulders.
'Come on, Paul. Let's leave the poor sod in peace. Want a coffee at Bentini's? Some of the others might be
ere.'
'OK. Why not? And we'll put that jukebox on, play some records. This place gives me the willies.'
'Me too.'
The two friends strolled back to Michael's motorbike.

'Here we go again,' Michael said, fighting to make himself comfortable in the oversize trousers borrowed
om his understanding 'uncle.' A safety pin did its best to make the waist fit. Gritting his teeth he straddled
e machine.
'Does it still hurt much?' Paul asked.
'Yeah, a bit, but this helps.' He prodded a blue candy stripe cushion strapped to the bike's seat. 'Takes
me of the pressure off.'
Paul sighed. *Pity. I was hoping you were in a lot of pain.*
He still loved his mother, but the thought of her in bed with Michael sickened him. His father had been the
iggest loser in the affair but Paul's immature emotions failed to see it that way.
'Ain't so bad walking about,' Michael said. 'But it's them bloody potholes does me in. Like being kicked
n the goolies all over again every time me bike hits one.' He tugged at cavalry twill slacks, a garment never

intended to be worn with a finger-tip drape jacket. 'I'll be glad to get shot of these, I hate being seen wearing them, the crutch is almost down to me knees.'

'Huh! Don't know why you're worried. Take a look at *these* stupid trousers; I look just like me dad! And who wears check shirts? Yeah, I know, Roy bleedin' Rogers in them cowboy films, but apart from him who else? At least you got decent clothes; I wish I could get some.'

'Well, why don't you? We still got some of that teacher's dosh stowed away; you can always have a bit more of your share. And Tony lets you keep that rock 'n' roll zip jacket of yours round his house don't he? So get a suit made at Burtons and keep it at his place.' Michael eased down onto the cushion. 'Bugger me, you *are* sixteen. Bit of a funny age that, old enough to legally have a shag but too young to buy a drink. But Christ, surely you can dress as you like. Anyway yer mum probably won't find out, and if she does I can always put in a good word for you.'

'Don't start all that again, you promised you'd leave her alone. Remember?'

'OK. Keep yer hair on, mate. You can trust me.' *Well, trust me not to get caught again, anyway.* 'Any new about your dad?'

'No. Mum looks for a letter on the mat every morning. But I don't think we'll hear from him again, thank to you.'

Michael didn't reply. Painfully kicking the Road Rocket into life he waited for Paul to get on behind, then roared off toward the coffee bar.

Inside Bentini's coffee bar, cigarette smoke drifted lazily across the tables. A girl in a mauve pencil skirt stood bathed in the glow of the jukebox choosing her records. As she walked back to her table Little Richard screaming about *Long Tall Sally!* was replaced by the seductive tone of Elvis, pleading with his girl to *Love me tender.*

Michael rocked his chair back to rest against the wall, the crepe soles of his shoes pushed firmly against the floor. 'Should be good tomorrow.' He grinned. 'Hope the seats are soft; give me bollocks a bit of a chance!'

When he was a child, an aunt had remarked that with a grin like that and his ears protruding as they did, he would make an ideal Pixie. A hairstyle and sideburns copied from Elvis had changed his looks, but the grin had stayed the same.

'Christine's really looking forward to the show. You going on your bike?' Paul asked.

'No. I'm coming with you lot on the bus. Now, make yourself useful for a change, go and get the drinks.'

Waiting for Paul to return with the coffees, Michael flicked open his knife and began clearing the dirt from beneath his finger nails.

Chapter 3

e queue for the Gaumont wound around the block, the star line up of rock 'n roll stars acting as a magnet
teenagers from miles around. Velvet collared drape jackets, bootlace ties, skin tight
users and brothel creepers singled out the teddy boys from the rest of the crowd.
I've had enough of this, we've been here for ever, we'll all grow roots at this rate. I'm going for a mince
out, stay here you lot.' Michael, now back in his role of undisputed leader of the gang, took it upon himself
look out for the others, especially when they had their girls with them.
Do you want any of us with you?' Paul asked.
No, mate. Just keep my place.' Michael brushed dandruff off black velvet as he began to stroll back down
 queue, shrugging the shoulders of his jacket, studying the faces of impatient youngsters shuffling forward
line.
There were always old scores to be settled, insults to be answered. Suddenly, Michael lunged out, grabbed
eather jacket, and dragged its owner from the ranks. Another youth moved swiftly to counter the attack.
Suds! Didn't expect to see you! How's it going?'
'Wotcha Mike! You still walking the streets? Thought they'd have banged you up by now!'
What do you mean by that? Michael's mind raced. *Surely Paul hasn't ....*
Yeah! What for? Talking to idiots?' Michael punched Suds gently on the shoulder. 'And talking about
iots, what are you still hanging about with this no hoper for, Jimmie?'
Jimmie, or James as his mother insisted he be called, spat his chewing gum out.
Hiya, Mike! Someone's got to do it; he ain't safe out on his own.'
Michael looked up and down the long line. 'Bloody hell, there must be hundreds here tonight. Come with
e, we're a lot nearer the front.'
As Suds and Jimmie walked off with Michael toward the head of the queue there were muttered objections
 queue jumping, objections that tailed away when the three youths turned to face the people complaining.
'Cor! Just like the old days,' Jimmie said, hooking his thumbs through his belt and exaggerating a swagger.
'You should come back and hang about with us,' Michael said. 'Get the old gang back together, just like it
as before Deiter turned up.'
'That'll do me! It was only that German nutter you had with you that put me and Jimmie off. That right,
mmie?'
'Yeah! Lucky he didn't get you all nicked; the things he got up to. Me and Suds, well we like a laugh, but
me of them stunts *he* pulled ...'
'Tell me about it. Come on then, them doors will open soon; let's get back to Roy and the others.'

'Look who I found,' Michael laughed, pushing his new found companions into the queue.
'Never mind who you found, mate. They ain't shoving in!'
The man pushed his chest forward. Military brass buttons accepted the challenge and struggled to keep his
nic closed. The girl next to him snuggled closer.
'You tell 'em, Boris. Bleedin' cheek! Who do they think they are?'
Michael took a step forward, his face inches away from the soldier's, a hand in his pocket curling around a
ife.
'What you want to tell us, Boris, mate? You forgot we was all in the queue when you arrived? All *six* of us
d our birds? I think you made a mistake, don't you?'
The soldier swallowed as he looked at the youths. 'Might have done,' he muttered. 'Don't worry, Mags,
e've got our tickets. Just ignore them.'
Michael grinned, 'That's what I like, a bloke with a bit of sense.'
A grating noise announced the doors being swung open. Something trapped beneath one of them was
raping across the marble floor of the foyer, setting teeth on edge. The manager kicked the door in an
tempt to dislodge the offending object. Before he could finish this maintenance, the crowd swarmed in.

After the concert the excited crowd spilled out onto the pavement. Young men playing imaginary guitars, hoping to impress teenage girls flushed from watching their heroes. Heroes clad in tight trousers that bulged enticingly as hips suggestively caressed the microphone stand, miming the promise of pleasures still to come Tony, who as an aspiring guitarist had spent much of the show studying the chords being played, swiped a comb through his hair. 'What yer think, Kay? Told you it would be great, didn't I?'

'Terrific!'

'Terrific!' Michael and the others chorused. Kay blushed, knowing her Cheshire accent still amused the gang.

'Take no notice,' Tony said, 'If brains were two a penny, you'd still get change from tuppence for this lot.

Roy pushed Tony playfully. 'So you're the expert on brains now, are you? Think you can work out whose round it is when we get to the pub?'

'Mine, I suppose.'

'Got it in one,' Roy laughed, tugging at his shirt collar with both hands, copying the style of his rock 'n ro idols.

'Come on lads,' Michael interrupted, 'there's Suds and Jimmie, give 'em a shout.'

The air in the pub could be cut with a knife. Pipe and cigarette smoke joined forces with the stale musty smell of spilt beer. Floorboards, scuffed by countless pairs of working men's boots added the smell of wood to the blend.

Paul coughed. 'Blimey! Hustles a bit in here, don't it? What a stink.'

'Yeah, not like the King's Arms is it.' Roy moved a chair for Elaine to sit on. 'Good show tonight though, he said to Suds. 'You and Jimmie like it?'

'Brilliant, fu …, er, flipping brilliant I mean.'

Elaine gave him a look that could have killed.

'Mike, do you miss that German geezer?' Jimmie quickly tried covering up for his friend.

'Only when we get in a bit of bother, he was a handy bloke to have around then. You should have seen him when he hit someone; they never hung about for more.'

'Well I don't miss him,' Elaine chimed in, 'I don't know what you ever saw in him, Chris. He was such an arrogant so and so.'

'You not supposed to speak ill of the dead, my dad always said. Not that I ever met him. Deiter I mean, no my dad. Roy told me lots about him though, while we were working together in the record shop.'

'You were lucky, Kay. That was the worst day of my life when he turned up and muscled in. I wish I'd never clapped eyes on him.' Michael's eyebrows met as he frowned. *And then I wouldn't be in this position now.*

'I second that!' Paul nodded.

James nodded. 'What about you, Roy? You feel the same?'

'I thought that was obvious, it's why you and Suds ain't been hanging about with us, ain't it? Anyway, that's enough about him. He's gone now, and good riddance I say.'

Michael thumped the table, empty glasses jumped and rattled. 'Tony, get the drinks. All this nattering is giving me a thirst. And make sure they don't put ice in me coke.'

Tony tapped his pocket before nudging his way through to the bar, the chink of coins re-assured him. Standing at the bar he waited - and waited - and waited. Becoming impatient he removed his cowboy boot from the brass foot rail and tried further down the line of beer swilling men. Waving his money in the air and shouting for service finally brought results. The bar tender, having run out of customers to serve, reluctantly asked him what he wanted.

'Four pints of lager and lime. One pint of lager, *no* lime. Three Babychams and a coke *without* ice.'

The barman spotted two new customers and served them before returning with Tony's drinks. Plonking
em down he said. 'Tell your mates to get 'em down then get out, I don't want the likes of you in my pub.
ou hear me?'
Tony started to protest, saw the look the scar faced man was giving him and nodded. 'Got a tray, *please*?'
: asked. The man turned away to serve another customer.
Tony tried to carry three pint glasses back, the lager lapped and spilled. Michael spotted his friend's
edicament and pushed his way through to the rescue. 'Give us 'em here, Tony. Go back for the others. I'll
: with you in a mo, give you a hand.'
'Cheers, Mike. Think we've got trouble, that geezer behind the bar don't want us in here.'
'Why? Now what we done?'
'Dunno, we ain't done nothing. Perhaps he just don't like Teds.'
'Well, I was just thinking, this is a strange boozer ain't it? Ain't no one our side of forty, more like an old
lks home. Go on, get them other drinks. I'll be with you as quick as I can.'

'Cheers, Tony.' Suds held his glass up.
'Yeah, cheers, mate,' Jimmie echoed. 'Nice one.'
The girls sipped at their drinks as the boy's throats made short work of the pints.
'I'll get these,' Jimmie said, moving toward the bar.
'No. Leave it, we're off.' Mike swallowed the last of his coke.
'Do what! What's got into you?'
Michael explained about the run in Tony had with the bar tender. 'We've got girls with us so we don't want
get into a bundle. Maybe we'll come back another time and teach him some manners.'
'Sod it! I've just realized; that thievin' git didn't give me my change!' Tony glared at the bar, fists
enched.
'Come on! All of you, let's go.' Michael grasped Tony's sleeve. 'Leave it!'
The gang forced their way through the crowd toward the double doors. When the others were all safely
tside, Suds swept his arm across one of the tables. Glasses flew through the air to crash against a wall with
shower of splinters. Unfinished drinks began adding to the stains on the floor.
'Pick the bones out of that, mate!' he yelled, dashing out into the night.
'You crazy bugger, Suds! Run!' Roy grasped Elaine's hand and pulled her along. Men began pouring out
the pub into the street, looking for the troublemakers.
'Christ, what we going to do, Mike? We can't get far with your birds in tow.'
'You should have thought of that, Suds, before you got us into this.'
Six or eight men were running toward them, some removing their jackets.
Christine stumbled, reached down and removed her shoes.

'Wotcha mate! What's going on?'
Michael groaned. *The Chieftains! That's all we need! Shit, I haven't seen you lot since Deiter got killed.*
3it of bother in that boozer!' he blurted out. 'They're going to sort us out; trouble is we've got our birds
ith us. Don't want them getting done over.'
'Bugger off then, leave it to us, we've had trouble in there ourselves. We owe 'em one.' Turning to the
hers he waved them forward. 'Come on lads, let's get stuck in!'
The leather jacketed youths advanced wielding chains and coshes. A brass knuckle duster glinted in the
reet light.
'We helping?' Paul asked, his young face revealing that this was the last thing he wanted to do.
'No, mate. Looks like they're out looking for trouble anyway. If they want a fight let 'em have it.'
'But it don't seem right, leaving …'
'Go on then, go and join in. Write and let me know how you get on.' Michael scowled. 'Come on, you
ow Chris can't run, grab her other arm. I'll give you a hand. Let's have it away on our toes!'
'ithout waiting for Paul to reply, Michael grasped Christine's elbow. She was hobbling, the pain in her leg
inging back fresh memories of being thrown from Deiter's motorbike. 'I'm sorry, Mike. I can't run.'

Michael glanced down the road to where the Chieftains had locked horns with the locals. The fight was in full swing. Broken beer glasses were being swung viciously at the gang who were busy lashing out with their favourite weapons. He shook his head in disbelief. *Bugger me! We only wanted a beer, not world war three!*

Christine curled an arm around Michael's neck. 'Sorry,' she sobbed, 'I'll be OK. If you can just take my weight a bit, I can manage.'

'Don't worry, Chris. We won't let anything happen to you. Paul! Grab hold of her; give me a hand for god's sake! Hurry up you waste of space, move it!'

Elaine and Kay heard the anger in Michael's voice. They stopped and turned around, concerned for their friend.

'Keep going!' Michael shouted. 'Leave her to us!'

A bus passed, slowed and pulled up. The elderly couple that had flagged it down stepped on.

'That's our one! Run on, Suds! Tell the conductor to wait!' Roy yelled.

Back down the road, the sound of a window breaking was almost lost amongst the shouting and swearing.

Chapter 4

That roll was bloody handsome, you can't beat them crusty ones. Talk about a café, this one's top notch. Ma's place is a great gaff ain't it? It's one thing Deiter did us a favour with, making us come here to get out of his way.' Michael slumped back in the sagging armchair, picking at his teeth with a spent matchstick, brushing crumbs and bits of cheese from his shirt.
'Yeah, can't argue with that.' Tony crossed his outstretched legs, letting a cigarette dangle from the corner of his mouth, imitating his hero, James Dean.
Michael flinched as he changed position.
'What's up, Mike? That looked as though it hurt.'
'It's OK. Just a bit sore, that's all.'
'Oh, still playing you up, is it. What *did* happen? You've never really said much.'
'Ain't nothing much to say. I was just in the wrong place at the wrong time.'
'How many of them were there? Funny you getting into a fight without us lot.'
'There was only two others there, but they caught me with me trousers down if you know what I mean.'
'Two! They must have been big buggers! Ain't like you to let two blokes beat you up so bad you end up in hospital.'
'Well, there's a first time for everything, as they say. Now, be a mate, get down them stairs and get Ma to make us another cheese roll. Oh, and a coffee. No, hang about, make that a tea. Cheers!'
'Make your mind up! And *just* remind me, what was it your last servant died of?'
'Cheeky bleeder! You wait till I'm fit. Go on, get that grub, I'm starving!'

Michael flicked through the pages of a "Flight" magazine while he waited for his tea; there wasn't anything else to read. 'Saw that one at Biggin Hill last year,' he muttered staring at a picture of a Spitfire. 'Bloody good air-show that was.' Hearing footsteps on the bare wood stairs he hurriedly stuffed the magazine back in place beneath the coffee table and eased himself back into the armchair. But instead of Tony, two other youths appeared, one wearing a finger tip drape, the other a cream coloured, hand knitted, fisherman's jumper.
'Wotcha, Mike! Tony said you was up here. How's it going mucker? Been in any good fights lately?'
'Up yours, Roy! And *what's* that you got on now, Paul?'
Paul's cheeks flushed. 'Me mum made me wear it, said it would keep the cold off me chest. Who'd have my mum?'
Michael grinned. *I would!* 'You gotta do something about your clobber, mate. You'll get us lot a bad name, walking about like that in broad daylight. And who needs a jumper in September? Blimey, what she going to dress you like when winter starts, a bleedin' eskimo? Tell you what, let's finish our grub then we'll go down to Burtons. Get you rigged out with some decent gear.'
'What I'm supposed to pay for it with? Shirt buttons?'
'You don't have to pay until it's ready. Well, only a deposit and I can sort that out.' Michael winked.
'OK then, let's go!'
'Hold your horses, mate. Tony and me got our teas to finish. Then we'll go.'

The youths strutted through the crowds in the high street, taking more than their fair share of the pavement. Men, sauntering alongside mothers proudly pushing tall, well sprung prams, stepped aside. A newspaper seller held out the latest edition to the passers by, **'Extra! Extra! Judge condemns race riots!'**
Michael laughed. 'So Notting Hill's made the headlines. Deiter would have liked to have seen that, I bet.'

Tony stopped outside one of the many shop windows and called the others back.

'Here! Take a look at this lot!'

Black bras and panties, trimmed with pink and red lace, dominated the window display. Suspender belts adorned with roses, bows and hearts hung alongside various patterns of fishnet stockings pulled taut over clear plastic legs. An explosion of intimacy, in sharp contrast to the recent wartime rationing, tantalised many of those who stopped to look.

'I remember my mum taking me to see my aunt when I was a nipper. We went on a trolleybus and there was a shop like this next to a toy shop. I wanted the "Lone Ranger" cowboy gun in the window, but my mum couldn't afford it.'

'What *are* you on about, Tony?'

'Nothing really. Just that I used to think what a waste it was having all those fancy knickers to wear when nobody ever saw them. Now I know better!'

'Silly bugger! Come on, put your tongue back in. We gotta get Paul sorted. Save your drooling till we get down the youth club on Wednesday.'

'OK, Mike. Let's go.'

Reaching the tailors, Roy bowed. 'After you m'lord!'

Michael strutted in, followed by the others. Oak tables displayed large swatches of materials alongside heavy books of patterns. Chairs dotted around the highly polished parquet flooring offered customers the chance to sit while perusing the styles. A subtle scent of beeswax and lavender pervaded the store. Overhead a fluorescent tube blinked, distracting from the soft glow of the wall lights.

Eagerly the youths began examining the samples, feeling the cloth between thumb and finger, turning pieces toward the daylight from the store windows.

'Come on then, make yer mind up, mate. We ain't got all day yer know.'

'There's too much choice, Mike. I dunno what'll look best. What do you think?'

Roy held out a sample. 'I like this charcoal grey, might get it for me next whistle.'

'Oh thanks a bunch, Roy. I was thinking of having that, but not if you're getting it.'

'I only said I *might*, you get it if it's what you like.'

A short, portly man, patiently waiting, tape measure at the ready, interceded.

'Has sir considered these? The Prince of Wales check is very popular.'

Paul took the proffered book of cloth samples and laid it down beside the others.

'Cheers, mate!'

With an audible sigh, the weary salesman left the group studying the materials, crossed the store and smiled ingratiatingly at a man nearer his own age, studying the racks of ties.

'What about serge?' Michael asked.

'Serge? What's that, Mike?'

'You don't know what serge is? Oh, don't bother! Choose yer own.'

'That's smart. Look at this one, Paul. Its got some sort of, I dunno, some sort of sparkle I suppose. Don't know how they done it, but it looks great.' Tony handed over the squares of fabric.

'Yeah, that's the one! Thanks, Tony, I didn't see that.'

The sound of the till opening and shutting signalled a sale. The salesman wrapped a tie and with a smile and deferential nod of the head passed it to the customer. Taking a white cotton handkerchief from his pocket he wiped his forehead and glanced up at the store clock. Inhaling deeply, he composed himself before returning to the youths. His practised smile and natural demeanour usually managed to carry him through each working day, but sometimes, on days like today, he wondered if it was all worth it. These last few years had brought a new set of clients through the portals of Burtons, young men with more money than sense, or so he thought. *Is this what we fought a war for?* Their brashness and disregard for traditional values disturbed him; he yearned for times gone by.

'Has sir decided?' The sycophantic voice intruded.
'Yeah, I'm gonna have this one.' Paul pushed the sample book across the table, his finger resting on Tony's oice.
'And has sir chosen the style?'
'Yep.' Paul held open the book of illustrations, 'That one. And I want a three piece.'
'Certainly, sir. Now, would sir kindly remove the pullover.'
Paul tugged at the creation lovingly knitted by his mother; Tony helped him pull it over his head.
'Oi, watch the Barnett,' a muffled voice protested. Red faced, Paul ran a comb through his hair and glared his friends. 'It's all right for you lot. Go on, laugh.' He hurled the garment to the floor and kicked it.
'Arms up, please, sir.'
The tape measure was wrapped around Paul's chest.
'Thank you, sir. Now the arm. Straight out, please.'
'Go on mate, click yer heels! Reminds me of someone that does! Good job Deiter ain't still with us!' Roy ighed. Paul glowered.
'Now the waist. Thank you, sir. And the leg. That's fine. And the inside leg.'
'Watch him, Paul. Oh, I dunno know, could be your lucky day. There's a lot of it about according to the pers!'
'*Piss off, Tony,*' Paul mouthed. With the tape measure pushed firmly into his crotch, he was not feeling mfortable.
'All finished, sir. Now let us begin with the jacket. How would sir like it?'
'Top pocket and two side, no flaps. Three buttons, and *no* vent.'
The man ran the tape down Paul's back and used a finger to indicate length.
'How's that, sir?'
'No! Finger tip, I want it down to here.'
A sigh.
'As sir wishes.' The man licked the end of his pencil and made notes.
'Sir wishes a waistcoat?'
'Yep. Double breasted, two pockets, no flaps. That's right, ain't it, Mike?'
'That's what we got, should be good enough for you.'
Paul's face grew flushed again. 'Got to make sure it's right, Mike. Blimey, no need to have a go at me.'
'Get on with it, I'm only kidding.'
'Now the trousers, sir. Turn-ups?'
Paul stared at the man as if he couldn't believe his ears.
'Turn-ups! They're only for old far ...' Paul remembered where he was and stopped himself. 'No! No, I on't want turn-ups. And I want fourteen inch bottoms.'
'I'm sorry, sir. The smallest we can supply would be eighteen.'
'Eighteen! How am I gonna see me shoes? Eighteen.' Paul wrinkled his nose.
'Just take 'em, mate. Me mum'll sort 'em out. You'll have to pay her for the zips though,' Tony said.
'Anything else, sir?'
'Yes, I don't want side pockets! I want them straight across.' Paul drew his finger horizontally across the ont of his trousers. The assistant raised his eyes toward the ceiling and closed them momentarily.
'Did sir wish for a zip, or a button fly?'
'Sir wants a zip,' Michael mocked. 'No hold on, he's only young, probably manage with a button or two.'
'Do they sell tweezers here?'
'No, Roy,' Michael laughed. 'But we can always take him to Boots.'
The youths were attracting attention, one prospective customer had already left empty handed. The lesman wanted this ordeal over. Quickly.
'Well, that's all, sir. If sir would leave a deposit and call back in two weeks for a fitting ...'
'Two weeks! Blimey, I thought I'd have it for the weekend.'
'Give him a chance, Paul. You want it to look right don't you?'
'Yeah, but ...'
'Come on, here's the dosh. Let's go back to Ma's, I need a coffee.'

'OK, Mike. Thanks for coming with me. Should look smart, shouldn't it.'

'If it don't, tell 'em to stuff it. There's other tailors we can try. That fifty bob one for a start.'

The man took the money to the till, wrote on his pad and handed Paul a receipt.

'Thank you for your custom, sir. Please recommend us to your friends,' he forced himself to say. *No, PLEASE don't*, he thought, *You teddy boys will be the death of decent fashion.*

Outside, Michael gave Paul a friendly shove, causing him to bounce off the plate glass window.

'There! That weren't too bad, was it? Soon have you looking like one of us.'

'Me jumper! I forgot me jumper! Mum'll have me guts for garters!' Amidst laughter and ribald remarks, Paul slunk back inside to retrieve the missing garment.

'How we ever gonna make a man out of him,' laughed Roy. Michael didn't comment.

Chapter 5

'What's up, Paul? Cat got your tongue?'
'Eh? What did you say mum. I missed that.'
'I asked you why you're so quiet lately. Not like you at all. Got something you want to tell me?' *Don't tell me you've got some girl in the family way, I couldn't bear it. Especially after your sister letting the side down.*
'No. I'm OK. Leave me alone, don't keep on at me.'
'No need to be rude. I am your mother don't forget.'
'Sorry, mum. Got a lot on my mind, didn't mean to be rude to you, honest.'
'That's better. Now, eat your toast. Oh, by the way, I forgot to tell you, I'm going to see about a job this morning.'
'A job! What sort of job? Where?'
'Cleaning. It's at one of those posh houses up by the common.'
'You can't! I don't want you to! You're my mum, not somebody's skivvy!'
'Oh, that's nice. But darling, we need the money. What with your dad running off and you never able to settle in a job. The rent's behind, I owe for the milk and ...'
'Oh, mum. Why didn't you tell me? I'll get a job, promise.' *Wish I could give you some of our money, but you'd only ask where I got it. And that's something I can't tell you, you'd go straight to the coppers.*
'I know you will, my darling. But the bills won't wait. I have to go. Anyway, I might not get it. Tell you what, you find yourself a good job and stick at it and I'll give up this cleaning malarkey. I've got to go now, got to walk to the shops and catch the bus. I'll see you when I get back, wish me luck.'
'Good luck, mum.' *Hope you don't get it.*
'Well, you could sound as if you mean it! Bye, love. Try the labour exchange, they might have something.'
'Yes, mum. I will.' *Bloody money, wish I'd never gone along with Michael and the others. I'd turn myself in but the bastards at the cop shop would torture me 'till I gave 'em all the names. I can't do that. I'm too young to hang, but the rest of the gang aren't. What a mess! And there's me mum having to go out to scrub floors when I've got enough dosh to sort things out. Life ain't fair. Bloody Deiter! Bloody teacher! Bloody knives! Bloody, bloody, bloody everything!*
As the front door closed behind his mother, Paul dropped his head into his hands and sobbed.

Chapter 6

'It's been two weeks, Mike. Do you think you could run me into town this afternoon to see if me suits ready
'Yeah, but it'll cost you.'
'How much?'
'A cheese roll and a cup of rosy at Ma's place should sort it. Right?'
'Yeah! Cheers, Mike. I can't wait to see it.'
'Don't bet on it. You know how slow they can be. Still it won't take us long, I've been tuning the bike. B
interesting to see what it'll do now.' Michael sauntered over to his beloved machine.
'What time then, Mike?'
'No time like the present, as they say, jump on, let's go.'
'But I ain't got me helmet.'
'So? We can call in at your house can't we?'
'Oh yeah, course we can. Cheers! But you can wait outside, I ain't asking you in.'
'Anything you say, mate.' Michael held his hands above his head.

Sitting astride his bike outside the council house, Michael lovingly ran his fingers over the rocket-ship
transfer on the fuel tank. A front door opened and Paul stepped out, adjusting the strap of his helmet.
'You could have come in after all, me mum's out,' he mumbled.
In answer, Michael kicked the machine back into life and began revving the engine unnecessarily, knowin
it would annoy the neighbours. Paul climbed on behind and the pair roared off.

The high street was busy, buses disgorging passengers and picking up queues of others. A few cars and
cyclists played dodgems with the public transport. Michael rode the bike fast, keeping to the centre of the
road, weaving around any pedestrians bold enough to try and cross. Paul used two fingers to answer any
shouts of protest or profanities hurled at them.

Once inside Burtons, they sat and waited while the rotund man went to retrieve Paul's order from the
stockroom. On the man's return Paul jumped to his feet, eager to try on his new clothes. The assistant
escorted him to a cubicle and stood outside as the clothes were put on, running his tape measure back and
forth in his hands. Finally the door opened. A wolf whistle pierced the air.
'I don't believe it! Paul, is *that* you?'
'Course it is you daft bug ... Who do you think? What do yer reckon?' Paul tugged at the jacket as if tryin
to increase its length still further.
'Apart from those flappy legs it looks great. Never mind, Tony's mum'll soon sort 'em out. The jacket's
great and that waistcoat's something else. You look the bee's knees.'
Paul looked over his shoulder, studying the rear view in the cubicle mirror, nodding approvingly. The
assistant began fussing around, checking the order, taking measurements. 'We will soon have it adjusted, sir
Shouldn't take more than a week or two.'
'Adjust what? Seems fine to me, I want to take it now.'
'But, sir, it needs taking in across the shoulders and –'
'It's fine,' Paul shrugged the jacket up. 'What do you say, Mike.'
'Looks OK to me, but this guy's the governor. I had mine adjusted like he said, fits like a glove.'
'Well, I think it's brilliant. I want to wear it now. Can you stick my other clobber in a bag, mate. Cheers!'

'As sir wishes.' The assistant shook his head as he walked away. *Why have a suit made to measure then :cept it at the first fitting? What is the youth of today coming to?* Folding Paul's clothes carefully he placed em in a bag and left them beside the till.

Returning to the youths he asked, 'Will there be anything else, sirs?'

'Yeah, them raincoats you got over there. Give us a butchers.' Michael pointed to the rack that bore a sign oudly pronouncing, *NEW LINE.*

'Certainly, sir. Would you walk this way?'

The pair dutifully followed, doing their best to imitate the assistant's rolling gait.

'We have them in black or tan, sir. The tan has a brown corduroy lapel as you can see but the black doesn't ve a contrasting collar.' He took down a black coat and held it out, 'Perhaps sir would like to try it on?'

Michael slipped his arms into the sleeves and pulled it around him, tying half a knot in the casual belt. Iow's that Paul? I like the length, just long enough to cover me drape but shorter than me dad would ever ear. Brilliant.'

'Looks great, Mike. You should go for that. Do you think the brown one would look good on me? I don't ant to copy you.'

'Try it on, mate. It's the only way to find out.'

Paul slipped the proffered coat on over his new suit and walked up and down. 'Well?' he asked.

'Take it. It suits you. The others will wet themselves when they see us wearing these.'

'OK, mate. We'll have these as well. Bung 'em in a bag will yer, don't want 'em getting caught up in the ke, do we.'

Paul handed the raincoat back to the flustered assistant. 'Come on, Mike. Let's see what the damage is. Can ju pay for mine out of you know what?'

'Cheeky so and so. I can, but remember you've had this money. Don't start moaning when you ain't got as uch left as you thought, will you.'

Much to the relief of the beleaguered assistant they left the store, strutting back to Michael's bike clutching eir bags.

'What on earth!'

Paul spun around at the sound of his mother's voice.

'Where did you get those clothes! Who said you could dress like that? What will your father say?'

'Don't know, but he ain't around, is he.'

'Don't you cheek me, my lad. All the time you live under my roof you'll do as I say. Is that clear?'

Paul stared down at his feet. 'But they're only clothes, mum. Mike wears them, and nobody has a go at m.'

'That's as may be. I'm not his mother, but I am yours. You'll be wanting a motorbike next I bet. Well, you n forget that before you start. I'll …'

'Excuse me butting in, Mrs. P. I don't want to be rude, but don't you think it's time you let Paul grow up. I ean, he's always getting picked on, wearing them jumpers and things. I can't always be there to keep an eye it for trouble. Why don't you cut him a bit of slack?'

Paul glanced at Michael, pleased to be defended by him, in spite of all that had happened between his friend nd his mother.

'That's all very well, Michael,' she said, trying to avoid his eyes. 'That's all very well, but who's going to ay for them? You know Paul never keeps a job for more than five minutes.'

'I am. I'm paying. He said he's going to get a job and pay me back. I trust him, so perhaps you should give im a chance too. Let him grow up.'

Paul listened in amazement. *Get a job? What for?*

'That's right ain't it, Paul. And you said I could start coming around your house again, didn't you.'

Paul felt trapped, he knew his mother was capable of banning his new clothes and that Michael seemed to e winning her over. But at what cost?

Paul's mother dived in her handbag and began dabbing powder on her face; she could feel the warmth in er cheeks. 'Well, if that's the case. Michael being allowed back in our home I mean, then perhaps it is time for you to let go of my apron strings. You can wear those clothes if you must, as long as Michael says it's OK. I'm sure he'll look after you.'

Yes! And you too, given half a chance! Paul thought.

'Good! That's settled then. Come on, Paul, let's get going. Bye, Mrs. P. See you soon.' Michael winked and turned away. With a sigh of resignation, Paul followed but the spring had gone from his step. 'Bye, mum,' he mumbled. The fact that he had just been outmanoeuvred exasperated him.

'Oh! Paul.'

He winced as he heard his name.

'Don't make any plans for Monday, I need you!'

'What for, mum?'

'The coal man's coming, remember? And remind me to order the sweep. We've got to get the chimney swept before the winter sets in.'

Waiting until Mrs Parker had walked off Michael mimicked her. '*The coal man's coming.* What's that all about?'

'Me mum don't trust the coal man, says he fiddled her last time. She wants me to be there and count the sacks as he delivers them.'

'On the fiddle is he? Well we wouldn't want her being diddled by a coalman, would we?' Michael grinned. 'Wonder if he wants to buy any fags? Me uncle's got another load to flog.'

'Cor! You don't never give up, do you. Wouldn't have thought you'd bother with them now. After all, we got money now ain't we.'

Michael caught hold of Paul's sleeve, 'Shut it!' he hissed. 'You never know who's listening.'

'Sorry, Mike. I didn't think.'

Chapter 7

he last bars of the *Rock & Roll Waltz* died away, the jukebox whirred and the next record dropped into lace. Gene Vincent raised the tempo. The door of Bentini's coffee bar opened and two youths wearing ather jackets entered. Michael pushed his chair back in alarm.

'Watch it, Roy, it's the Chieftains!'

'Now that's what yer call music, go for it, Gene!' one of the pair yelled as they walked to the counter and rdered drinks. Chrome studs on the back of their jackets changed colour as they reflected the lighting. Michael and Roy knew the crossed tomahawks motif well. It was this rival gang's challenge to race, just veeks ago, that had given Michael an opportunity and cost Deiter his life.

'Wotcha, you two. On yer own?' The youth's breath made Michael sit back.

'Yeah, why? We ain't looking for bother.'

'Didn't think you was. Just asking.'

'How did it go the other night?' Roy asked, trying to ease the situation.

'What? Oh, that punch up you started. Great! One of me boys is in hospital, but it was worth it. Don't think ve'll be going in that boozer again though!' he laughed.

Roy swallowed a mouthful of coffee. 'Christ! Sounds like it got a bit rough!'

'A bit? You can say that again. Look,' he pulled his swollen lip to one side, exposing a mouthful of rotten ceth. 'See? Lost a tooth. Bugger me, that bloke could hit. Well he could, until me bonce floored him!' The outh rubbed his forehead, a grin crossing his face.

'Thanks for helping us out that night, appreciate it. Don't like to admit it but we was in trouble there. Bleedin' birds are a nuisance at times.'

'Yeah, you're right, Mike. Reckon we'd have got done over good and proper,' Roy said quietly.

The other Chieftain leered. 'Reckon you lot owe us one.'

Michael and Roy nodded in silent approval.

'Talking of birds; how's that one who started our race? Cost me a good fifty yards she did, flashing her tits ke that!' The memory of those milky white breasts being suddenly exposed caused a stirring in Michael's oins. He winced and moved in his chair, trying to ease the discomfort.

'Problems, Mike?'

'Yes, Roy. And you know why. Shut it.'

Bad Breath leaned toward Michael. 'What's up, mate? Got a dose?'

'No! At least, I hope not.'

'Well then, what's up? Got crabs?'

'I gotta kicking, me bollocks still throb at times.'

'That all! You don't want to worry about things like that. Happens in our gang all the time, don't it?' He urned to his companion who was busily raking through a grubby handful of coins.

'Do what? - Hang on, just going to feed the jukebox.'

'Stick Bill Haley on, and Gene again!'

Michael grinned. 'Like yer taste. *And* your secret weapon, that bird of yours.'

'Watch it squire, she's ours.' Bad Breath sneered, menacingly.

Michael raised both arms in the air, 'Keep yer hair on. I didn't mean nothing.'

Bill Haley and The Comets broke the tension with, *Rip it up.*

'Come on Roy, let's go. We're supposed to be meeting Tony, remember.'

Roy didn't, but stood up anyway. 'OK, Mike. Just finish me coffee.'

To Michael's dismay, Bad Breath also got to his feet. 'We're thinking of bombing down to Leysdown oon, you know, that place on the Isle of Sheppey. Interested?'

Glancing quickly at his friend, Michael swallowed hard. 'What yer going down there for? What the leedin' hell's out there?'

'A decent club for a start, bloke plays our sort of music, don't shut till midnight. And then there's some aity roads. Course, if you're scared ...'

'Sounds great. When?' Michael listened to someone speaking, someone who sounded just like he did, someone who could easily be getting the gang into trouble. With a jolt he realized it was him.

'Oh, no hurry. Couple of our bikes need working on. We'll let you know. You use this place a lot?' Bad Breath glanced around Bentini's.

'Yeah, most evenings, and the weekends. We're either here or at the King's Arms.'

'Then we'll be back. And don't get any ideas, she's ours!'

'Who? The girl with the big ...'

'Who else?'

'Wouldn't dream of it, mate. See yer.'

Outside, Roy gripped Michael's sleeve. 'What you getting us into now, Mike? That lot are bleedin' hard! We don't want to mess with them.'

'Do what? Thought you'd like a day at the seaside. We could leave the birds at home, see what the talent's like down there.'

'You're incorrugated, er, incorrogitated. Bugger! What do I mean?'

'Incorrigible! Big word for you ain't it, Roy, you cheeky git! Anyway, let's hope it's not too soon, got to get me tackle sorted first.' Michael winced.

'See what I mean? You never learn, Mike, do you. And what's with that, *meeting Tony*, rubbish.'

'Don't know, had to think of something. Just wanted out of there. Didn't want to get into a bundle and get us banned from Benito's, did I?'

'Oh, scares you, does he?' It was Roy's turn to grin.

'No, he don't! *And* I'm going to have that bird of theirs!' Michael shrugged, moving the shoulders of his jacket toward his ears.

Chapter 8

lfred pulled back the wet, oily smelling tarpaulin cover and stood back as water cascaded onto the path.
eiter's motor bike saw the light of day for the first time since it had been recovered from the police station
llowing his death. He ran a hand over the seat, a contact of some sort with his lost brother.
'Why?' he asked, although there was no one to hear.
The Norton now bore little resemblance to the original. Shattered headlight glass, handlebars and brake
vers bent by impact. Paintwork scraped back to bare metal, rust filling in the missing pieces. Alfred shook
s head. *This is not the bike my brother was so proud of.*
He leant his walking stick against the wall of the house and used his hand to help swing his gammy leg
ver the bike. Sitting astride it he rubbed at the damage with the sleeve of his jacket. Aladdin rubbing a
agic lamp, but, sadly, no genie to offer help this time.
Tugging the handlebars, trying to force them back into position, he sighed when they didn't move. Pulling
e bike upright, freeing it from its stand, he tried rocking it back and forth. Squeezing the brake levers he
as surprised when the rear brake failed to operate. *Strange, the front one is fine. Perhaps the other has been
amaged in the crash.* Alfred sat and let his mind wander. *That crash. A brief moment, but it has changed our
es forever. What happened, brother?* He wiped a tear from his cheek and patted the bike. *I will restore
ur motorcycle. It will be your memorial. Perhaps Michael will help me? He is a mechanic and he was your
iend.*
'What are you doing? Cover that up, I hate the thing!' His irate stepmother stood wiping flour covered
ands down her apron.
'I am only looking.'
'I don't know why your father wanted it returned, it upsets him so. I said it should be melted down or
hatever they do to wrecked things, but he wouldn't listen. It's horrid. I'm going to speak to him again, I'm
ire he will see my point of view this time. After all, your brother is dead and buried, so what use is that pile
f junk now?'
'I think it would be better for all of us if you two hadn't married,' Alfred snarled. 'Deiter was right. We
hould have returned to Germany, I see that now. My father should have re-married someone from the
atherland instead of an Englander. You never liked my brother, did you! You are pleased he died! I warn
ou, do not interfere or there will be trouble!'
Alfred turned away from the confrontation and swallowed. *I will do this thing for you, my dear brother.
Perhaps someday your bike will live again!*
Oil wept from the heart of the machine, dark tears staining the concrete beneath. He let the bike settle back
nto its stand and struggled to get his leg clear. Removing his jacket, he rolled his sleeves back and tugged at
e stubborn mass of metal, testing the practicality of moving it. The weakness of his leg, combined with the
eight of the machine, prevented his efforts, the bike resisted him. *There is only one solution; I will have to
sk Michael to help. I cannot do it alone.*

The rhythmic tapping of a walking stick interrupted Michael's thoughts.
'Hello! Michael, please wait. I have to talk with you.'
The German accent sent a shiver down Michael's spine. His first impulse was to ignore the call and keep
alking, but it was too late. Turning, he saw Alfred approaching, doing his best to catch up.
'Thank you. I'm not as quick as you, even in those strange shoes you wear.'
Michael glanced down, 'Nothing wrong with brothel creepers, mate. Got 'em in Bata's, reduced. Look at
them soles. Crepe, last a lifetime. Mind you, had to change the laces, red looks better against blue suede I
reckon.'
    Alfred shrugged, 'I choose black leather, more practical.'

'Well you would, wouldn't you? Anyway, what do you want, I'm on my way to Paul's house.'
'It's about my brother's bike. I need …'
'Blimey! Deiter's bike! You still got it? Thought you'd have had it down the scrap yard by now. It was right mess last time I saw it.' *And after bouncing off the road, then sliding down the dual carriageway like that, no bloody wonder!*
'Yes. My father kept it, my stepmother hates it. They have a lot of trouble about it.'
'So? Why not get shot of it?'
'My brother. I want to repair it for him.'
'But he's dead. He don't need no bike.'
'You do not understand. I wish to keep it in his memory. Will you help me?'
As the two stood talking, Paul joined them. 'Wotcha, Alfred. Wotcha, Mike. How's it going then?'
'I was just coming round your place to call for you,' Michael said.
'Saved you a walk then, ain't I?'
'Hello, Paul. Nice to see you. I was just asking Michael to help me mend my brother's bike.'
'What on earth for?'
'That's just what I said. Sell it for scrap. Get rid of it.'
'Please, Michael. You are a good mechanic. I know you could do this thing.'
'Sorry, mate. Too busy. Take my advice, dump it.'
'Yeah, Alfred. It ain't worth fixing. Mike knows what he's talking about.'
'Think about it, Michael. Perhaps you will change your mind.'

Paul and Michael stood and watched as Alfred resumed his walk. When he turned the corner and disappeared from view, Paul cleared his throat. 'Why did he ask *you*, Mike? Do you think he suspects something?'
'No! Why should he? Bikes crash all the time. Nothing new, is it.' *But you could be right, Paul. Why me Plenty of garages around here that could have a go at it.*
'Come on, Mike. Forget it. Let's go down the boozer, mum's give me ten bob. Here you go, now you ca buy me a pint.'

Michael stopped outside the King's Arms. 'My shoelace is undone, sort it out for us will yer. I can hardly bend in these trousers.'
Paul dropped to one knee and tied a double bow, 'Them laces look great, Mike. You really don't give a toss what people think, do you?'
'Why should I? This is my life and I'm going to live it how I like. Anyone don't like it, tough tittie!'
Paul opened the door to the public bar and stood aside while Michael stepped inside. He mimed having to use a stick as he approached the bar.
'Blimey, Brian. How do you see in here? This smoke gets any thicker it'll be like that smog last year.' H coughed loudly. 'Give us a pint of mild, a coke and two masks.'
The barman ignored the remarks, placed a glass under the pump while wrestling the top off a bottle. The beer spat, stopped, then spat again. 'Sorry, Mike, looks like the barrel needs changing. Want something els instead?'
'Yeah. Why not. Give us a Woodpecker.'
'There you go, Mike. The cider *is* for you, isn't it?'
'Course it is. We know the law.'

Over in the corner, out of sight, Paul sipped at the cider. 'Cor! Not bad, Mike. You should try it, better than that fizzy muck you drink. Cheers!'

Michael took a mouthful of coke and nodded. 'You know I don't drink, *and* why. I'll be glad when you're eighteen, you can buy your own booze then.'

'Only a year and a bit now, Mike. By the way, when's your mum coming home? She's been at her sisters a long time. Don't she get bored?'

'Me dad's been to see her, they …, her sister said she will be home soon.'

'Oh.'

'What about your dad? Heard anything?' *I hope not, I can do without any more bother from him.*

'No, I don't suppose he'll show his face again. The rozzers still want to feel his collar, don't forget.'

'Well, if it'll do any good, tell him I won't be giving evidence, that's if you hear from him of course.'

'Thanks, Mike. But me mum will.'

Michael spread his hands and shrugged. 'Life's like using Vaseline for sex, you never know when some bugger's going to put a bit of sand in it.'

'What's that mean?'

'Nothing. Drink up. Let's go round Tony's place, see if your trousers are ready.'

Chapter 9

The office door swung open. 'Oi! Mike! Come in to my office will you.'

'Coming!' Michael wiped greasy hands down his overalls. Putting feeler gauges back in his tool box resting on the running board of the car, he strolled across the floor of the garage. *What's up now? Not more bleedin' overtime I hope, I done enough this week already.*

The young man waiting with the boss behind the hardboard partition that served as an office, sat with one leg stretched out. Even in the poor light Michael recognised him at once.

'Wotcha, Alfred. What you doing here? Didn't see you come in.'

'Hello, Michael. I did not know you worked here. I have come to have my brother's motor cycle restored. This man,' Alfred nodded toward Michael's boss, 'said that you are the person to ask if it is possible.'

'You know this customer, Mike?'

'Yes. He's already asked me about this before. I told him to scrap it. It's going to cost a bomb, be cheaper to buy another bike.'

'But I do not wish another one; I want only this one repaired. I will pay.'

'Sounds like it's right up your street, Mike.' Turning to Alfred he said. 'Yes, sir, bring it in by all means. If it can be fixed then Mike's your man, right, Mike?'

'If you say so, you're the boss. But it's going to be bucket loads of work, don't say I didn't warn you.'

'That's settled then. Back to work, Mike. I'll sort out the details with your friend here.'

Michael walked slowly back to the Austin Ten, his stomach churning. Deiter's bike had returned to haunt him, bringing with it nightmares to invade his day light hours.

Chapter 10

'Not going out, son?' Michael's father pulled the front room curtains, blocking out the setting sun.
'Might do. Why? Why are you always on my back? What's it got to do with you anyway?'
'No need for that, I only asked. You seem worried lately that's all. Anything I can do to help?'
'Why are you so interested all of a sudden? You don't usually bother about what I do.'
'I'm sorry, Mike. But it's all this business with your mother. It's getting me down.'
'They'll soon get her sorted out, they did last time. Dried her out like a kipper.'
'I know, son. But for how long? As soon as I'm out of the house she's off down the pub cadging drinks.
I'm not sure how much more I can take.' He lit a Woodbine without thinking to offer them to Michael.
'See, there you go again dad, can't even spare a fag. I knew you couldn't really be bothered about me.
Well, don't come to me with all your problems. Probably your fault me mum drinks like a fish in the first
place!'
'You cheeky … I've a good mind to …'
'To do what? Fancy your chances do you? I'm not a little kid now, you just try it.'
His father slumped into a saggy armchair, the cigarette dangling from nicotine stained fingers.
'What did I do wrong? Why have you turned out like this? I fought …'
'Shut it, dad. I've heard it all before. Don't try and dump all that on me. I've got to live in this world you
helped create. Thanks a bunch!'
Michael stormed out of the room. Snatching his drape from the coat stand he left the house, slamming the
front door behind him, emphasising the division between father and son. Heaving his bike off its stand he
kicked it into life and rode down the front path. On the road the thrill of riding way beyond the speed limit
soon dissipated the anger he felt. By the time he reached Bentini's he was his usual self once more.

'Handsome!' Michael said appreciatively as the smell of coffee combined with cigarette smoke greeted
him as he opened the door. He blinked to adjust his eyes. Neon tubes, set high up, cast pools of pale pink
and blue light, merging the ceiling with the walls. The owner, Bentini, an ex P.O.W. had attracted the
offspring of the men who had captured him in North Africa by catering for them. Business had been slow
to start, but the wise investment in a jukebox had changed all that. Now it was a popular haunt for teenagers
from miles around.
He waved to Paul and pushed his way through to join him at his table.
Putting his empty cup down, Paul reached into a back pocket and tugged at a folded paper.
'Here, Mike, take a look at this. Me mum bought it, it's Dalton's Weekly.'
Michael pulled the paper toward him, saw an advert that had been circled with a pencil and began to read
out loud. 'Two berth caravan, close to beach, shop on site … Yeah, OK, Paul, so what's it all about?'
'Think me mum's trying to save up, maybe take me on holiday.'
'What! You don't want to go, do you! You and your mum in a bloody caravan! How much fun's that
going to be! Tell her you don't want to go.'
'Can't. She ain't asked me yet.'
Michael screwed the paper up and threw it at Paul. 'Go and get some more coffees, you twit. Caravans!
What are you going to come up with next?'
'Butlin's?'
'Sod off! And hurry up with them drinks, I got to go round my uncle's place. Got some gear to pick up.
That reminds me, did you ask that coalman if he wanted any fags?'
'I forgot, sorry, Mike. I was busy counting sacks. And he tried it on, just like me mum said he would.'
'What! How? The cheeky bleeder, wish I'd been there.'

'He had an empty sack on his shoulder to rest the coal on. When he dumped the last lot into the coal bunker he added the empty one to the others. Thought I wouldn't see him, but I did.'

'Oh.' *I thought you meant he'd chatted her up.* 'That's alright then. Now, go and kick Benito's arse into gear, I'm in a hurry. Play your cards right and I'll drop you off at your place on the way to my uncle's.'

'Why do you lot call him Benito? It's Bentini ain't it?'

'You daft bugger, of course it is. But we call him Benito to wind him up. It's what that wop, Mussolini, was called. Surely you know that?'

Paul pushed back his chair without answering.

Michael accelerated hard as he tore through the streets, leaning the bike far more than was necessary on the bends, sending sparks up from the concrete. His experiences of seeing friends and acquaintances die riding bikes had no effect on Michael. Like them, he too believed he was immortal. The motto, *"Only the good die young!"* gave him an exaggerated sense of confidence.

Outside his uncle's house he dismounted and placed the machine onto its stand, brushed his hair back in place with a sweep of his hand and rang the door bell.

'Hello, Michael! Haven't seen you for a while. Feeling better?'

'Hello, Aunt Nell. Yeah, I'm getting there, thanks. It's still a bit sore though, if you know what I mean. But that cream you gave me's doing the trick.'

She nodded. 'You come to see Jim? I'll give him a shout. No, better still, come on in. I got the kettle on you want a cuppa.'

'Cheers! Got any cakes?'

'Silly question! When's this house never got cakes! No point being a baker's delivery man if you can't have a few cakes. Get in there, I'll tell 'im you're 'ere.'

Michael hung his jacket in the hall, entered the front room and sprawled in one of the armchairs, putting his feet up on a multi- coloured leather pouffe. A tall lamp stand, with a hammered copper band halfway up the teak leg, sported a pink pleated shade. The light was on, its homely glow casting a circle of light onto the highly polished linoleum.

Someone had spent a lot of time making a rug, a thatched cottage surrounded by rose bushes set against a biscuit background. It took pride of place in front of the open coal fire set into a peach and green tiled fireplace. The polished brass fender surrounding the hearth was complemented by a three piece fire companion set, poker, brush and shovel. Gurgling and knocking noises from pipes were an indication that the back boiler was busy providing hot water for the household.

A warm, electrical smell wafted from the radiogram. The illuminated front panel offered a choice of stations from around the world, but today the Billy Cotton Band Show was in full swing.

'Wotcha, Mike! How's the wedding tackle?'

'All right for you to laugh, could have happened to any of us *couldn't* it.'

'That's enough of that, don't you let Nell hear you say anything.'

Michael looked at his uncle and mouthed, *No, Dad, of course not!*

'Cut it out, Mike. Don't you ever call me that again, we agreed didn't we. It's *uncle*, right?'

'OK. Keep you're hair on. Anyway, I've come for the fags, what you got this time?'

'More Yank ones, Lucky Strike, Black Cat, State Express and Pall Mall. Wotcha think?'

'Well the other lot all went, the punters will smoke anything if the price is right. Same as last time?'

'Yeah, get what you can. I've got some English ones to pick up from a bloke in Woolwich but haven't had time.'

'I could get them for you, nip over on me bike. Where's he live?'

'Dunno. But he's got a book stall in the market; I'll give him a ring and tell him you're coming. Thanks, Mike, save me going over there. I don't get a lot of time now what with working and managing Roy's band. Getting bookings for them is bloody hard at the moment. How's that Paul getting on? Don't see much of him lately.'

'He's trying to get out of being dragged on holiday with his mum.'

'Why don't you take her instead!' Jim laughed, lit a cigarette, coughed and laughed again.

'Don't think I'm not tempted, but I think I'll let the dust settle for a while. Anyway, who wants to stay in a caravan?'

'A caravan? Is that where Paul's going? Where abouts?'

'I dunno, by the sea somewhere. Why?'

'Oh, nothing really. Just that the bloke who's got the fags, he's got a caravan up in Norfolk. Lets it out. Says it's a nice racket. He only takes cash and says the caravan's somewhere to get away to at times. Between you and me, I think he needs somewhere to hide now and then, so it suits him down to the ground.'

'He sounds like a bit of a lad. Is he?'

'Let's put it like this, there ain't much he can't get his hands on. He's got a brother who works in the docks. Surprising what falls off them boats at times! Want a fag while Nell gets the tea?'

Jim held out a crumpled, pink, packet. Michael took a cigarette and sniffed it.

'What are these? Russian?'

Jim held out his lighter. 'No. Turkish, here, try it.'

Michael drew deeply and blew the smoke down his nose. 'Bugger me! What do they make these out of? Camel shit? That's the worst bleedin' fag I've ever had.'

'They're what they call an acquired taste, Mike. You get used to them.'

'I don't think so; I'll stick to my Players, thanks.' Michael ground out the offending object in the belly of the china reclining nude girl ashtray his uncle pushed toward him. 'Can you phone that geezer? I gotta get going, said I'd meet the lads up the field by the allotments, they'll be wondering where I am.'

His uncle nodded and went out into the hall. Michael couldn't hear much of the whispered conversation but did hear Jim call out, 'Hold the char, Nell. Give us five minutes. I'm on the dog and bone.'

Coming back in, Jim placed a finger to the side of his nose. 'All sorted, had to keep me voice down, don't want Nell to know. Dodgy, he's the bloke with the fags, Dodgy said make it next Saturday. He's got the stall next to the bloke selling snake oil, just tell him who you are and he'll give you the gear. Can you sort out the cash? I'm a bit strapped, just changed the telly.'

'How much?'

'Not sure, depends on how many he can get his hands on. Just do your best, any you can't pay for, just leave. We can always pick 'em up another time.'

'OK. Leave it with me. I'll go Saturday morning, save me having to go to work for a change.'

At Paul's house, his mother asked. 'Did you go down the exchange, my darling? Did you manage to get a nice job?'

Paul spread the dripping on two thick slices of toast, stirred his tea, stretched his arms above his head and yawned.

'Yes, mum. I can start on Monday. Painting and decorating.'

'Oh well, you've always liked painting haven't you!' Paul's mother smiled at her attempt to make a joke out of her son's inability to find suitable employment and his love of art.

'How's your job, Mum? Bet they get you doing everything, lazy so and so's.'

'It's not too bad. I quite like it really. They've got some lovely things in the house and the garden's like a park, even got squirrels.' She lit a cigarette and blew the smoke toward an open window. 'And when they go out they've got a man to drive their car. Now that's what I call posh!'

'Blimey!'

'Don't say that, darling. It's so common. Listen, when I get my wages I'm going to try to save a little towards a holiday next year. You'd like that wouldn't you.'

'Yes, Mum.' That was the second lie, the first being the job offer. Fabrications tripped effortlessly off his tongue, deceit becoming a necessary survival tool since the murder of his teacher.

Chapter 12

Michael parked his bike and used a strong chain to anchor it to a lamp post. The market was in full swing, crowds of bargain seekers thronged the temporary stalls as stall holders busily vied with each other for business.

Defunct tramlines, crossing the cobble stone square, picked up a strange new set of travellers. Live eels making a bid for freedom. Open trays, containing countless writhing bodies, ensured that they were constantly escaping from one of the shops fronting the area occupied by the market. A boy, on his hands and knees, was trying to extricate one of them with a pencil.

The sweetness of hot sugar permeated the air as homemade sweets were produced in front of a crowd of incredulous children. Large lumps of hot, various coloured concoctions were fed into a set of rollers from one side by a woman while a man cranked a handle. A slab of small squares emerged, falling onto a tray dusted with icing sugar. After allowing it to cool, the woman attacked it with a small metal hammer and began bagging up the pieces in white paper bags. Eager young hands reached out clutching pennies, sweet on ration coupons still a vivid memory.

Complete tea sets and dinner services were tossed into the air and deftly caught while the seller kept up a steady stream of patter, the longer he talked the lower the prices dropped. When the price reached the correct level, an accomplice pushed his way to the front waving money. The effect was remarkable. People standing watching the free show now surged forward, all eager to purchase. The man smiled as he passed the goods over. Human nature was very predictable.

Pushing past stalls piled high with bed sheets, eiderdowns, pillows and towels, Michael made his way toward a voice he could hear proclaiming the virtues of snake oil. Having tracked the vendor down he stared in amazement at jars and bottles containing a reddish orange liquid with pieces of snakeskin suspended in them.

He listened as the man listed the ills it could cure; they were as diverse as they were many. Its uses, it appeared, were limited only by the imagination of the swarthy man selling it. A close inspection of his shirt collar would have exposed at least one deception, the dye used to create the illusion that the man was of foreign origin.

According to the fakir, or faker, the fluid had been extracted at great expense and danger from King Cobras. A suspect looking scar on his forearm was offered as proof of the risks involved in producing this precious cure all. He described being bitten and how his Indian servant had nearly died sucking poison from this wound.

Having finished haranguing his potential customers, he held out a flat sided bottle of the magical fluid on the palm of his hand. Gullible men and women parted with hard earned cash in the hopes of relieving aches and pains, stimulating libido, building up stamina and a hundred other things the elixir promised to cure.

Tearing his eyes from the fakir's hypnotic gaze, Michael saw a man lounging in a deckchair behind a makeshift table stacked high with books.

Well thumbed paperbacks, magazines, battered leather bound editions. Anything and everything. A cloth cap pulled down shielded the man's eyes from the sun, a red scarf knotted around his neck soaked up the sweat that trickled through stubble that hadn't seen a razor for days. His thumbs were tucked behind grey and white striped braces, an off cream collarless shirt adding to the unkempt look. But appearances can be deceptive. These were Dodgy's work day clothes. At the races, his dress sense and style provoked flattering comments.

Michael stepped across and picked up a dog eared copy of 'Future Science Fiction Stories.' On the cover a gigantic spider with hundreds of eyes was creeping up behind a scantily clad, well endowed woman.

Christ, she must be Titsaleaner's mum! Look at the size of those!

'One and a tanner to you, squire.'

Michael looked up from his fantasy lover. The man who had spoken pushed his cap up a little and smiled. A gold tooth winked in the sun. 'You like Science fiction? Got some good ones here. Or how about something a bit unusual? Young feller like you should be interested, get the sap rising if you know what I mean.'

'No. No thanks. I'm here for me uncle Jim. He sent me to pick up some ...'

'Oh, Jim! Why didn't you say so. You got the lolly?'

'Probably. Jim didn't know how much. What you got?'

'Not here, too many eyes. Got 'em in the motor. Come on, I'll show you.'

Throwing a grubby cloth over the piles of books the man placed a piece of corrugated cardboard on top. The message, scrawled in red crayon, was short and to the point. **'Back in 5 minutes.'**

Dodgy led Michael across the market to where a two tone Dodge car stood parked in the shade. Opening the boot he pulled back a blanket and waved a hand at the boxes. 'How many does Jim want?'

'Dunno, I've got this,' Michael walked around the American monster as he pulled a wad of notes from his jeans. 'I'll take as many as I can.' He continued to admire the feast of chrome and leather. 'This is a real beauty, I love the bench seats.'

The deal done, Michael shook hands. 'Suppose you couldn't give me a hand with these could you?'

'Do what! Bring yer motor over here; we can load the stuff straight in.'

'Motor? I ain't got a motor, I come on me motorbike. I got Jim's rucksack, they ought to fit in.'

'That's up to you. It's your funeral. I got the dosh, you got the fags. How you get 'em to Jim's your problem.' Dodgy put his fingers up under his cap and scratched the side of his head. 'Why don't you get a jam jar? Make things like this easy, and be great for pulling crumpet.'

'A car, get a car? Where? And how much would it set me back?'

'Well, seeing as how you're a mate of Jim's, I might be able to do you a favour. I've got one I'm thinking of selling; you can have it for what I paid. Interested?'

'Might be. Is it a Yank, like this? Can I see it?'

'No, it's British. And yes you can have a look. Jump in, I'll run you round to me yard.'

Michael sat in the car Dodgy had for sale. No extravagant tail fins, no abundance of chrome, but the mixture of smells would have driven a bloodhound crazy. Tobacco, beer, dust, petrol and oil, the working man's potpourri. Under instruction from Dodgy, Michael cautiously drove around the yard, the grating of the gears proving this was his first attempt.

'Well?'

'Brilliant! I'll have it. Do you think I could get me bike in the back?'

'Leave it out! It's a "Flying Nine" not a bleedin' rag and bone man's cart. Tell you what, I'll drive this over to Jim's place and you can follow on your bike. Then you'll have to give me a lift back, OK?'

Michael nodded. 'Cheers! Jim'll pay you for it later and I'll settle up with him. I can't wait to show the lads! Blimey, we'll be the only gang with a car, be a bit like Al Capone.'

Half an hour later Michael began following his new acquisition through the streets. At the second set of traffic lights he pulled alongside the car and gestured to Dodgy. Dodgy wound the window down and rested his elbow on the door frame. 'What's up?'

'Too slow mate. I'm going on; I'll see you at Jim's.'

The lights changed and without waiting for a reply, Michael roared across the junction and accelerated away. There were a few vehicles on the road but he weaved around them without losing any speed and w. soon back on familiar territory. Seeing the next set of traffic lights were green, he opened up the throttle. The lights changed to amber, then red. Michael began braking hard, smoking tyres squealing all the way. He stopped with his front wheel over the white line. 'Shit!'

Looking to his left, Michael grinned. Four motorbike riders sat astride their machines, revving their engines. He lifted a hand in salute. The lights changed and the bikes tore across, the riders crouching low.

I bet I know where you're going, you crazy bastards! Trying for the ton down the mad mile! His excitement at this thought was tempered by recent memories and the death of a fellow gang member.

The lights changed and he rode the rest of the way to his 'uncle's' house with his mind conjuring up images he had been trying to forget. The race, a result of a challenge from a rival gang, should have been just that, a testosterone fuelled duel of nerves and riding skills. But one of the riders was doomed from the start. Michael had seen to that.

Pulling up in front of the house, he wiped beads of sweat from his forehead. Shaking his head, he tried in vain to erase the vivid pictures from his mind. He felt sick.

Inside the house, he was telling Jim about the car when a horn sounded outside. Jumping up he dashed outside.

'There you go, squire. Bet you ain't been here long, the old girl goes like a dream.' Dodgy patted the top of the car. 'Remembered about the paperwork on the way over, I'll stick it in the post for you.'

'Cheers! Can you send it here though, me dad might get the hump about me having a car.'

'No problem. Right, I'll just come in for a cuppa then you can run me back, OK?'

'Sure. Oh, one other thing, Jim says you got a caravan and that you let it out for holidays. That right?'

'Yeah, but I'm fussy who I let have it. Why you asking, got some bird in tow?'

'No. Just that a mate of mine's mum is trying to get one but she's strapped for cash.'

'Is she? Well, come on in, we can talk while we drink our tea. And don't forget all them fags in the boot Jim won't be best pleased if you drive off with them.'

'It's all right. I sell 'em for him. It's a sort of business arrangement we got going.'

'Yeah? Well just make sure he pays you, I've known Jim a long time.'

'That's nothing. I've known him all my life.' *But I never knew he was me dad! Not until a couple of weeks ago, when I was in hospital!*

'Well, what you think? That's a good deal; she won't get it any cheaper.' Dodgy used a dirt filled fingernail to dislodge a piece of cake wedged between his teeth.

'Don't know, never thought about caravans before. Seems fair enough to me.' Michael took out his cigarette case, extracted a cigarette and tapped it on the chrome lid. Lighting it, he leaned back in his uncle's armchair. A smile crossed his face as he expelled the smoke across the room. 'I've just had an idea Dodgy. How about letting me and my mates have it?'

'You kidin'? You can pull the other one. I don't want me 'van smashed up thanks.'

'Cheeky bugger! We ain't all like the papers tell everyone. We got the cash, what's the problem?'

'Mike's all right, Dodgy. Him and his mates are a bit full of themselves, but they're OK.'

'So *you* say, but what if they're not?'

'Charge 'em a deposit to cover breakages, that way you can't lose. I'll cover it if that helps.'

'No, it's alright, don't bother, Jim. I know you're a bit short at the moment, and you already owe me for the jam jar.'

Jim turned to Michael. 'There you go then, sorted!'

'Great! Thanks, Dodgy. I'll talk to my mates then get Jim to phone you with the dates, that be OK?'

'Shake on it, Mike. Wish I was younger, I'd come with you. All that sea air and fish straight off the boats. Best I've ever tasted.' He ran his tongue around his lips. 'The van's got all you need, apart from sheets and towels. How you going to get there? Coach?'

'What! No, we got a motor now ain't we. I'll drive up.'

'But you ain't passed your test yet.'

'So what? No problem, there's lots of things I ain't done yet.' *And things I wish I hadn't done too.* 'You old blokes always see the black side of things, no wonder you're all so square. If someone drops the bomb we can all kiss our arses goodbye, so enjoy today, it may be your last.'

Dodgy frowned. 'Do you really believe that? You really think there'll be an atomic war?'

'Why not? They said the First World War would end war forever didn't they? So how come we had that last one? My dad goes on about it at the drop of a hat.'

'Oh, Gawd. Hang on, I'll just go and slit me wrists. Christ, you're a bundle of laughs, that's for sure. C'mon, get me back to Woolwich before it's too late. I think I can hear the bombers coming already.'

'Sorry, Dodgy, you silly sod. But it makes you think, don't it.'

'What I think is, thank god for boozers, that's where I'm off to tonight. Six pints of Mild and Bitter'll soon put the world to rights. - See yer, Jim. Let us know if you need anything, fags, stockings ... You know.'

'Yeah, cheers, mate. I'll be in touch. Now, Mike, take it easy. Dodgy ain't used to bikes, don't you go mad.'

'Me? Go mad? Come on; soon have you back safe and sound. Take no notice of Jim.'

Paul pushed himself up from the grass, brushed the backs of his trousers and held out his hand.

'Pass the cider, Roy.'

Roy poked him in the ribs. 'You're too young to drink.'

'Give it here, I need a drink.'

'You alright, mate? You been a bit of a misery just lately. Got problems?' Michael shielded his eyes from the low evening sun.

'No, Mike. I'm OK. Just 'cause I want a drink don't mean nothing. Crikey, you sound just like me mum.'

'Keep your hair on! Drink yourself to bleedin' death for all I care.'

'Sorry, Mike. Didn't mean it.' Paul held his hands up to the side of his head, blocking out the conversation. Roy passed him the bottle.

Michael took out his cigarette case and offered it around. 'Tell you what, Paul. And you two. That bloke I bought the car off, he's got a caravan; said we can hire it. What do you think? Be a laugh won't it? It's near the sea and the town, think of all those birds up there just gagging for it.'

Paul dropped his hands from his ears 'Yeah! Let's go! Get away from me mum's nagging for a while. That'll be great. When we going?'

'Right, that's Paul coming. What about you, Tony?'

'Count me in.'

'And me; can't trust you lot on your own. I might bring me guitar.' Roy half clenched his left hand and strummed the air with his right.

'That's settled then. Sort out your holiday dates and let me know. I'll be OK at work; he's alright, my governor.'

Paul pushed his plate away, folded his arms on the table and lowered his head to rest on them. His mother stood at the sink, up to her elbows in soapy water, washing underwear and stockings while listening to the Archers. Her pinafore, tied in a bow at the back, pulled her dress in at the waist. Hair curlers and tied piec of cloth gathered her hair, exposing the white scalp beneath. The radio station faded and she turned to tun it in again. Reaching out to the set with one of her bright red forearms she saw Paul slumped over, his me barely touched.

'What's up, my darling? You haven't eaten your dinner. Aren't you feeling well? Corned beef and chips that's one of your favourites. And I bought that brown sauce especially for you.'

'I'm just not hungry, mum. Leave me alone.'

'I'll get the cod liver oil, and then I think you'd better have an early night for a change.'

'Oh, mum. Don't keep on at me. I'm OK; just don't fancy anything to eat.'

'I hope you're not sickening for anything.' She crossed towards him and placed her hand on his forehead 'You feel alright, perhaps you've just been working too hard.'

Paul lifted his head and nodded. *Not bleeding likely! Though walking around all day without me mates just so you think I'm at work is really boring.*

She fiddled with a curler that had worked its way loose. 'How's Christine? How's her leg, is it getting any better? You haven't bought her home lately; haven't had a row, have you? She's such a nice girl. I lik her. What she ever saw in that German hooligan, Deiter, I'll never know.'

'He was alright, a bit strange that's all. Chris is fine, just that sometimes I prefer my mates. Anyway, her parents wouldn't let her come to the caravan so I have got to go on my own.'

'Well of course her parents won't allow her, I should think not! That's the difference with girls, you just think yourself lucky you're a boy.'

The sound of a motorbike pulling up outside finished the discussion. Paul walked slowly through the front room, into the hallway and opened the door.

'Wotcha, Paul. Fancy a coffee? I've arranged to meet the others at Benito's, come on.'

'Not tonight, Mike. I don't feel like it.'

'What's up? You've got a face like a smacked arse. Come on, I'll pay.'

'I don't want to see anyone.'

'How about a pint instead?'

'No.'

'Please yourself. I'll see you later.'

The hall door opened. 'Hello Michael, nice to see you. You taking my Paul out?'

'I was, but he don't want to come.'

'Why not, my darling? Do you good. Wait there, I won't be a minute.'

'Now what's she up to?'

'Beat's me, Mike. She's been on at me ever since she got in from work.'

Stepping back in to the hall she held out her hand. 'There you are, two shillings. Go and enjoy yourself with Michael.'

'Yes, come on. Get your jacket and let's get going.'

'Can we sit outside, Mike? I want to talk.' Paul wobbled his glass from side to side, watching the lager lap up the side.

'We can talk in here. What's up?'

'I can't tell you. People might be listening.'
'Oh, alright. I'll just get another; you go and find us a seat.'
'Cheers, Mike.'

'Now. What's bugging you? You need some more dosh?'
'No. Not yet. It's just that I'm just getting really pissed off lately.'
'So? I do sometimes. What's the problem?'
'You know.' Paul looked around the beer garden. 'My teacher!'
'Oh.'
'It's all my fault. The poor bugger would still be alive if it weren't for me.'
'Leave it, Paul. We can't change things.' Michael leant forward and studied the grass at his feet. 'How do you think I feel? I know Deiter was a bastard who still worshipped Hitler but …'
Paul shook his head from side to side, put his glass down by his feet and stood up. Looking down at Michael he said. 'My brain's driving me crazy, I can't stop thinking. If I hadn't been out of work I wouldn't have been down the labour exchange that day. Then I probably would never have met my teacher and both of *us* wouldn't both be in the shit.'
Michael swallowed then placed his empty glass on the ground. 'Drink up. I've had enough of all this. I'm going. They're both dead and nothing can alter that. Just thank your lucky stars we ain't been banged up for murder, or hanged in my case.'

Michael knocked on the glass, his boss tossed aside the newspaper he had been reading and beckoned him in.

'What's up Mike? Problems?'

'No, nothing like that. Just want to book a week of my holiday if that's OK.'

'There's the calendar, and here's a pencil. Help yourself. By the way, got a bloke coming in to work here on Saturday mornings. Says he'd like to learn the trade.'

'Saturdays? Why only Saturdays?'

'He's a copper at the moment but he wants to chuck it in and try something different. I ain't paying him, if that's what's worrying you.'

'Who said I was worried? Hope he plays cards, might take a bob or two off him in the tea-break.'

'Well, you'll soon get your chance, he's starting this week.'

Michael drew a moustache on the pretty model posing on the calendar, chose his dates and wrote his name across them. Tossing the pencil back onto the desk he turned and left. 'Cheers, boss. I suppose you want me to help this new bloke if he turns up, do you?'

'As long as he don't stop you working, yes, I'd appreciate it.'

'No trouble, but it'll only be this Saturday. Another week then I'm off, got a caravan up near Lowestoft. Should be a right laugh!'

'OK, Mike. Just let me know what you make of him. If he's hopeless, I'll tell him not to bother.'

'Will do, leave it to me.' *I'll make sure he's no bleedin' good. The last thing I need right now is a coppe looking over me shoulder. Christ, with him working here I'd have to think twice before I said a thing. No, he'll have to get the elbow a bit smartish.*

'Hello, Mike. We've met before. Remember me?'

'No, - I don't think so? - You the bloke that's with the police?'

'Yes, that's right. But we have met, you were at a dance above Burtons and I warned you about that German guy you were hanging around with.'

'*Oh, yeah,* now I remember. Bit dark in there, didn't recognise you. How's things? Boss says you want t try your luck in this game, that right?'

'As I told you that night, I'm bored with police work. I don't know what I want to do really. But I've got a motorbike and done a bit of work on it so I thought I'd give garage work a try. Nothing ventured, nothing gained as they say.'

'It's alright here, but the first thing you want to get is some overalls. This is a bit of a mucky job, that clobber of yours will get filthy.'

'Got you. I'll get some ASAP. How's your kraut friend? Not well, I hope.'

'Haven't you heard? He's dead. I thought you lot kept each other informed of things.'

'Dead! I can't believe it, big bloke like him. How did he die? An accident? Or did somebody murder him? That wouldn't surprise me.'

How did you guess! 'No. He came off his bike. We were racing and Deiter lost it on a bend.' Michael shrugged. 'He ain't the first and he won't be the last, not all the time we got bikes.'

'I'm not sorry, serves him right. The Germans killed my dad, so the more the merrier I say.'

'Come on, that's enough chat, it's time we got started.'

Michael pointed to an NSU moped. 'There you go. Start on that one. It's in for a de-coke. Simple job, don't know why the geezer didn't do it himself. Probably doesn't like to get his hands dirty.'

Leaving the newcomer to strip the bike, Michael began adjusting tappets beneath the bonnet of an Austin Seven. Minutes later he was interrupted by a tap on his shoulder.

'Sorry, Mike. Can I borrow an adjustable spanner; I'm having problems getting the exhaust off.'
'Help yourself, just dive in my toolbox, there's one in there somewhere. Do you need a hand?'
'Thanks, but no, I can do it. Just that none of the spanners seem to fit. Trust you to give me a kraut bike!'
Michael smiled and turned back to his work.
'Got one,' the newcomer said. 'I'll bring it straight back.'

Wiping his hands on some rag Michael dropped the bonnet and turned off the engine. As he did so he heard the sound of his spanner being returned to his box.
'There you go, Mike. I've wiped the muck off. It's a new one isn't it? I see you haven't got your initials on it like all your other tools.'
Michael swallowed and nodded. When the time came to clock off he did something out of the ordinary, he lashed his toolbox to the back of his bike and took it home.

Later, he rode to the common, parked beside the pond and carried the ex-army, khaki coloured burden to the edge of the water. He looked all around. Summoning all his strength he swung the box back and forth before releasing it to fly out into the depths. A column of water rose up before crashing back down, ripples spreading ever wider, his precious tools lost to sight. *Even if he puts two and two together, he can't prove nothing now! Trouble is; I don't know if the coppers even found my spanner that night, but it ain't worth taking chances.*
Next day he 'phoned in sick, rode into Woolwich and spent the day replacing the box and tools.

Chapter 15

Michael coasted to a stop and applied the handbrake.
'Are we there yet?' Tony quipped.
'Dad, I feel sick.' Roy did his best to mimic a young girl.
'Watch it you two, and watch your language, Paul's mum's sure to come out to wave him off.' Getting out of the car, Michael stared in amazement.
'You can take those back indoors, mate. I told you, *one* case each. This ain't a coach you know.'
'Sorry, Mike. Me mum did me packing, and she said I wouldn't take enough jumpers and things.'
'Well tell her to start again, tell her you don't need much. Bugger me, it's only for a week, we ain't emigrating.'
'OK, Mike. Won't be long. She's making me some sandwiches for the journey.'
'While you're about it, tell her to put the kettle on, might as well have a cuppa while we're waiting.'

Twenty minutes later the four of them struggled back into the car.
'Why have we got to have your case in the back, Mike? It's bad enough with our own,' Roy complained
'Oh, sorry, your majesty. Pass it over; I'm sure I'll be able to drive with it on my lap. Paul can tell me when to turn, that's if he can see over the top of his, which I doubt.'
'Yeah, right. OK. We'll shove it in between us then, Mike.'
'Silly pair of buggers. I know there ain't much room, but I can't help that.'
'I heard that Yarmouth's a fishing place but I didn't think we'd be travelling like sardines to get there.' Tony tried to light a cigarette while balancing a suitcase on his knees.
'Watch it! Here's your mum, Paul. Come to kiss you goodbye. Mind she don't spit on her hankie and wipe your face!'
'Leave it out, Roy. At least she let him come with us.' Tony held his cigarette down out of sight.
'You will look out for him, Michael, won't you.' Paul's mother smiled as she leant forward, allowing he dress to reveal just the hint of her breasts. 'I wish I was coming.'
Michael smiled at her choice of words. *I wish you were too!*. 'I'll keep on at him until he sends you a postcard Mrs P. And I'll make sure you get a stick of rock as soon as we get back.'
Her cheeks flushed, she stood back and waved.
'Bye, Paul. Be a good boy now.'
Paul slumped down in the front seat of the car. 'Get a move on, Mike! *Please!*'

'Look! Must be a café! Get ready to stop, Mike.' Paul pointed ahead at the large, hand painted sign board. 'Trukkers Rest, 2 miles.'
'Hope they can cook better than they can spell,' Michael sniffed.
'Why? What's up with it?'
'You doughnut. That ain't the way to spell truckers.'
'Might be someone's name.'
'Shut it, smart arse.'

Minutes later the solitary building appeared, delivery vans and a lorry parked out front. Good, bad or indifferent it was the only place to eat the gang had seen for over an hour. Michael swung off the road and stopped the car. Immediately, four bursting bladders struggled out and raced inside.

'... *saved her from the endless sleep!*' Roy and Tony snapped their fingers and sang along with Marty Wilde.

'Did you put any more on, Tony?' Roy asked; using his reflection in the window to check his shirt collar was still erect.

'Yeah, Pat Boone.'

Mike spat out a mouthful of tea. 'Pat Boone! You're having a laugh. Why'd you waste your money on him?'

'I like him, Mike. That's why. Thought our band might try a couple of slow songs some time. Rock 'n roll is our thing I know, but birds like the slushy stuff as well.'

'Worth a try, I suppose. But if you and the band get booed off, just remember it was your own great idea, OK? Now, get us another tea, and tell that bloke to put it in the cup this time, not slosh it in the saucer.'

'Blimey, who rattled your cage! Perhaps Pat Boone wasn't such a good idea after all.'

'No, but this trip was! Been brilliant so far hasn't it.' Michael lit a cigarette and blew smoke across the table.

'It has, but I was glad we stopped at this caff. That tea at Paul's house was definitely a mistake. We should have brought an empty bottle with us. What makes it worse is because it don't half rock in the back.'

'Well, swap with Paul then. You don't mind swapping with Tony, do you?'

'No, Mike. Let him have a go with that bloody choke. Made my fingers go numb. Look.'

'You big girls' blouse! Leave it to a man, ain't nothing to it.' Tony pushed his chair back and went to the counter.

'Get some more rolls, Tony. We can eat 'em on the way. And tell 'im not to be so stingy with the butter, it ain't still on ration.'

Tony raised two fingers by way of reply then ordered the teas and rolls.

'Come on you lot, push!'

'It's alright for you, Mike, you've only got to steer,' Roy gasped. Paul was red in the face, his back against the car, feet trying to get a purchase on the loose gravel, pushing hard. A bored delivery driver managed a smile as he sat watching their efforts through the grimy window of the café.

'Bloody car,' Tony managed to pant. 'Why didn't we get the coach?'

With a lurch the engine spluttered into life and the three pushers wrenched open the doors and scrambled in. 'Grab hold of that wire, Tony. Keep pulling it, keep it taut. I gotta take a look at that choke when we get there.'

'If we get there,' Paul said under his breath.

'It's a good motor, this is. Just got a few teething troubles that's all.'

'I think that bloke saw you coming.'

'Christ, cheer up Paul. I've had more fun at a funeral. What's up with you lately?' Roy glared at his friend, hunched up in the corner.

'Nothing. Keep your nose out.'

'Cheeky little sod. Stop the car, Mike. Let's have him out of here. Bloody misery.'

'Leave him, Roy. Probably the wrong time of the month.'

'And you've been a bit moody too, Mike. Don't know what's got into the pair of you lately. You ain't been the same since Deiter bought it. Miss him, do you?'

'Why don't you lot shut it. Open that cider you brought along, let's start enjoying ourselves. And keep the bottle to piss in. I don't want to have to stop again if I can help it.'

Tony began coughing, theatrically.

'Now what's up, cider gone down the wrong hole?' Michael took one hand of the wheel and began thumping him on the back.

'No! It's this bleeding smoke and fumes. And it's getting hotter and hotter. We'll be like a load of smoked kippers if it carries on like this!'

'Don't know how you can smell anything, what with all the smoke from our fags. Wind your window down, let some fresh air in.'

Tony used his free hand and began furiously turning the handle. The glass began to slide down then suddenly, with a thump, it disappeared into the body work of the door.

'That's it, you daft sod! Now you've buggered it!' Michael glared. 'That's another job I've got to do. Supposed to be a holiday, this is. I might as well have stayed at work.'

'You better hope it don't rain, Tony. Unless smoked kippers can swim of course!' Roy laughed.

'Ha, bleeding ha! Very funny. If wit was shit you'd be constipated,' Michael retorted. 'OK, you lot, sort yourselves out. It's not far now, about another hour I reckon.'

'Do what! We've been going for hours already!'

'You want to drive, Tony? All you gotta do is sit on your arse. My bleedin' arms are going to drop off soon.'

'No. You're doing a great job, well apart from backing into that geezer's wall. Couldn't he run! Though he was going to catch us.'

'If Tony here could read a map I wouldn't have had to turn like that. Tosser! And those coats blocking the back window don't help!'

'That wasn't my fault. The map was folded wrong.'

'Yeah, yeah, yeah. Of course it was. Funny that Paul never had any bother with it!'

The gang lapsed into silence, muscles ached, joints were cramped, boredom set in. Paul and Roy stared at the passing countryside without interest, Tony glared at the road, determined not to make another mistake. Each roadside sign was scrutinised and checked against the map. Finally, a sign proclaiming that the caravan site was only five miles away galvanised the youths back to life.

'Thank gawd! Let's hope there's a chippy nearby, I'm starving.'

'Yeah, me too, Tony. Sausage in batter and double chips. Handsome!' Roy wiped his lips with the back of his hand.

'First we gotta find the caravan, get the luggage sorted. Then we can go out and get some grub.'

'OK, Mike. Shan't be sorry to stretch me legs. What about you, Paul? You're a bit quiet ain't you?'

Paul nodded.

The car bumped over the ruts lining the gate way, the gate itself resting at a drunken angle, one end digging into the grass, soaking up moisture, slowly turning green. Weeds, thrusting through the bars, showed just how long one of the hinges had been broken.

'Christ, Mike! Slow down! I just hit my head on the roof.'

'Good. Might have knocked some sense into you then.'

Roy gingerly felt the top of his head. 'What's the van look like, Mike? There's dozens of 'em here.'

'It's red, cream and green. On the edge of the field nearest to the sea, Dodgy said. That's all I know.'

'Just drive round, Mike. We'll all keep a lookout. But watch the bleedin' bumps.'

Michael drove slowly around the field, passing many caravans that had the appearance of being abandoned, cracked windows, flat tyres and paintwork that had not seen a bucket of water for months.

'Hang about! There you go, that must be it over there. But it's a bit old ain't it?'

'Think you're right, Roy. Well spotted. Hang on I'll get as close as I can.'

The car doors opened and four weary travellers clambered out, suit cases dropped onto the grass and promptly sat on.

'Glad to get out of there, like a can of bloody pilchards in the back.' Roy rescued his cigarettes from his pocket and offered them around while Michael began struggling with a key in the lock of the caravan door

'Perhaps it ain't this one,' Paul suggested.

'Can you see another one painted like this? No, of cause you can't. It's got to be the right one.'

The door opened suddenly and Michael fell off the steps. 'Bollocks! That was my shin that was. Bloody good start to me holiday. Had to fight that bloody car all the way, had to listen to you lot all moanin' and now I've bashed me bleedin' leg. I'm pissed off!' Michael turned and kicked out at the car. He was ewarded by the sight of a wing mirror falling off in slow motion. 'Now look! Sodding car! I'll have Dodgy's bleedin' guts for garters when we get back.'

'Got to get back first,' Paul muttered under his breath.

Michael stopped rubbing his leg and picked up his suitcase.

Tony stepped toward the caravan. 'Come on; let's sort out who's sleeping where. I bags first pick.'

'You can bags what you like, mate. But I bought the car, I arranged the trip and I get first choice, *right!*

'OK, Mike. You're the boss. It's only fair I suppose. Let's hurry up though, I could eat a horse.'

A damp smell, the smell of wet washing waiting to be hung up to dry, met Michael inside the van. He wrinkled his nose. 'I think something's died in here.'

'No, it's probably just a pair of Noah's socks,' Paul laughed. 'This thing looks like it came out of the ark.'

Michael wrote his initials and the date in the mould above the fold down bed.

'That's not right, Mike. You should have put B.C. How we going to live in this wreck?'

'Good job my mum's not here. She's fussy she is. This grotty van would drive her nuts,' Paul said, using his handkerchief to wipe the draining board.

Michael snorted. 'Well I ain't turning back. I'm knackered from all that driving. We'll have to stop for one night at least. Paul, see what you can find then get this place cleaned up a bit.'

'Why me?'

'Why not?'

'There's no answer to that. But it don't seem right, or fair.'

'Neither's a blackman's left leg so just get on with it. We'll sort out who's sleeping where, get the beds made, then go out for something to eat.'

Tony called out from the back end of the van. 'Here, Mike, take a look. This sodding bed's only got one leg. It's fixed to the wall at the back, but someone's propped it up on house bricks! Paul better have it, he's the lightest.'

'Talking about bricks, where's the shit house?' Roy asked.

'There's a building in the middle of the field, I saw it as we drove in,' Michael said. 'That must be it. Anyway, there's no one much here is there. Just piss out the door, or around the back. But no big jobs, this place stinks enough already.'

Paul jammed the cupboard door back in place, its one remaining hinge not strong enough to do the work of two. 'That's one we can't use,' he muttered to himself. 'And these cushion covers won't be up to much by the time I've finished cleaning with them.'

'What a doss house. How much did we pay for this?'

'Too much, Roy. Don't worry I'll have a chat with Dodgy when we get back.'

The odour of cooking, wafting on the breeze, led the gang by their noses. A parody of the 'Bisto Kids,' but this time in Edwardian garb.

Tony ran a hand around his stomach. 'Crikey! Listen to my belly! It's growling.'

Roy pulled his shirt collar upright, spread his legs and sang. '*I just want to be your teddy bear.*'

'Silly sod! I'm starving!' Tony chased Roy down the road.

Rounding a corner the gang were rewarded by a small illuminated sign displaying a mermaid and the legend, "Bill's Plaice." It projected out over the pavement above a blue and white striped awning, faded by the sun and locked in position by two steel arms. Rust lines from the elbow joints stained the tired white paint.

The shops on either side were both closed, trading finished for the day. In the distance the local pier stood out against the darkness of the sea, pinpoints of light reflecting on the gentle waves lapping around its skeletal supports, a giant metal centipede venturing into the sea.

'Last one there's a poofter!' Roy shouted as he led the charge.

Inside the shop fly papers twisted lazily in the heat rising from vats of seething fat. Flies that had yet to become ensnared inspected jars of pickled onions, rested on the pile of newspapers, marched over the serving tongs. Moths danced around the fluorescent tube fixed to the ceiling, irresistibly drawn to the light much the same as customers were enticed by the smell of fish and chips.

A grimy poster, showing a tramp stealing a bottle of drink from a boy while he was fishing, was attempting to free itself from the tiled wall. The two cartoon characters were not aware of the large blue-bottle crawling across the advert for "Vimto."

'Oi! Pass the salt. And the vinegar. Come on, they're getting cold!'

'You want the vinegar, Roy?' Tony held it out but as his friend reached for it he withdrew his hand and squirted the plastic bottle. Roy leapt to one side, narrowly missing the stream of amber liquid.

'You stupid sod! You could have ruined me drape!'

'Can't you take a joke?' Tony laughed.

Seizing the salt off the counter, Roy began vigorously shaking it over Tony's hair. The small crystals stuck to the Brylcreem.

'You bastard, Roy! Watch the jacket! I'll get you for that!'

The man behind the counter stopped turning the wire basket of chips and looked up. 'Not in here you don't! Get out! All of you! And don't come back or I'll call the law! I *just knew* you Teds would be trouble. You hooligans are all the same.'

'Watch it mate, and get this pigsty cleaned up.' Michael tore open the newspaper parcel he was clutching and scattered the contents. The others looked at the mess the greasy chips made on the highly polished red tiled floor. Tony took a run at them, slid across the shop and out the open door, copied immediately by Michael and Roy. Paul grabbed the salt and vinegar and rushed after them.

The man raised the flap in the counter and began chasing them, his off white apron flapping around his knees. 'You lot! Stop! Come back!'

Michael turned to face him. A flick-knife snapped open; the blade glinting in the light from the shop window. 'What do you want, Grandad? Go back inside, if you know what's good for you.'

'Leave it out, Mike. We've had our fun. Let him go, he ain't done nothing.'

'You made me lose my supper.' Michael stepped toward the frightened shop keeper. 'I think you better get me some more, don't you?'

The man swallowed, 'Yes, yes of course. I'll get them straight away.' Michael followed him back inside and waited.

Swaggering back out he offered the huge parcel towards his mates, 'Help yourselves, lads. Seems he has a ton of cod he didn't want. Come on, get stuck in. Paul, chuck the salt and vinegar on. Loads of it!'

Laughing, the gang sauntered down the road toward the lights on the seafront.

'That's better, *now* the holiday's started. Let's see what the local crumpet's like. I've got me starter, now let's get to the main course.' Michael stuffed another handful of greasy chips into his mouth.

A few minutes later Roy stopped and motioned to the others. 'Quiet! Listen. There! That's "*Sweet Little Sixteen,*" must be a jukebox. Lead on, Mike, this place is getting better and better.'

After finishing their meals, hands were wiped with the outer newspaper wrapping; the inner white paper that had held the chips now translucent with grease. But transferring black print to flesh could hardly be called cleaning. Going to the side of the road, Tony pulled up a handful of grass and rubbed his hands, moderating the grimy look.

'Leave it, we can clean up in the first pub,' Michael said.

'Good idea, let's get going. The first pint ain't going to touch the sides.'

'Here! Look! Blimey, wonder what Deiter would have made of this!' Paul held out the crumpled front page he had been using to remove the grease from his hands. The smeared headlines were still legible, *"Colour: A bold plan. No ban at hotels or dances."*

'I'll be buggered if I know. Anyway, he seemed to have lost interest in that right wing mob he was with up London. Still, makes you think don't it. Where's it going to end?'

The sea washed over the pebbles producing a rhythmic sound as it tumbled them back and forth. Lights from the pier danced in the foam. Across the road a few of the many amusement arcades were open, beacons of light amongst their shuttered neighbours. The penny machines beckoned to the gang but lost out to a pub.

'There you go, *"The Ship Inn."* That one's open, come on, let's get a drink.' Tony quickened his pace.

'Three pints of lager, mate, two with lime and one without. Oh, and a coke.'
'Hold it, Roy. Make that four pints, two with and two without.' Michael yelled across the room.
'But you don't drink, Mike. I've ordered you your usual.'
'There's a first time for everything, ain't there? Bring 'em over to the table next to the window, I'm nipping in the gents to wash my hands. Coming, Paul, Tony?'

'Cheers! Here's to the first of many! We'll have a couple in here then go and find that jukebox we heard,' Michael sipped his beer, shuddered then took a gulp. 'Not bad. Not bad at all. I could get used to this. Roy, let's try yours, without the lime.'
Roy pushed his pint across the table. Michael took a swallow. 'Yeah. That's better, I'll finish mine but then I'm going to change to the same as you.'
'Yeah, OK Mike. But why are you starting to drink? I've never seen you have a beer before.' Paul frowned.
'It's a free country ain't it? Mind your own!' *Perhaps it's what I need to drown those bloody nightmares, something's got to. I need a good nights kip.*
'Cut it out you two, if we wanted to hear arguing we could have stayed at home. Don't know what's got into both of you. Used to be a laugh, all of us hanging about together.'
'You're right, Roy. Sorry. Here, get another round in, then we'll push off. Need to find some birds and some music. It's like a morgue in here.'

'This place is better! Sick some records on, Tony. I'll get the beers in.'
'Right you are, Mike. You seen them birds in the corner?'
Michael stepped to one side, staggered and lurched into a table. 'Oh yeah. Cor, they look tasty. Bring the drinks over; I'll start chatting 'em up.'
'Give us a hand, Paul. Roy, you better keep your eye on Mike. He don't look too steady on his pins.'
Michael made it to where the youngsters were sitting and slumped into a chair. The girls giggled. Placing his arms on the table he let his head drop.

'Well you were about as much use as a chocolate fireguard last night! God knows how we got you back. Them birds laughed their tits off, and no wonder!'
'Cheers, Roy. Now leave it out will yer.'
'How you feelin', Mike?'

'Bloody great, Paul, I don't think! Did any of you get anything?'

'No! Me and Tony tried, but nothing doing. They said they already had boyfriends.'

'Oh, never mind. We can try again tonight. Anyone got any aspirin? My bleedin' head's thumping.' Michael put a hand on his forehead. 'Now we know how far it is we'd better take the car. I probably won't drink so much next time, don't want brewers droop, do I? But first I gotta take a look at the jalopy, wasn't running that good, was it.'

'No, I said to Paul I thought it was a bit iffy. Anyway, while you was laying in me and Roy been walking round. There ain't *no* bugger here. Oh, tell a lie, there was one old geezer painting the steps outside his van.'

'What did you expect? It's out of season. Probably why it's quiet in town too.'

'Didn't think of that, Mike. But what do the locals do for a laugh, there ain't much here is there.'

'Well there's the pier, and …'

'And?'

'Oh, I don't know. But that boozer was OK, the one with the jukebox I mean. The other one was more like a rest home. Shove halfpenny, dominoes, cribbage and darts. They want to be careful; someone could have a heart attack with all that excitement!'

Tony smiled. 'You want a hand to look at the motor, Mike?'

'If you like, cheers mate.'

Michael wiped the dipstick on a rag then pushed it back in place. Withdrawing it again he glared. 'Christ! Look, Tony. Nothing! Wonder it didn't seize up! Blimey, all those pints of oil we bunged in on the way up here; now look. Empty!'

Tony wrestled with the cap on the radiator; but rust had made a home and was reluctant to give it up. Wrapping the rag around it he tried again and with a sudden jerk it came loose. Bending over the engine Tony stared into the radiator as intently as he had peered at "What the butler saw," on the pier.

'I know I don't know much about cars, Mike, but shouldn't there be water in here?'

'You're pulling my pisser ain't yer! Can't you see the level?'

'What level? I'm telling you it's as dry as a bone. And it stinks something chronic.'

'The tosser! He's sold me a right pig in a poke. Well that's it! I ain't letting him get away with it! This motor's going straight back, soon as we get home and I'll get my money back off him. Thieving git!'

'So what now, Mike?'

'Shove the rest of that can of oil in, but we'll have to get some more. I'll get the kettle out the van and top the water up. I can't believe it! He's supposed to be a mate of me dad, I mean uncle.'

'What? That bloke, Dodgy, he knows your dad does he?'

'No! I meant me uncle. Talking of uncle's did yours bring you them records?'

'Not yet. He's due back in port next week. Last time he was home he told me his mates were bringing them home but didn't think about me. Bloody typical, I might as well be the invisible bleedin' man for all the notice people take. As if I wouldn't want American rock 'n roll records!'

'Well, if he don't bring 'em you can always join the merchant navy. Then you can get some for all of us!'

'On your bike, I feel sick on the Woolwich ferry. All that warm sickly smell coming up from the engines. You can stick all that.'

'While I'm getting the water I'll get Paul out of his pit. Then we'll drive into town and get something to eat, that's if I fancy anything by then. Bloody lager!'

'Perhaps you should go back to drinking coke. Leave the beer to us men!'

'You cheeky bastard! I'll drink you under the table when I get the hang of it.' *At least getting pissed stopped the nightmares, best night's sleep I've had for ages! Apart from chucking up that is.*

The sea front was almost deserted when the gang arrived. A lone angler on the pier was checking his line while gulls stomped about the beach, inspecting the debris from the last tide. The tang of seaweed, left high and dry on the shingle, filled the air.

As the car braked to a stop clouds of black smoke drifted past. 'Christ! Is that us?'

'No, Paul. It's bloody rain clouds! Don't be so bleedin' daft, cause it's us. Where do you think all that sodding oil we keep putting in is going?'

'I don't know, Mike. You're the mechanic.'

'Right. And you're the grease monkey from now on. It's your job to check the oil and top it up every morning, understood?'

'Why me?'

'Cause I said so, besides you're the youngest.' The logic of this was lost on Paul but he knew better than to argue with Michael.

'When you two have finished, how about finding a café? Me and Tony are starving.'

'Come on then all of you; pile out. Let's let this place know we're here.'

As a few diehard holiday makers sauntered along the promenade, they tried not to make eye contact with the teddyboy gang strutting along toward them. National newspapers had recently been full of stories regarding this anti-social group of youngsters. Teenage killers, gang fights, people frightened to walk the streets at night, the reporters were having a field day. But, unknown to two of these high spirited youths, their companions deserved this public censure. And more, much more.

A light in a shop window at the entrance of the pier attracted Paul's attention. 'Hang on lads, just going to have a look. Coming?'

'No, leave it out. It's all tacky souvenir stuff.'

Paul ignored Tony's jibe and pushed the door open. The gang strolled on.

Inside, Paul stared all around the crowded shop. China cruets, plaster dogs, boxes and figurines made from sea shells. Comic postcards and paste jewellery. Brightly painted tin buckets sporting pictures of Mickey and Minnie Mouse, sat alongside others with brightly coloured fish and sea horses. Spades and rubber rings, dried starfish and nets for shrimping. Hand-held fishing lines wrapped round wooden frames came complete with a large lead weight and wire arms trailing barbed hooks.

'Good morning. Can I help you?' The woman with the florid face smiled.

'I'm looking for something for me mum.'

'Anything special, luvvy?'

'I don't know. What do you think she'd like?'

The woman bent down and withdrew a tray from the display cabinet.

'How about one of these? They're very popular.'

Paul picked up a piece of the imitation jewellery from the dusty mauve velvet. It sparkled as it caught the light from the shop window.

'Yes, I'll have this one, please.'

'Certainly, I think your mother will like this very much. Would you like a box for it? I usually charge extra but you can have one for nothing.' She smiled again. 'I'm sure she'll love it to bits. She's so lucky to have a thoughtful son like you.'

Paul frowned. *If only you knew!*

'Well, what did you buy?'

'Nothing.'

'Well it took you long enough. Come on, show us. Bet it's something soppy for Christine!'

'I told you, Roy. I didn't buy anything.'

'Then what's that bulge in your jacket? What you got? Let's have a look, lads.'

'Get off! Leave me alone! You'll rip something in a minute. - Alright, I give in. Here, this is what I bought.' Sheepishly, Paul pulled the box from the inside pocket of his jacket and opened it. Peeling back the cotton wool he held it out for inspection. His cheeks reddened.

'M-U-M! It's for his mum! Arrrgh, is diddums missing his mummy?'

Michael grabbed Roy's lapels and leant forward, 'Leave him alone!'
'OK, Mike, leave it out. It's only a bit of fun, mate.'
'Let's have a look, Paul. I won't laugh, honest.' Tony held out his hand.
Paul held out the box. The brooch, three letters joined together and set with imitation diamonds, sparkled in the sun. 'Nice. She'll like that. That'll suit your mum. Now, let's go and find a café. I'm starving.'

'This'll do, come on. Let's get some grub.' Pushing the door open, Roy stepped into the thin blue smoke of hot cooking fat and cigarettes joining forces to defeat the fresh sea air outside.
Michael took one breath, retched, and stepped back. 'Not for me, I'll sit on that wall and have a fag.'
'Please yourself, Mike. I'm having the works; fried bread, two eggs, two bacon and two sausages.'
Michael put a hand to his mouth and walked away, quickly. The others followed Roy inside while Paul added to the list. 'And beans! But no farting in the van tonight. It's bad enough already,'
'That was you, mate. I told you not to have that cider.'

The three lads sat at a table in the window. A young girl sashayed toward them, pouting her bright pink lips. Standing in the aisle she licked the end of her pencil, scribbled down their order, while nimbly avoiding groping hands.
When their meals arrived, Roy tipped sugar onto a slice of bread and margarine and bit into it with relish. The sound of teeth crunching made Paul shudder.
Picking up his knife and fork he sawed at the blackened sausage, popped a piece in his moth and chewed. And chewed. Removing the skin and gristle he placed it on the side of his plate and reached for his tea. The sight of red lipstick on the cup put him off. Standing up, he rummaged through his pockets.
'Pay for mine, Roy. I don't fancy it after all. Here's ten bob, make sure I get my change and don't give her a tip.'
'What's up? You was hungry a minute ago.'
'Nothing's up. Just going to sit with Mike if that's OK. What's it matter to you?'
'Now what have I said? Cor, you're touchy ain't yer? Go on, sod off, I'll finish yours.'
Paul made sure the door slammed behind him.

Outside, resting on the rust bubbled rail, Michael gazed out to sea. *Wonder how that copper is getting on. Why did he have to pick the same garage as me? Does he know about my spanner? Christ! What a mess!*
'Penny for 'em, Mike. What you thinking about?'
'Blimey, you made me jump. You finished already? That was quick.'
'I wasn't hungry after all. Thought I'd join you for a fag. Come on, tell us what's up.'
Michael offered his cigarette case. Paul took one, cupped his hands around it, shielding the flame of the match from the sea breeze. Not long ago he smoked to be part of the gang, now he depended on cigarettes to calm his nerves.
'Nothing. Just that this holiday ain't what I thought it would be.' Michael turned his head from the breeze and blew smoke. 'I was hoping we could get away from things, know what I mean?'
'Yeah. Me too.' Paul looked up and down the promenade. 'I been thinking of giving myself in. getting it over with. Trouble is me mum. She's only got me now.'
'Sorry, Paul. That's my fault, I know. But don't go to the coppers, let them go on thinking Deiter done it. What's done is done, can't change things now. Going on about it won't bring your teacher back. Dead is dead.'
'What about Deiter? How do *you* cope? He didn't really do anything. Well a bit of grievous bodily harm now and then, but he never killed anyone. Apart from when he was in that "Hitler Youth" thing of course.'
'I know that now, smart arse. But I thought he'd get us all hung the way he was carrying on. *And* I thought he murdered your teacher. You should have told me what you did a bit sooner, then Deiter would still be alive.'

'Yeah, go on! I suppose it's all my fault. Why didn't *you* tell me what *you* was planning? I would have told you then.'

'Shut it, here come the others!'

'Enjoy your breakfast? Why you wearing that egg on your face, Tony? Doing a bit of advertising for the caff?' Michael grinned, masking his true feelings.

Tony wiped his chin with his hand, then removed the handkerchief from his top pocket and wiped it once more. 'No. But as it happens I've got a date with the girl taking orders. So shove that in your pipe and smoke it!'

'Can't be very fussy up here. In fact, they must be desperate if it was that easy.'

'Yeah? Well let's see you get sorted then.'

'I might, if I can be bothered.'

'What's the matter then? Fallen in love with your wrist!'

Michael scrambled to his feet and began chasing Tony along the sea front, Roy and Paul joining in the fun.

Laughing loudly and a little out of breath, they stood looking around.

'Not much going on here, is there?' Paul said.

'There's more life in a tramp's vest!' Tony chimed in. 'Let's get in the motor and cruise about a bit. See if there's anyone under thirty in this place.'

'Yeah, right, Tony. Good idea.' Michael led the way back to the car. There was the usual tussle to avoid sitting up front and manually control the troublesome choke, but finally the youths settled down to see what the day would bring. Turning right, to enter the back streets of the town, Michael put his hand out the window and raised two fingers at the motorist behind. 'What's up with him? Must have got a new horn for Christmas. I signalled, what more does he want?'

'The signal arm is pointing left, Mike. We turned right.'

'Bollocks! I indicated right, I know I did. Anyway, what's it still sticking out for?'

'Must be stuck. Want me to see if I can pull it back down?'

'No! You'll snap the bloody thing off. Leave it. I'll pull over and see what the problem is.'

'Don't bother, mate,' a voice from the rear of the car said. 'It's just dropped off! Paul, you'll have to stick your arm out now whenever we go left! Mike will have to do it when we turn right.'

Michael hastily wound his window down. 'Oh, for Christ's sake! Now the bleedin' window handle's come off in me hand. How am I going to shut it? *Right,* that's it! Keep yer mince pies peeled for a phone box. I'm going to have a word or two with Dodgy!'

After stacking all his pennies, Michael lit a cigarette and leaned back against the side of the phone box. Inserting his finger he rotated the chrome dial, repeating the numbers out loud. Hearing the dialling tone he began inserting the coins. A voice spoke and Michael pushed button 'A.' The pennies dropped inside and Michael answered.

'Is Dodgy there? What? I dunno, my uncle Jim always calls him that. Anyway, is he there?' Michael began picking at the red paint around the windows.

'Is that you, Dodgy?'

'Right, now listen, mate! That bleedin' car you sold me is a pile of … '

'Bollocks! I work with bikes and cars and I'm telling you that this … '

'Will you shut up and listen!'

Michael's face reddened, he bunched his free hand into a fist and pounded it down onto the telephone directory. 'When we get back I'm bringing it straight over. I want my money back, and more, to pay for the oil we've had to buy.'

Outside the box the other three stood listening. 'Looks like there's going to be a bundle when we get back,' Roy grinned, throwing a punch at an invisible foe.

Michael kicked out at the phone box door, but crepe soles proved no match for the glass. The others lea against the kiosk, desperately trying to hear more of the row going on inside.

'Please yerself! But don't forget it's still yours legally.'

'No, I ain't sent the papers off, why should I? I ain't even got a licence. So it's still registered in your name.'

'Do what you like, you old fart! You're going to regret crossing me!'

Michael slammed the telephone down and pushed at the door. Turning, he pushed button 'B' and was rewarded by two pennies being returned. 'Tosser! If he reckons he's gonna dump that pile of shit onto me he's got another think coming!' He looked at his reflection then ran a comb through his hair. 'Come on, let's go and see what's in the next town, can't be any worse than this dump.'

The engine started at the third attempt, black smoke brought an equally black look from a young mothe pushing a pram. Indignantly she pulled the hood up, straightened the matching apron and tugged at the blankets covering her baby. Tony grasped the wire attached to the choke, coughed, and dabbed his eyes. 'It's getting worse, Mike. Blimey, how's it going to get us home?'
'Don't ask me. I'm not a bleedin' miracle worker. Have to make sure we've got plenty of oil and water, then it's fingers crossed.'

Despite the protestations of the car, Michael drove to the neighbouring town. Tony slumped down furth in the passenger seat, trying to avoid the fumes while clutching the twisted wire, pulling it when instructe to. As they entered the resort, Paul snorted. 'Needn't have bothered, Mike. Looks deader than the last place.'
'There's *got* to be something going on, it's *still* September. Look, there's some amusements and a coup of pubs.'
'Right, Tony. But are they open?'
'How do I know? Drive along a bit, Mike. Let's take a butchers.'

The family saloon drifted along the seafront, all eyes trying to spot somewhere to liven up the day.
Michael thumped the steering wheel. 'Nothing! Every bloody thing is shut! I ask you, what's the point? I'm starting to think we should head back home. I'm getting right brassed off.'
'It ain't that bad, let's give it another chance tonight, then decide. What do you reckon, Roy?'
'Yeah, Tony, it's a long way to come. Why give up? Might find some birds tonight. If you pulled that o in the café this morning there's gotta be a chance for us more handsome ones!'
'Dream on. You got to have a bit of finesse. Shoving your hand up her dress like that, what did you expect!'
'Bit of fin … bit of bloody what? Where d'you learn words like that? And what's it mean, bet you don't know.'
'Cause I do, but I ain't telling you. It's French.'
'The only French you know is French letters, and they don't make 'em small enough for you!'

'Girls! Girls! Cut it out! You can take each other on with powder puffs at ten paces when we get back. hoot out at the *not* so OK caravan corral!' For the first time that morning, Michael laughed.

Chapter 16

The owner of the garage uncrossed his legs and swung them down from the desk in front of him. 'Come in!' he called. Putting a newspaper down he picked up a grimy mug and swallowed the last of his tea.

'Sorry to disturb you, but I thought you might like to look at this before I start.'

'What is it? What's the problem.'

'It's the bike that German bloke brought in for repair. Something strange about it. I know I'm new to all this but I'd like your opinion.'

It was Saturday morning, and the young police officer training as a mechanic in an attempt to change his career path was the only person in the workshop, apart from the cleaner who was a distant relative of the garage owner and employed out of charity.

The title of cleaner was the only one he had ever won. Loser of too many fights in the ring he now lived in a world of his own. He turned up every Saturday, talked to his broom for hours on end, took it for rides in a wheelbarrow, and sometimes managed to do as he was asked. A harmless young man in his twenties, courted when his talents were in their ascendancy, cast aside when punches scrambled his brains.

'Seen better days, I'll give you that. But apart from the obvious, what's wrong?'

'The brakes. Look, the front one works, as best as you'd expect anyway. But the back one? It's not even trying. I know it sounds daft, but you could almost say that it's been slackened off. What do you think?'

Taking hold of the badly damaged motor bike the boss rocked it back and forth, applying and releasing the brakes. 'You're right. That shouldn't be like that. Leave it alone, I'll get in touch with the bloke who brought it in, perhaps he's been messing about with it. If not, something's wrong alright.'

'Good morning. My father read the note you left for me, he said you wanted to see me about my brother bike. Can it not be fixed?' Alfred's accent was still strong, despite living in England since being captured during the war.

'We just wanted to know if anyone had worked on this bike before you brought it in to us.'

'No. I was going to try, but I could not get any person to help me. Why is it that you ask this question?'

'Watch this.' The garage owner demonstrated the brakes. 'See? The back one doesn't do anything. It's a if your brother slackened it off by mistake.'

Alfred nodded his head from side to side, 'But it was repaired here, a head gasket I think. Michael would surely have tested the brakes. My brother rode it many times since; there could not have been anything wrong.'

Scratching the side of his head, Michael's employer stared at the machine. 'I think that as your brother was killed on this I had better inform the police of what we've found. I take it you have no objections?'

'Nein! I mean no. Certainly. If you think that the authorities should be informed...'

'OK. It's probably nothing, but you never know, it could be something serious. If it had been just an accident I wouldn't bother, but when someone's killed that's different. Leave it with me, I'll deal with it and then we can get on with the repairs.'

'Thank you. And thank you for your concern. I will wait to hear from you.'

The policeman rested the "sit up and beg" bike against the wall of the garage, bent down and removed his cycle clips, tugged at his uniform jacket and entered the workshop. Sparks from an enthusiastic mechanic wielding a hand grinder caused him to step back. The sight of the blue flame of a welding torch lancing through the smell of petrol made the hairs on the back of his neck rise. He decided to get this visit over as quickly as possible.

'Morning officer, I take it you're here to see the bike I reported.'

'Yes, sir. That's correct. Where is it?'

'Follow me; it's at the back of the workshop. Do you know much about motorbikes?'

'Yes, I've got one myself. The wife and I take it down to Hastings at the weekends, she loves the sidecar. But let's take a look at this one. I've been informed that you have some concern about it.'

'Only because it was involved in a fatality. I can't see why the brakes are like they are.'

The uniformed officer inspected the machine thoroughly before standing up and wiping his hands on a piece of rag. Ridges formed on his brow as he stared at the rear of the bike.

'It's a puzzle, I give you that. Whoever rode that stood no chance. That's *if* the brakes haven't been adjusted since the accident. I say *if* because I can't understand how it wasn't spotted at the time. It was logged as a traffic accident and would have been checked over. Most odd.'

'So what happens now?'

'Nothing. The state of the brakes doesn't change anything; they could have been altered by anyone at anytime. But *if* it was before the accident then we're looking at a possible suicide, or even murder. Then again, if it was afterwards …'

'It doesn't prove a thing. Yes, I see that. Sorry to have wasted your time officer, but I felt I should report it.'

'Quite right, sir. I have my doubts as to the truth of the matter, but it's too late to act now.'

'I take your point. Would you like some tea before you go?'

'Thanks, but no thanks. Got to go and investigate a possible body in the pond. A young lad reported seeing a man throwing a large box into the water, he's sure there was a body inside. Probably been watching Dixon of Dock Green, or reading too many Sexton Blake books, but we have to check.' He touched the edge of his helmet. 'I'll leave you to your work now. Thank you for informing us about the motorcycle. As I said, I think you're probably right, but that's unofficial. Good morning, sir.'

Dunking a biscuit in his tea the garage proprietor flicked through his paper and began studying the greyhound racing page. He was interrupted by the sound of something being leant against the corrugated iron clad wall. A knock on the office door was quickly followed by the policeman who had left minutes earlier.

'Sorry to interrupt, sir, but while I was cycling to the pond on the common I began thinking. I am of the opinion that the motorbike I inspected should be examined once more. Taking into account your concerns, and my own, I think it prudent to take the matter further.' A note book appeared and pencilled notes began being scribbled.

'Of course! I'll see that no one touches the machine until you take another look.'

'No, sir. I want the bike removed from here for a proper study to be carried out. Please make sure it remains exactly as it is until I can arrange collection. If you would give me the owner's address I will make sure he is kept informed.'

'As you wish. I'll put a tarpaulin over it and tell my mechanics not to touch it. Will there be anything else?'

Snapping his pad shut the policeman shook his head. 'No, sir. That will be all for now, thank you.' Smiling, he added, 'I'll get back to *the case of the body in the village pond!* now!'

Chapter 17

'Bit quiet in here ain't it, squire?'
The barman didn't answer and carried on pulling another pint.
'Oi, mate! Do you reckon that fish died of boredom,' Roy said, nodding toward a large pike, stuffed and mounted, glaring out of a glass case hanging high up on the wall behind the bar.
'There you go, four pints. You tearaways up from London?'
'Course! Don't think we'd live in this dead and alive hole do you? Got any crisps?'
'Four packets?'
'Yeah. And let's hope they've all got salt in. Make this beer taste better.'
'If you don't like …'
'Whoa! Hold your horses, mate. Just that it ain't what we're used to. But when in Rome as they say. Got a tray?'

Roy bounced back across the public bar balancing the drinks and crisps.
'What was he on about, Roy?' Paul asked, sipping his drink.
'Nothing much. The moustache suits you, Paul. Almost makes you look old enough to be in here.'
Paul dragged the back of his hand across his mouth, removing the white froth. 'That better?'
'Yeah. Right, Paul, I got the beers, so you can stick some records on.'
'Why me?'
'Just do what Roy said. And watch what you're doing, we don't want any rubbish.' Michael pushed a mixture of coins across the table.

Paul stood with legs astride in front of the jukebox, the coloured lights reflecting the sparkle of his suit. Running his finger down the play-list, he paused to select any of the music that appealed to him and knew would be acceptable to the others. The memory of the time he had become confused and played Alma Cogan still haunted him, the gang had taken great delight from his embarrassment.
He watched as the first record was selected from the mechanism, rotated through ninety degrees and laid onto the turntable. The Big Bopper was in full flow before he got back.

'OK?' he asked.
'Yep. What else did you pick?' Michael asked, clicking his fingers in time to the music.
'*Chantilly Lace* …'
'I can hear that you clown, what else?'
'*Pink Shoelaces* – and *Splish Splash* and … Oh, I can't remember the last one.'
'*Pink Shoelaces!* Where'd you drag that one up from?'
'It's good, Mike. Honest. Oh, blimey, the Big Bopper just reminded me, I promised me mum I'd phone her. Can we stop on the way back if we see a phone box?'
'Missing mummy?' Roy laughed. 'Need her to tuck you in at night?'
Paul crumpled his crisp packet and threw it at his friend. Roy raised a hand and batted it back.
'Still no crumpet then.' Tony tried to defuse what might lead to an escalation that could get them thrown out. 'Who's ready for another?'
'I'll get these,' Michael pushed down on the arms of the carver chair. 'It's my round.'
'Cheers, Mike. Get some more crisps will yer. Anyone would think we was still on rationing the stingy amount they put in these packets. Salt must be cheaper than spuds, I got three packets of that and a dozen crisps!'

'How do you know they wasn't a new type of crisp, blue ones?' Roy asked, smiling. 'Them scientist blokes are always mucking about with things.'

'Silly bugger! I hope you bite into one. That'll take that silly grin off your face.'

Michael hooked his thumbs into his belt and sauntered up to the bar.

'You lot here for the fight tonight?' The barman wiped his hands on a wet cloth that doubled as towel and mopping up rag.

'Four pints and four more crisps, squire. What fight?'

Feigning surprise, the man pushed a glass under the pump and began pulling the first drink.

'Thought that's what you Teds had come here for. Everyone knows the fishermen love a punch up when they get back from a trip.'

'Well, we never knew. How many of them?'

'Four or five usually. Tough lot. See that stain on the wall beside the jukebox? That's blood, that is. Seems they didn't like the music someone was playing. Four packets of crisps was it?'

'Yes,' Michael swallowed. 'What time they getting here?'

'Should be here by now, but perhaps they're not back yet, must still be out fishing. You lot'll have to come back tomorrow.'

'You can bet your life we will. We'll show your locals a thing or two.'

Michael took the drinks and turned to return to the others. *Bugger me, that lot sound like a lot of hard-nuts. Roy and Tony are OK, but I can't be sure of Paul. Don't like the sound of this.*

'What's that sour faced git on about this time, Mike?'

'Nothing. Come on, I've had enough of this place, get these down your necks and we'll try our luck somewhere else. Ain't nothing going on here.' Michael drained his drink and looked all around. 'Where do all the birds in this place hang out? And what happened to that one from the café, Tony? Thought you had a date?'

'No, just winding you up. Didn't fancy her at all. Anyway, you're right, let's go. Beer's like gnats piss, crisps have emigrated, only thing any good here is the music.'

'What about you, Roy? You coming?'

'Might as well. Like you say, ain't much here, is there.'

Michael thumped his glass down on the table. *Thank god! Let's get out of here in case them bloody fishermen DO turn up!* 'See you tomorrow, squire!' he shouted, 'Tell your mates we'll be back!'

'Do what, Mike? What you on about? What mates?'

'Keep yer beak out, Tony. Got nothing to do with you.'

'Hang onto your syrup mate, for god's sake. Can't say anything to you lately. You and Paul make a fine pair. Miserable buggers, both of you. What's up?'

'Just ain't sleeping much lately. Come on, I'll be alright. Let's go and get pissed.'

Michael slouched against the car door and turned the key.

'You sure you can drive, Mike? You've had a bit of a skin full.'

'You want to try?' He slurred.

'Don't be daft, you know none of us have ever driven a car.'

Reluctantly, the youths got in.

Michael belched, turned the key, and drove off along the seafront. Mounting the kerb, the car narrowly missed colliding into galvanized bins.

'Pull up, Mike. I'm getting out. They're dustbins, not bloody skittles!'

'What's up, Roy? Lost your bottle? I didn't hit 'em did I.'

The car slewed to a stop and Roy stepped out. 'You lot coming? I'm gonna walk back.'

'Bloody long way, mate. I dunno, what do you think, Paul?' Tony yawned.

'I don't mind walking. I want to find a phone box anyway. See you, Mike.'

'OK, if you two are going I might as well come with you.' Tony joined his friends on the pavement.

'Chicken! The bleedin' lot of yer!' Reaching across, Michael slammed the door and set off once more back toward the caravan site. The youths stood watching the car as it did a reasonable imitation of a kangaroo.

'Bugger that! He scared the shit outta me. What's got into him? He ain't usually like this.' Tony scratched his ear. 'Don't ask me, Roy. Come on, it's miles to get back. Let's get going.'

'How about thumbing a lift?' Paul asked.

'*How about thumbing a lift?*' Tony mimicked. 'Who the hell's going to pick us up? Paul, you really are complete twat sometimes! Would *you* give us a ride?'

'Suppose not. Just that these beetle crushers ain't meant for walking.'

'Don't worry; you should bounce along with soles like that. Bit like Roy does! Anyway, I thought you wanted to find a phone?'

Tony and Roy were asleep long before fumbling at the door announced Michael's arrival. He tripped on the step and fell into the caravan. 'Shit! - Shit! Shit!'

'That you, Mike?' Paul asked.

'No. It's bleedin' Father Christmas, who else you expecting?'

'No one. Sorry. Where you been?'

'Got lost didn't I. Bloody country roads, couldn't see a thing half the time. Lucky to get here at all. Now shut up and let's get some sleep.'

Michael climbed into bed, made an attempt to rescue the sheet and blankets that slid off, partly succeeded and fell asleep. The nightmare returned. But this time it was different. A motorbike, tumbling through the air, lost its rider. Deiter rose up, menacing and bloody. With him were men carrying fishing nets and armed with knives. Michael held out both hands to ward them off, but still they marched forward. Deiter, eyes and mouth leaking blood, reaching out for him. Frantically, Michael lashed out, his blows ineffective. Deiter was getting closer. He sat bolt upright, shouting, 'No! No! No!'

'Bugger me! What's going on? You OK, Mike?'

'What's up? What's all the bloody row for?'

'It's Mike. Must have been having a nightmare,' Paul answered the questions fired at Michael. *Blimey, no Mike as well! Thought it was only me.*

'Nothing. I'm OK. Just had too much booze. Get back to sleep.' Michael tugged at the bedclothes and tried once again to cover himself up. The sheets stuck to his body, a clammy shroud.

'What's the time?' Tony knuckled his eyes.

Roy peered at the luminous numerals of his watch beneath the covers. 'Half past soddin' four!'

Tony grunted something undiscernibly and turned to face the caravan wall.

'Do you want a cup of tea, Mike? I'll make you one if you like.'

'No thanks, Paul. Come on, let's all try to get some shuteye shall we.'

Roy's nostrils twitched as the smell of bad eggs permeated the van. His eyes opened and he leapt out of bed. 'Paul! Is that you again! You dirty little bugger!'

'Open the bloody door! Quick! We'll all be gassed. Chuck him out!'

'Good idea, Tony. Here, I'll give you a hand.'

'Leave him,' Michael mumbled as he tried to pull the blankets up around his nose.

But Roy and Tony were already dragging Paul from his bed. 'Out you come, you smelly little git!'

'Get his pyjama trousers off, Tony. I'll hang on to him.' Tony and Paul thrashed around in the narrow confines of the van. The dirty cups and plates in the sink and on the small draining board rattled as the van rocked from side to side.

'That's it! I've got 'em! Now, let's chuck him out!'

Opening the door they bundled Paul out onto the grass, then slammed it shut and turned the lock.

'Let me in! It's bloody freezing out here!' The van rocked again as Paul hammered with his fists. 'And there's someone coming, walking her dog.'

'Pack it in you lot. You'll have this thing over in a minute!'

'OK, Mike. Here, Tony, give me his trousers,' Roy winked, conspiratorially.

Dumping them on top of the mounting pile of washing up, he dribbled water from the kettle over the crotch, opened the window and tossed them out. 'Here you go, mate. Better get 'em on quick; that dog might like sausages. Sorry, I mean chipolatas!' Laughing, they watched Paul hopping from one foot to another, trying to get the wet garment on with one hand while hiding his embarrassment with the other.

'You sods! They're soaking! I'll catch a bleedin' cold next! Let me in!'

'Say, please.'

'Bugger off!'

'Suit yourself. Stick the kettle on, Tony. I fancy a nice cuppa.'

'Come on, Roy. Hurry up, that woman's getting nearer. Open the door.'

'Didn't hear the magic word.'

'PLEASE! Now open the friggin' door.'

Roy flicked the catch and let the door swing open. 'There you go, easy wasn't it?'

Paul shoved his way past Roy. Pulling the wet pyjama bottoms off, he grabbed his pants and trousers. Michael turned over in bed. 'Blimey, Paul, you been down the seafood stall already?'

''Cause I ain't. What are you on about?'

'That winkle. Anyone gotta pin?'

The fun over, the four friends dressed, then sat drinking tea. 'Bleedin' long walk last night, weren't it.' Roy glared at Michael as he spoke. 'My feet are still throbbing.'

'That was your choice. I got the motor back, didn't I? It's not my fault if you lot chickened out.'

'Well, at least I spoke to me mum.' Paul said. 'She was a bit pissed off about getting out of bed to answer the phone though.'

'She's lucky to have a phone; my old dear would have had to have legged it down the road to the phone box!' Tony laughed at the thought of his mother with her hair in curlers, clutching her winceyette nightdress, rushing down the street to answer the phone.

Michael stirred his tea. 'What did she have to say, Paul?'

'Said her and Christine was missing me. And something about dragging the pond for a body.'

'Do what? What pond? What you on about, you clown!'

'The pond on the common. She said that some kid saw someone throw a chest into the pond. Now the rozzers are looking for a body.'

Michael leant back against the wall of the caravan, the colour draining from his face. *They'll find my bleedin' tools, I know they will. Just my luck to have some nutter murder somebody and chuck the poor sod in the pond. Now what? Wait until they drag me toolbox out? Give myself up? If I do that they'll beat me up in the cells until I split on Paul. Bollocks! What a sodding mess.*

'You alright, Mike? Look like you seen a ghost.' Roy sounded concerned.

'Bit of a hangover, that's all.'

'Should have chucked it up, Tony did. You should have seen him, on his hands and knees in the gutter.'

'Leave it out, I feel rough enough already.' *Oh, bugger me; them fishermen'll be in the pub tonight. We're in for a right hiding. This holiday has been a right cock-up from the start. Wish we'd never come.* 'I been thinking. I've had a bellyful of this bloody place, nothing to do, no crumpet. Why don't we pack it in and go back home?'

'Yeah! Then I can see Christine.'

'Hang about, Mike. If we leave now, what we going to do when we get back? We booked a week off work, remember?'

'Go up the field by the allotments, it's the youth club tomorrow, and I think there's a dance in the village hall sometime this week. Always go there and liven things up a bit. And you can get some extra practise with your band, Roy.'

'Not much point, Tony and me are thinking of jacking it in. We ain't getting nowhere. No offence, Mike, but your uncle's talents seem to be more in chat up lines than getting bookings.'

Michael managed a smile. 'No change there then. He's always chasing bits of skirt, dunno how me aunt puts up with it.'

'You can talk! Blimey, you've had more birds than I've had hot dinners.'

'Jealous? Thought you rock 'n roll stars were fanny magnets! Bet Elvis don't go short. Anyway, what about it? We going back or staying? Let's have a vote. Hands up who wants to go.'

Paul's hand shot up. Tony and Roy lit cigarettes and finished their tea. 'What do you think, Roy? I don' really care. How about one more night down the pub, if it's no better then we pack it in.'

'No,' Michael butted in, 'I say we go this morning.' *Another night at that pub might be our last!*

'This morning! Christ, Mike, you're in a bleeding hurry. What's up? You run some poor bugger over la night?'

'Sod off! No, I was just thinking about Paul. He wants to get back to his girl, don't you, mate.'

'Yeah, that'd be great.' Paul fished in his trousers and produced a packet of Woodbines. Extracting one from the crumpled box, he straightened it and put it between his lips. 'Anyone got a match?'

'Yeah! Your face and my arse!' Tony grinned.

'Ha, bloody ha. Where'd you get that one from? Last years' Christmas crackers?'

'Come on you two. Make your minds up. Do we go, or stay.'

'I don't know. What do you think, Roy?'

'I think it's time I had one of me mum's corned-beef shepherd pies. I'm sick of the sight of chips. I'm ready to go.'

'Right! Get packed; let's get out of this place.'

Suitcases were stuffed with clean and dirty clothes mixed together. A scuffle ensued over the rights to t toilet while Roy cleaned his teeth over the sink. 'What we doing with all these plates?' he asked before spitting to clear his mouth.

'Just leave 'em. Let Dodgy clean up.'

'Suits me, Mike.'

Roy and Tony settled themselves in the back of the car with their cases.

'Everyone got all their bits? Right. Come on, Paul, pile in. Let's get this show on the road.'

'Hang on, Mike. There's oil all over the place this side. Look at it! Looks like we've struck oil! Just like James Dean in that film "Giant." We're rich!'

Michael joined Paul and stared at the grass, glistening in the weak sunlight.

'Right! You've had your laugh, Paul. Now fill it up. Christ knows how we're going to get this crate hom I'll *have* that bastard when we get back.'

Paul retrieved the large can of oil, lifted the bonnet and began pouring. 'Going to have to get some more Mike. There ain't much left.'

Michael kicked the car. 'That does it! Get out Roy, and you Tony. We're gonna teach Dodgy a lesson.' Dutifully, the lads in the back clambered back out.

'What you gonna do, Mike?'

'Come over here; get your shoulders against the van and push.'

'Do what? We can't move it, it'll tip it over.'

'Exactly! Now push.'

The caravan rocked but stayed put. 'Bugger! This bleedin' thing's heavy. We need something to lever it with.'

'I got an idea, Mike. Why not take the brick away from under the wheel on the other side? That way it'l be leaning a bit before we push.'

'Good one, Roy. You're not just a pretty face. Give him a hand, Paul.'

The two youths disappeared round the side of the van.

'It ain't going to budge!' a muffled voice called. 'We need help!'

Michael stormed round the caravan to where Roy and Paul were crouching down, red in the face, gripping the brick supporting the wheel. Taking his knife out he released the blade and stepped forward. A quick thrust and stale rubbery smelling air rushed out of the tyre. 'More than one way to skin a rabbit,' he smirked. 'Come on, get back round the front. It should go this time.'

All four youths placed their hands against the van and pushed. It moved but soon righted itself.
'Come on you bunch of pansies. Push!'
This time there was a lurch as the punctured tyre slid off the bricks and the van began to tip.
'Get your backs into it,' Michael gasped. 'It's going!'
With a crash the van toppled onto its side with the sound of breaking glass and crockery.
'Sort that out, Dodgy! Come on lads, get in the car. Time we had it on our toes.'
'Bugger me, Mike, what did we have to do that for? You'll be getting the dosh back for the car, why wreck his van? You never used to be like this, we've always liked a bit of fun but things seem to be different somehow.'
'Piss off, Tony, just leave me alone. And all of you; yell out if you see a garage, we gotta get more oil.'

Paul sniffed, his nose twitching from side to side. 'Mike, I can smell burning.'
'Cause you can, this bloody car burns oil faster than petrol. Let go of the choke wire, see if that helps.'
'There's smoke pouring in, worse than ever! It must be …' Paul's words were cut short as Michael pushed down hard on the brakes and swung the car to the right. Blue black clouds began billowing from beneath the bonnet, enveloping the car and everyone in it.
'Paul! Get your arse in gear! Get out! We're stuck in the back, let us out!'
While Paul helped his friends, Michael rushed to open the bonnet, then stood back as clouds of hot smoke greeted his efforts. He covered his nose and mouth with a handkerchief.
'What's up? We on fire?' Roy rubbed at his weeping eyes. 'Christ! We couldn't see a thing in there!'
'I know, I was driving, remember? Lucky I spotted this lay-by.'
Tony finished coughing and spat on the ground. 'What now, Mike? Can you fix it?'
'My guess is that we've dropped a piston. This old crate ain't going nowhere.'
'We'll I am,' Paul said. 'I need a leak. Be back in a minute.'
'I'll come with you; it's all that bloody tea we had.'
'Yeah. Me too, Roy.'
Paul shrugged. 'It's a free country, do what you like.'
Michael used his handkerchief to wipe the dipstick, pushed it back then pulled it out again. He examined it and threw it onto the ground. 'No bloody wonder! There's no soddin' oil. Bloody engine's probably locked solid. Right, that's the end of that and no mistake!'
Roy sauntered back, staring down at his trousers while trying to close the zip, a cigarette dangling from the corner of his mouth. 'Any luck?'
'Didn't you hear me? It's knackered, *kaput*, as Deiter would say. Get the cases out; we'll have to start walking. Try and grab a lift.'
'Four of us? A lorry might stop, I suppose.'
'Well it's that or spend the rest of our lives living here. Come on, give the others a shout. Sooner we get started the better.'
'What about the car, Mike?'
'Bollocks to the car. Let Dodgy sort it out. Unlucky for him it's still registered in his name.'
Roy laughed, 'Serve the bugger right.'
Paul appeared, being chased by Tony. 'What's up?' Michael asked. 'You two better save your energy; we're going to have to walk. The car's had it.'
'It's that silly sod,' Tony glared at Paul. 'He splashed me suedes. They better not mark or he'll owe me a new pair!'

'Leave it out you two. Grab your cases and let's get going. God knows how we're going to get home now.'

Half an hour later four dejected youths sat on their cases and swapped cigarettes. 'Bloody hell, Mike. How much further?' Tony rubbed the backs of his legs.

Michael began turning his pockets out. 'No, sorry, can't tell you. Must have dropped me crystal ball somewhere.'

'Very - bloody - funny!'

'Well how am I supposed to know?' Michael blew smoke down his nose. 'It could ... Hold on, what's that? Listen!'

'It's a train! There must be station somewhere. Come on, let's get going.'

'Hang about, Roy. Finish your fag first, it could be miles yet.'

Tony tossed his cigarette end to the ground and watched as a breeze blew it along, shedding sparks as it rolled on its way. 'What's going to happen to the motor, Mike?'

'Don't care, Tony. That's his problem now. If he wants it, he can come and get it.'

'Are you still going to sort him out? What with the caravan and everything.'

'No. I reckon we're quits now. Weren't really my dosh anyway, was it. Got enough problems, without giving the rozzers a chance to nick me. Right, let's crack on; see if we can find this bloody station.'

Gathering around the ticket office, they waited for someone to serve them. 'Come on!' Michael rapped the small counter. He was tired; it had been a long walk carrying luggage. Blisters were nothing new to him, but today they were not from working in the garage.

A flustered man appeared behind the glass partition, 'Sorry about that. We're one short today.'

Michael placed both hands on the counter, 'How much is a third class single to London, mate?'

The man ran his finger down a grimy page in his book; he knew the answer but always checked. Pride in his work prevented him from not doing so.

'How much!' Paul stepped back in surprise.

'You're *having* us on, mate. We only want to ride in it, not bloody buy it. You must think we just fell out of the trees.'

Roy moved closer to Michael, sensing trouble.

'What if we hang on the sides or ride on the roof like the cowboys do in films! How much then?' Tony taunted.

'The next train is due in two minutes. Do you want tickets or not. If you don't then I suggest you go away before I call the police.'

'Go and wait by the doors, I'll sort this.' Michael watched as the others made their way toward the platform. 'Give us two singles and two platform tickets, granddad. We'll toss for who goes and who stays, alright?'

Michael handed the tickets over to be clipped and the gang strolled onto the platform. With a great hiss of steam the train pulled in and the youths surged forward.

'Not yet!' Michael shouted. 'Move further down the platform.'

'Why?'

'Just do as I say will you! Move your arse toward the engine.'

Doing as he said they began running along the platform.

'This one do, Mike?'

'Yeah, Roy. Pile in.'

Yanking the carriage door open, Paul jumped into the corridor falling over the case he had just tossed on.

'Get in, you idiot! The train's going.' Roy threw his case on top of Paul and forced his way into the carriage followed by Tony. Michael swung his case aboard and joined the melee. A shout from the man at the station door rang out and he began to run down the platform.

'Oi! You lot! What do you think you're playing at!'

'Take no notice,' Michael panted, 'Shut the bloody door quick!'

The train began to move and Michael wiped his forehead with his handkerchief. 'Phew! That was close!'

'What's going on, Mike. What was that geezer on about?'

'These!' Michael grinned as he held out the tickets.

'There's only two! The others are only platform tickets! What happens when the inspector comes along?'

'Shut it, Paul. Ain't my fault if the bloke gave me the wrong ones, is it? He's probably on the fiddle, charged me for four and pocketed the dosh. Thieving git.'

'Did he really, Mike?' Roy asked.

'Well let's put it this way, the inspector's either going to believe me or he's going to have to start checking with that bloke in the ticket office. I don't think he'll bother, too much like hard work.' Michael stretched out his legs and put his tired feet on the seat opposite. 'Don't worry, I'll sort it. I always have, haven't I?'

Chapter 18

The four youths sprawled on the grass, tight trousers eased up to prevent the knees from bagging. Cigarette smoke drifted aimlessly. The sound of grasshoppers filled the evening air. Paul reached out slowly for one swinging on a stalk, but the insect launched itself into the air. High above their heads a hawk hovered, seeking its next meal. In the trees that bounded three sides of the field, bird song signalled the end of one more day.

'God, it's good to be back. You can stick Norfolk where the sun don't shine. I've never been so bored, and that's saying something!' Michael stretched his arms above his head.

'Yeah, me too! What's it like at your place, Mike? Seems to be a honey-pot for coppers lately. First you got that flat foot who had it in for Deiter working with you, then the law turned up and took Deiter's bike. Why'd they do that?' Roy flicked the ash off his cigarette. 'You want to watch it, there'll be fitting you up for the *headless body in the pond* mystery next.'

'What headless body? That's all a load of bollocks that is. All because some kid swears he saw a bloke toss a trunk with a body in it into the pond.' Michael blew smoke down his nostrils, 'Bloody hell, Roy, I couldn't even lift some of those birds we was dancing with up Burtons last night, let alone chuck 'em in the bleedin' pond. You'd have to be Charles Atlas or something.'

'Who's Charles Atlas?'

'That muscle building bloke on the back of magazines, Paul. He looks like he's got bigger tits than your Christine. The advert says, *You too can have a body like mine!* They show you someone getting sand kicked in their face on the beach, tell you to take his course and then you can fight back. But you don't need muscles when you've got one of these.' Michael flicked open his knife.

'Leave her out of this. You're only jealous. At least I've got a girl.'

'Yeah, one of Deiter's cast offs!' Tony jeered.

Paul got up, walked to the wire fence surrounding the allotments and leant against the wire. Cupping his hands, he lit another cigarette and watched as the sun sank down behind the trees.

'So what do you think the coppers will find? What do you think the nipper really saw?'

'How the hell should I know?' Michael struggled to his feet and walked across to join Paul.

'He's off again! Christ, you can't say anything to him lately. Come on, Tony. Let's go down to the swings, see if there's any talent about. And bring the cider, there's four pence back on that bottle.'

Michael and Paul watched until their friends were out of sight. Michael kicked at the dusty ground, half heartedly trying to dislodge a stone.

'What's up, Mike? They having a pop at you too?'

'No, not really. Just that they keep on about things. How do I know why the police took Deiter's bike? And I'll let you into a secret, you know that kid, the one that told the coppers about a body? Well it was probably *me* he saw. I chucked my tool box in the pond.'

'Why?'

'Oh, don't you start!' Michael scowled. 'Sorry, Paul. Didn't mean to jump down your throat. It's just that everything seems to be crowding in on me. You got a fag?' Paul hurriedly pulled a crumpled packet from his jacket and held them out.

'Lucky Strike? Didn't know you smoked these.'

'I don't, usually. I scrounged 'em off Tony. He says they're what James Dean smoked. You know what Tony's like.'

'I got rid of the tools because they all had my initials on them, remember? Anyway, when that copper came to work at the garage he noticed the one I'd replaced because I hadn't got round to marking it. Stood out like a sore thumb.'

'Oh, bugger! So if they find your gear they'll think it was you killed my teacher.'

'I don't know. There's never been anything in the papers about finding the spanner I lost that night. Could be that someone found it and took it.' Michael blew smoke through his nostrils. 'Anyway, the police ain't looking for anyone now. They believe Deiter did it. But them taking the bike away does worry me.'

'God, it's a mess. Seems to be one bloody thing after another. How did you explain your new tools?'

'When that smart arse copper who works at my place asked, I told him me uncle borrowed them. Told him that he was fixing his car and left my tools out overnight. Some one must have nicked them.'

'Clever! Especially as your uncle don't have a car.' Paul rummaged in his pockets. 'Got any dosh, Mike? I fancy a pint. Let's go down the King's Arms.'

'Cheeky bleeder! Go on then, let's drown our sorrows as they say. Tell you what, why don't we go back to your house afterwards? We could listen to Radio Luxembourg or perhaps your mum would like a game of cards, or something.'

'I dunno, she's been a bit ratty lately. Think her job's getting her down. She walks two miles each way usually. But sometimes the chauffer drops her off at the top of the road. I don't think she enjoys riding in a car, she looks all red in the face when she gets home.'

Michael frowned. 'I'll have a chat with her if you like, try and cheer her up. Probably missing your dad or something.' *Might be your dad, but it don't sound like she's missing 'something'. That randy bloody chauffer sounds as though he's got his feet under the table!*

'OK. Try if you like, anything to stop her keeping on at me. It's almost as if she knows ...'

'Don't start going down that road, it'll do your head in. *No one knows.* It's finished. We've just got to try and forget it ever happened. Come on, let's get down the boozer.'

'Hang on, mate. You've got something crawling up your back.'

Michael twisted his head around trying to see over his shoulder.

'Stand still a minute. - There, got it! It's one of them blood sucker things. I'll chuck it over the allotment, let them have it.'

'Cheers, Paul. Come on. Let's get that drink.'

'Wotcha, Brian. Still watering the beer?'

'Cheeky sod, Mike. Ain't seen you lot for a while, been in nick?'

'No. But we might as well have been. We went to Norfolk.'

'Oh.' Brian nodded and picked up a glass. 'What you having? Coke?'

'No. Beer, but it'll have to be two pints of mild. I'm a bit strapped at the moment.'

'Since when did you start drinking beer?' Brian shrugged. 'Anyway, have what you like, pay me next time. Now, what's it to be?'

'Lager please. Cheers, Brian. You're alright, you are.'

Sitting in the corner of the public bar, Michael and Paul sipped their drinks. 'What's this chauffer geezer like, Paul? Have you seen him, you know, close up I mean.'

'Just an old guy, must be at least forty. Wears a smart uniform and a peaked cap, looks full of himself. I saw him tap me mum on her arse one day, expected her to slap him one but she didn't.'

Michael's eyes narrowed; reaching into his pocket he fondled his knife. *I think it's time I had a word with him.*

'Fancy a short, Paul? Rum and black, gin and lime or a whisky mac? You lot got through enough up Norfolk.'

'I don't mind. Whatever you're having. I'll have the same.'

'Two rum and blacks, Brian. Put 'em on the slate. Do you want a drink?'

'Cheers, Mike. I'll have half of Toby, if that's alright.'

'Course it is, give us two halves of that as well. Never tried Toby. Must be good if you drink it.'

'You sure? Not riding that bike of yours are you?'

'No. We've been up the field, you know, the one up by the allotment. We're walking.'
'That's alright then. Don't want anyone else getting killed, do we.'
'No, we don't.' Michael gulped. 'Got a tray for this lot?'

'Blimey, Mike. More beer? And shorts. You trying to get pissed?'
'Get it down you, help you sleep tonight.'
'If you say so, I could do with a decent night. I haven't told anyone, not even me mum, but I get nightmares. Horrible ones.'
'You're not the only one, Paul. Come on, let's get these drunk then go and cheer your mum up.'

The sound of motorbikes outside was swiftly followed by two youths in black leather entering the saloon bar. Michael put his glass down and listened to them as they spoke with the barman who seemed to be reluctant to serve the newcomers.
'I *know* that voice. Stay here, Paul. I'm going next door to see what's going on.'

Entering the saloon Michael saw the new arrivals, fur lined flying boots resting on the brass foot rail, scruffy jackets emblazoned with motives that he knew well, CHIEFTAINS.
'Everything OK, Brian?'
As he spoke the two turned to face him.
'Wotcha, mate. Ain't seen you for yonks. Where you been hiding?'
'Nowhere. Been crumpet hunting up Norfolk way.'
Michael flinched back from the smell of bad breath as the larger of the two laughed. 'Wasting your time up there. You should've been there last week; I shagged this bird on a table round the back of a pub. She loved it, dirty bitch!'
'Less of that in here.' Brian eyed the two strangers as he vigorously polished a glass. 'This is the saloon bar. People come in here for a bit of peace and quiet.'
'These two are OK, Brian. They won't give you any bother, *will* you.'
'No mate, just called in for a pint, then we're off home. You and your mates going to join us down at Sheppy sometime?'
'Why not? How about this weekend?'
'Can't. Big bundle arranged with some lads from Charlton. We're meeting 'em on Woolwich common. Fancy it? Use what you like, coshes, chains, knives, razors, anything. We done 'em good last time so they're looking for revenge. Going to be a good one.'
'No, we'll give that a miss. Don't know the Charlton lot. How about the week after?'
'Yeah, that'll do us. Meet us at that coffee bar you use, Bentini's? Three o'clock on the Saturday, OK? Should be a right laugh.'
'We'll be there. Now, me and me mate are off. Do us a favour, go in the public bar. Make poor old Brian here happy.'
'Why not? Anything to oblige. I can see this is your local, don't want to queer your pitch.'
'Cheers. Brian, their first drinks are on me. See yer.'
'Right, Mike. Be good!'

'Hello, Mrs. P. Got the kettle on?'
'It's just boiled, Michael. I'm making myself a cocoa and then going to bed, got to be up bright and early.'
'That's a shame; we thought you might like a game of cards. Didn't we, Paul?'
'Yes, but I don't feel too good, Mike. Think I'm going to be sick. I'll see you tomorrow if ...' Paul made a dash for the stairs; the sound of retching from the bathroom filled the hallway.

'Are you alright, my darling? Try not to make a mess; I've just cleaned up there.'

'That's a shame, it's a bit early to go home yet, my dad will still be up. Don't need another row.'

'You can have a quick cuppa if you like. Don't think we'll be seeing Paul tonight. Pity, I would have enjoyed a game. You should have got here sooner. Listen to him, what on earth have you been up to?'

'Nothing. Must be something he ate.' Michael reached out and embraced her. 'Been a while, do you still fancy me?'

'Yes. Of course I do. But behave yourself, Paul's upstairs remember.'

'Leave it to me.' Michael winked and walked into the hall.

'See you, Paul. Bye Mrs. P.' Michael's farewells echoed in the confines of the narrow staircase.

Michael lowered his voice and leant forward. 'Shut the door so he thinks I've gone. Leave it a couple of minutes then open it again.' He kissed his fingers and touched them to her lips.

Standing outside Michael lit a cigarette and waited. The hall light went out and he wondered if she had changed her mind. The click of the door opening sent his heart racing. Throwing the glowing stub to the floor he ground it out with the sole of his shoe.

'Get in quick, and be quiet. I think Paul's gone to bed, he did sound bad. Anyway, come on, in the front room.'

'After you,' Michael whispered. After carefully closing the front room door, Paul's mother switched on the light. Michael blinked. Putting his arms around her waist he rubbed up against her. Snuggling into him, she offered up her mouth. Soon they were tearing at each others clothes.

'Michael, oh, Michael. I need you so much!'

'Just as well I brought this stick of rock back for you then!'

'Oh, Michael!'

Next morning light rain greeted her as she opened the door. 'Oh dear, I'm going to get wet. Where's that headscarf? And my umbrella?' Frantically she searched the coat-stand, found the square of paisley print, carefully arranged it over her hair and began tying it under her chin.

'Paul! Are you awake, darling? Have you seen the umbrella?'

A tired voice called back, 'Yes, mum. It's in the outside toilet. You put it out there to dry, remember?'

'Oh, yes. Thank you, dear. Sorry if I woke you. I'm just off to work, do me a favour, pull the front room curtains will you. I'm late already.'

'Yes, mum. Bye.' Paul's eyes closed at the same time as the front door.

The tall clock in the hall struck ten. Paul turned over, pulling the blankets up over his head, trying to forget. It had been the usual nightmare, the monster, arms outstretched, chasing him. He was running on the spot, getting nowhere, the thing-from-hell getting closer. He could see the wounds in its body. It was trying to speak but the words were lost, bubbling through blood pouring from its mouth. Paul soon realized he would not be able to get back to sleep, even though he was very tired.

Partly dressed, he hopped around on the landing trying to put his socks on, glaring back into his bedroom. Then, clutching his trousers, he made his way down the stairs. In the kitchen he finished dressing while waiting for the kettle to boil. Lighting a cigarette from the gas stove he inhaled deeply. *How much longer's this going to go on? I can't hack this much more.*

The cup of tea calmed him down a little as he sat, idly dunking biscuits. A ginger and white cat strolled in through the open door. Tail erect, it marched straight over to Paul and mewed. 'Wotcha, puss. I know you, you're from next door. What you after? Want some tea?' Paul poured a little from his cup into the saucer, added more milk and put it down on the floor. The cat lapped at it for a while then turned its back on Paul and left.

Putting the cup and saucer into the sink for his mother to wash up he remembered the curtains.

Opening the front room door he stepped into the gloom and tripped over a cushion. Picking it up, he tossed it onto the settee. After tugging the curtains back into place he turned and saw another cushion on the floor.

'What's being going on? We don't use this room much, who's been mucking about?'

Stooping to retrieve it, he saw a torn piece of paper, mauve and green. Immediately he recognised it, O: the same brand of contraceptive that he bought at the barbers.

'Not again, mum! Who was it this time!' Tears trickled down his cheeks as recent memories flooded back. Then he saw something else and bent down again. 'Half a dollar! Blimey, she could do better than that up Piccadilly. Still, it'll buy a couple of pints. Cheers, mum!'

Chapter 19

Paul read the card once more. Shaking his head he reached back across the counter to hand it back. The man in the pinstripe suit declined it.

'It's up to you, son. Either take the job or lose your money. It's your choice.' He began rifling through a pile of reference cards, ignoring Paul.

'Give us it here then. Slave labour I call it. Ought to be a law about paying peanuts. I seen this geezer, he's got a car he has. Now I got to go and earn the petrol for it I suppose.'

'A car is something you can afford only when you work for a living. Hanging about in coffee bars and such never made anyone rich.'

Paul sullenly accepted the card the man held out. *I hate this bloody labour exchange.* Ignoring the man's protest he lit a cigarette and blew smoke contemptuously toward the ceiling. 'What about Cliff Richard?'

'Who?'

'Oh, I give up. You old ones just don't get it, do you.'

Outside Paul glanced at the address he had been given. 'Suppose I'll have to. Funny, looks like I'm going to be painting and decorating after all! Just like I told mum!'

Paul walked away from the imposing building, its architectural features lost on him. Ivy clinging to its brickwork softened the austere façade. Trees, lining the pathway back to the road, competed with the height of the structure, but the tall chimneys on the roof outreached them.

Buses were lined up in a lay-by on the opposite of the road, drivers and conductors taking their break from the repetitive journeys. On the one nearest to him the conductor was busily winding the destination board; Paul watched as the place names and numbers changed.

'The 161, that goes to New Eltham, I can walk it from there. But it's a bit late now; I'll leave it till the morning. Might as well cut across the common, have a cup of tea and a roll in the tea shop. I've done enough today.'

His mind made up, he entered the cool of the woods. Masses of ferns surrounded silver birch trees that cast shadows over a dusty path. Pebbles, polished by countless feet, shone through the mixture of earth and leaf mould. Dank, woodland smells floated on the air. Paul pulled a packet from his pocket and shook it.

'Bugger! That's me last fag. Lucky I found that half a crown this morning. I'll have to stop at the tobacconists and get some more.'

Leaving the shade of the trees, Paul stood at the side of the main road waiting for a solitary bus to pass before crossing. Gazing across the grassy area on the other side of the road Paul's attention was drawn toward a policeman in the distance, standing beside the pond. Curiosity got the better of him and when the road was clear he crossed and made his way over to see what was going on.

The man in uniform stood on the bank of the pond, his bicycle resting precariously against a young tree that reached out across the water. As Paul approached he saw the man whirl something round his head, the strange action followed by a large splash. Paul watched, fascinated, as the man hauled on the rope, struggling with something he had caught. *Blimey! He's found the body!*

The grappling hook reached the bank and the police officer bent down. Huge clumps of weed, dripping mud, were pulled off and tossed back. Again the rope was twirled and the four pronged hook sailed out across the pond. This time it bounced off something before settling into the depths. Eagerly the rope was pulled taut.

'Got something this time!'

Paul held his breath as the contest continued, water sprang from the rope each time tension was applied, circles rippled across the pond as the droplets returned to their home. The police man stopped pulling, wiped his brow with one hand then resumed the battle. Finally, a rusty bicycle broke the surface. Paul laughed.

'Nearly as good as your one,' he mocked, before running off.

Outside the tobacconist shop Paul stood studying the display in the window. He admired the pipes carve with figures, human and animal, stared at long pipes and short pipes, both straight and curved. On the larg display area at the base of the window, pipe cleaners, lighters, jars of tobacco, boxes of cigars and cardboard cut-outs advertising cigarettes competed for attention.

A bell attached to a coiled spring jangled as Paul pushed open the door. He stood still and breathed in deeply. The combined aromas were delightful. Approaching the counter, with its glass top and front, Paul became distracted by yet another collection of smoking paraphernalia.

'Can I help you, lad?'

'Oh, yes please. Have you got any loose fa … sorry, cigarettes? I've left most of my money at home.' *Anyway, they'll be cheaper when I see Mike, that's if he's been around his uncle's place. AND I better ask Mike for some more lolly.*

'I'm sorry, we do not sell single cigarettes. Perhaps you should try the sweetshop at the top of the hill; I've heard he sells them from beneath the counter. Something ought to be done about it if you ask me. He sells them to children under sixteen. He should be prosecuted if you ask me.'

Paul guessed the man was about to launch into a tirade.

'I can't be bothered to walk that far. Give me ten Batchelors, please.'

'Certainly. Thank you for your custom.' The man slammed the till shut as Paul left the shop.

I give up, I go in for a few fags and get me lugholes bashed! What's up with all these old farts anyway?

Paul poured two cups of tea. 'Thank you, darling. How was work today?'

'I didn't go. That job wasn't any good. But don't worry, I've got another one. Supposed to start next week, but I persuaded the bloke down the labour to arrange for me to start tomorrow.'

'Oh! You're such a good boy. Well done! I'm so proud of you.' She searched through her purse. 'There you are, five shillings. Now you can go out with your friends tonight. Bring Michael back if you like; I'll make us all a nice cup of cocoa.'

Michael! Of course! I bet it was him last night! The sod, he promised he wouldn't do it again.

'No, it's OK. We're going to the bughutch, there's two cowboy films on, then I'll need an early night. Don't want to be late for my first day, do I?'

'No, dear. Of course not.' She tried to hide the disappointment in her voice.

'How did you get on, mum? Did you get to ride in that posh car again?'

'No, Bert's … I mean the chauffer, is in London this week. Business meetings I think.'

'Oh, it's alright for some. I have to walk everywhere, apart from when Mike gives me a lift on his bike.'

'Never mind, my darling. If you start saving, you'll have enough for a motorbike yourself by the time you're old enough to ride one.'

'I could get one now! Mike's uncle's bound to know someone.'

'No! I'm not having you riding a bike without it being legal and above board. You'll just have to wait.'

'But, Mum …'

'No, I said no, and that's final. Now, pass your mum a biscuit, there's a dear.'

Paul sat on an upturned bucket staring at the red raw fingertips clutching his sandwich. A wet border around the bare floor boards marked his progress. In one corner a pile of shredded wallpaper oozed milky water. Chewing the bread and fish paste he surveyed his work.

'Bugger me. This'll take for ever. Painting and decorating, that geezer down the labour said. Not, wear your bloody fingers down to the bone. I'd like to see him try it instead of standing behind a counter in his bloody lah – di - dah suit handing out cards.'

The door opened, its surface reduced to a patchwork of dull and bright varnish.

'Hello, lad. How you getting on? Nearly finished, I hope. We haven't got all day you know.'

'No, Mr Smith. I've nearly finished rubbing the paintwork down. It's hard work though.'

'Hard work?' He wiped hands covered in whitewash down his paint spattered boiler suit. 'Hard work? You youngsters wouldn't know a hard days work if it bit you on the arse! I don't know why they keep sending me kids. There must be proper tradesmen out there somewhere.'

Paul gave him a sullen look. *I know why; it's the bleedin' money you pay.*

'Well, hurry up and finish that sandwich, you've got work to do.' He sniffed. 'God help us, it stinks in here, what you got; sardines?'

Paul nodded and chewed, washed it down with a mouthful of water from the chipped enamel mug and stood up.

'Soon have this done, Mr Smith. Don't suppose there's any sticky plasters, is there?'

The man raised his eyebrows and shook his head. 'Give me strength,' he muttered.

Paul scuffed his shoes in an attempt to rid them of pieces of wet wallpaper, gave up and sank to his knees. Wrapping fresh sandpaper around a block of wood he began rubbing at the layers of paint on the skirting boards.

'Bloody work! Who invented it? I should be painting master pieces, not bloody council houses. Mr Attwood said I was good and he should know. He was a bloody good art teacher, he was.' Paul's eyes welled up; a tear trickled down his cheek. 'Bollocks! Why did we do it?'

The door opened again.

'Do what, lad? What are you on about? It's not healthy to talk to yourself, first sign of madness that is. Anyway, here you are. Bring your own tomorrow.' Mr Smith held out a strip of plasters, dark red fingerprints on some told their own story.

'Cor, you made me jump, never heard you come back in. Thanks, Mr Smith, I'll ask me mum for some.'

'When you've finished that you can start the undercoat. Then it's the cream for this room, I'll fetch the cans for you.'

Paul put plasters on two of the tenderest fingers and began rubbing again. Before long one of the plasters came loose.

'Fat lot of good that did!' Paul rose to his feet and crossed to his jacket lying on the floor. Lighting a cigarette he gazed up at the freshly papered ceiling, one of the wet patches resembled a dog; another looked like a hen or cockerel.

'You can put that out! You haven't got time to smoke, there's work to do. Get on with it. And stop staring up at the ceiling, that's a job for tarts!' He massaged the white band of skin on one finger and scowled.

'Yes, Mr Smith.' Paul dropped the cigarette and ground it out. *Yes, Mr Smith. No, Mr Smith. Three bags full, Mr Smith! What am I doing here? Mum earns enough to feed us and pay the bills. And I'm alright as long as our money holds out. This work lark will be the death of me.*

'Here's the paint, be sure to stir it really well. I don't want to see any lumps in it. Oh, and when you finish, before you go home, put the lid back on and turn the can over. That way the skin will be at the bottom when you open it again.'

'OK, I'll try and remember.'

Dropping the piece of wood to the floor, Paul straightened his back. 'Oooh! Christ that hurts. And me knees, I know what me mum feels like now when she scrubs the lino.'

Looking at the tins of paint, he scratched his head. 'There's got to be a short cut, can't face going round this room two or three times.' Using a screwdriver he levered the lids off both tins and tipped the paint into the bucket he had been sitting on. After thoroughly mixing it he began the laborious job of painting, using a newspaper to cover the floor where he was working. Paul kept at it. When it was time to go home he put the brush in a jam jar full of turpentine, gave his hands a quick wipe with a rag dipped in the same jar and looked around the room.

'Get that door varnished tomorrow and that's me done. All ready for the paperhanger.'

Chapter 19

The throaty sound of the Road Rocket reverberated from the walls of houses as Michael tore through the estate. A man pushing a lawnmower glanced up as Michael shot past. A shake of the head was followed by a suck on his pipe before the click clack of blades cutting grass resumed.

Outside Paul's house Michael sat astride his machine and revved the engine. The noise brought an immediate response.

'Leave it out, Mike! Turn it off! – That's better. Want a cuppa?'

'Nothanks, Paul. I'm meeting the others at Ma's, you coming?'

'Can't. I'm seeing Christine tonight.'

'That's OK. I think Roy's bringing Elaine. Why don't you join us?'

'Where?'

'Ma's, I said didn't I? There ain't much else to do, is there. Come on the bus, I'll see you there.'

Michael kicked his bike back into life and roared away.

'Lucky bugger! You wait until I get a bike!' Paul kicked the empty milk bottles off the polished red step before stepping back into the house.

Michael carried a bacon roll in one hand and a mug of tea in the other. As he reached the top of the stairs he licked at the tomato sauce leaking through his fingers and waited for Roy to vacate the larger of the armchairs.

'Hello, Michael.'

'Wotcha, Elaine. Didn't see you there. How's he treating you?'

Elaine dropped her gaze. Michael's grin did something to her, something delicious, something she knew she shouldn't like.

'Fine.' She shifted position, tugging at the hem of her dress.

'That's alright then. Anyone got any ideas where to go tonight?'

'There's a dance at the church hall, Ma said. It's not far. Why don't we give it a go?' Tony dropped his feet from the coffee table to let Michael pass.

'A dance at the church hall! You're pulling my pi … leg aren't you?'

Elaine blushed.

'Could be alright,' she said. 'They've got a band, it's not just records.'

'Oh well, why didn't you say? A band! This place is really getting on the map.'

'No need to be sarcastic, Mike. Elaine was only trying to help.'

'I didn't mean it. Finish your drinks and then we'll go and liven the place up for them.' Michael put his feet up on the low table exposing bright pink fluorescent socks with black music notes.

Roy clapped a hand over his eyes, 'Ye gods, Mike! You got a license to wear them in public?'

He ducked to avoid the half of a roll aimed his way.

'Cheeky so and so!'

Back downstairs, Michael took his change and funnelled it into his trouser pocket. 'Do us a favour, Ma. If Paul turns up, tell him we've gone to the dance. Cheers!'

The vicar beamed, 'Good evening, please come in. Nice to see you all.'

'How much is it, mate?' Michael struggled with a pocket in his tight trousers.

'There's no charge, just a donation please.'

'Oh, right. There you go then. Come on you lot, I've paid for all of us.'

The vicar tried hard to maintain his smile as he watched the small change drop into the bucket. 'Thank you. Enjoy the dance.' *Hard to think of these tearaways as God's children, but I mustn't judge a book by cover.*

A waltz greeted the gang as they entered the hall. A quick glance around confirmed Michael's worst fears. Women, faces heavily made up to hide the ravages of time, sat on stackable chairs drinking tea, little fingers crooked politely. Men, still wearing the suits they were issued with when they were demobbed at the end of the war, lounged against the walls. Two couples gamely circled the dance floor. Red, white and blue bunting along with a picture of the Queen decorated the hall. The musty smell of tired floorboards was fast becoming masked by the cigar being smoked by a man in a double breasted suit.

Michael turned to his friends.

'Oh - my - gawd. Look at this! It's grab a granny night! After you, Tony. Help yourself!'

Tony held his hand to shield his mouth, 'Bollocks!' he said, quietly.

Elaine glared at Tony. 'What did you say?'

'Nothing. Just asking Roy if he fancied a tea.'

Roy smiled. 'Good idea, Tony, cheers. Two sugars in mine.'

'Yeah, me too. And tell 'em not to put too much milk in.'

'Looks like you've volunteered, mate. I'll have one, and see if they've got any of them squashed fly biscuits, if not, anything'll do.' Michael nodded to the table at the end of the hall.

Feeling very conspicuous in his drape suit, Tony edged his way past the men supporting the walls.

Standing beside a portly woman waiting at the folding table, Tony sniffed. *Lavender. And mothballs. Where's that coming from?*

'Yes, young man. What would you like?'

'Oh, four teas, one with two sugars, one with three and the other without.'

'Please!'

'Sorry?'

'You're supposed to say, please. Have you left your manners at home?'

'And a plate of them squashed fly biscuits, *please*.'

'Squashed – Do you mean Garibaldi?' She pointed disdainfully.

'Yeah, that's 'em. Cheers.'

The volunteer hastily filled the cups from a large cream and green enamelled teapot, placed a handful of biscuits on a plate and stood back. 'There's a box for money at the end of the table.'

'No, I couldn't missus, honest. You've been too generous already. Cheers!'

Waiting until Tony was out of earshot the woman turned to her companion. 'There'll be trouble tonight. You mark my words. The vicar had no right letting them in. Teddyboys! In here! What *are* things coming to?'

A weedy looking man, wearing tortoise shell framed glasses and a badly tied bow tie, grasped the microphone stand. Passing a hand across his head to check the remaining strands of hair were still there, he cleared his throat. 'Ladies and gentlemen. Please take your partners for the Valletta. Thank you.'

'What the bloody hell's a Valletta when it's at home? Oops, sorry Elaine. Forgot you was with us.'

'Didn't hear what you said, Roy.' Elaine searched her handbag, found her powder compact and examined her face in its mirror.

'We can't stay here, Mike,' Tony pulled a face. 'It's back to the caveman days. When Ma said there was a band I thought she meant a *band*. Not three old codgers. The one on the concertina, blimey, he must be fifty! And the guy on the trumpet thinks he's Eddie Calvert. What a mob!'

'I think they're sweet. Leave them alone, they're doing their best.' Elaine dabbed at her cheeks with her powder puff.

'Doing their best? They're doing my brains in. Look at them. It's like "Gone with the wind" but without the costumes, all this waltzing lark.' Michael glared toward the stage.

Roy spread his fingers and waved both hands from side to side. 'I ain't no good at birthing babies Miss Melanie. But don't you worry none, I's a coming.'

Tony swallowed his tea and laughed out loud.

'Cut it out, people are looking at us!' Elaine looked down at her feet.

'Yes, Miss Melanie. Don't sell me down south, Miss Melanie.'

Roy ducked the swinging handbag.

'Come on lads, let's have a dance,' Michael said.

'You lost your marbles, mate? We can't dance to this rubbish.'

'Course we can, Tony. I'll lead. Roy you hang on to my waist, watch the clobber though, and Tony, you get hold of him. Come on, we'll show 'em.'

Pushing their way through the seats lining the floor, the three of them left Elaine watching in disbelief.

'Right, ready lads? Aye, aye, conger, aye, aye, conger.'

Doing their best to lift their legs in the constraints of drainpipe trousers, the trio snaked around the bemused couples.

Tony's foot caught an empty chair and sent it, along with a pink cardigan, skating across the floor. The MC rushed over and grabbed him.

'Pack it in, all of you! This is a religious building I'll have you know, not a spit and sawdust pub. Now behave, or you'll have to leave.'

'Say's who, granddad? You?' Michael leaned toward him.

'Yes, me. I was in the commandos in that last lot. If you think you can handle it, be my guest.'

'Only having a bit of fun, mate. Come on; let's get back to Elaine before she dies of boredom.'

Elaine grasped Roy's arm, 'I want to go home please, Roy. I've had ...'

'There they are!' The voice from across the hall interrupted her.

'Paul! Over here, mate! You made it then.'

Christine hung onto Paul's arm as he weaved around people waiting for the next dance to begin.

'Christine! I'm glad you came, but I'm just leaving. This lot are playing up again, as usual.'

'What have they been doing?'

'The conger! Nearly got us thrown out.'

'What! In here! No wonder you're going, I don't blame you.'

Elaine tugged Roy's sleeve. 'Come on, let's go.'

'But it's early yet. There ain't no where else to go. Give us half an hour then I'll take you home, alright?'

'No. It's not alright. If you don't want to leave yet I'll catch the bus on my own.'

'We'll come with you, won't we, Paul.'

'Only if Mike and Roy are going, we've only just got here. Tell you what, Chris, why don't you go with Elaine. I'll call for you tomorrow.'

'Huh! OK, come on Chris, let's leave them to it.'

The two girls linked arms and left without a backward glance.

A tap on the microphone was followed by the voice of the MC. 'Please take your partners for The Gay Gordons. Thank you.'

Michael groaned. 'Perhaps we should have gone with the girls.'

'Bit late now, they've gone. And I bet I get it the neck when I see Chris next.'

'Leave it out, Paul. Just get her a box of Black Magic, always works with Elaine.'

'What with? Shirt buttons? I'm skint.'

'Thought you was working?'

'I am, but it's a week in hand and I only started today.'

Roy held his hand out. 'Here you are; here's ten bob. Pay me back when you get paid.'

'Cheers, Roy.' Paul ran the note through his fingers, straightening the creases. 'Mike, how about letting me have some dosh? Me mum thinks I've been working all last week but I got fed up with it, jacked it in. She'll be after some housekeeping on Friday.'

'Yeah, alright. But we all get the same, OK? Got to keep the books straight, if you know what I mean. Now come on, let's get this lot going again.'

'OK, Mike. But what about that commando bloke?' Paul's voice betrayed his fear.

'What about him? Thought you wanted a laugh?'

'Lead on McDuff, we're right behind you.' Roy pushed Michael toward the dance floor.

'Conger again, Mike?'

'No, we've done that, I gotta better idea. Form a square, facing in, OK?'

'I get it,' Roy laughed. 'Come on you lot, let's show 'em how to dance.'

Michael took a deep breath and began. 'You put your left foot in, your left foot out, you do the Hokey Cokey and you turn about ...'

The gang put their heart and souls into it, singing loud enough to distract the dancers.

'You put your right foot in, your right foot ...'

Suddenly Michael was grabbed from behind and yanked from the square. 'I told you lot. *Pack it in!* I'll have ...'

The man's words were cut short by Michael's head crashing into his face. Blood spurted, women screamed.

'Scarper lads! Get out of here!' Michael wrenched himself free from the stunned man.

'Now you've done it! Let's go!' Roy charged into the chairs, knocking them aside, heading for the door the others close behind him. Hands reached out to stop them but swinging fists prevented anything more than a token gesture.

Outside the hall the four ran toward a bus that was pulling away from a stop. Leaping onto the platform they raced upstairs.

'That was great!' Michael puffed. 'I gave him what for.' He glanced down at his shirt and jacket. 'And I didn't get any tomato sauce on me gear. That's a bonus.'

The others sat and sucked in gulps of air.

'Shit! I forgot me bike! It's still outside Ma's!' Jumping up, Michael rang the bell, three times.

Taking the stairs two at a time he rushed down.

'Fares, please.' The conductor held out his hand.

'Upstairs, mate. They got mine.' Michael jumped from the slowing vehicle and began running back the way the bus had come.

'Wotcha, mate. Knew it was yours, not many Rockets around here, is there? Anyway I'd recognise that sign anywhere, N.F.N.R. And you're right, no fanny, no ride. Fair enough ain't it?' Bad Breath shrugged his shoulders, chrome studs in his leather jacket reflecting the light from the café window.

Michael nodded. 'Don't seem to put 'em off, that's for sure. Where's your mates?'

'Only one here and he's gone inside, needs a leak. You lot still coming to the island? We're all up for it.

'Why not? Change of scenery will do us good. You taking birds?'

'Only one, need her to start the races.'

Memories of the last race Michael had seen her start in her own unique style set his blood racing. It collected in its usual place and he tugged at his crotch.

'Great! Look forward to it. Not sure if any of ours will be able to come. You know what parents are like. It's alright for blokes to stay out all night, but daughters, they're something else.'

Bad Breath nodded. 'Know what you mean. Still, our girl's OK. Her parents don't give a toss. You wouldn't believe some of the things she gets up to. Real sport she is!'

Michael glanced toward the café, 'Think I'll grab a tea before I get going, you coming?' *I can't ride me bike till this goes down, that's for certain!*

'No. We're off as soon as me mate's finished. Think he must be shaking it once too often in there. Dirty bugger.'

'OK. See you at Benito's, er, Bentini's.'

Chapter 20

Paul walked up the path toward the open door clutching his lunch bag.
'Morning, Mr Smith.'
'I'll give you good morning! What on earth did you do yesterday? I've never seen such a mess.' The
foreman held up his hands in despair.
'Mess? What mess? I only did what you said; rub the old paint down, then undercoat and gloss.'
'Come inside and take a look. I still can't believe it!'
Paul trailed behind as Mr Smith led the way to the upstairs bedroom.
'What do you make of that?'
'Nothing. It's cream isn't it? That's what you said.'
'The undercoat was white. Why is the woodwork cream.'
'That's the topcoat, like you said.'
'Touch it.'
Tentatively Paul prodded the paint, the end of his finger turned cream.
'It ain't dry yet, that's all. I only finished just before I left. I wouldn't have got it finished at all if I hadn't
had a good idea.'
The foreman clenched his fists. 'Go on. Tell me what you did. Undercoat would have been nice and dry
by now, ready for you to put the gloss on.'
'I thought it would be quicker if I mixed the undercoat and gloss together, get the job done quicker.'
'You did what! No bloody wonder it's not dry! It'll never dry, you idiot! What do they teach you at
school these days? I thought you told me you could paint?'
'I can, watercolours, charcoal, I've even done some oils. Not many though, I can't afford the paint.'
'And I can't afford to employ idiots and bits of kids like you! You're finished. Go on, get out of my
sight.'
'What about my wages, I worked all day yesterday.'
'Wages! I've got to pay someone to clear up all your mess! You should owe me money.'
Paul decided not to push his luck further and went back down the stairs. Spotting a packet of tea and a
blue paper bag of sugar in the kitchen he picked them up and walked out. *That's something for me mum at
least. Tight git! How was I supposed to know? He never said. Bloody hell, nothing ever seems to work out.*

Paul watched housewives queuing for fruit and vegetables on the pavement outside Michael's home.
King Edward potatoes were being weighed on large scales inside the mobile shop van. A stern looking
woman nodded and the vegetables were tipped into her wicker basket. Paul turned away as he heard
Michael's front door open.

'Here's five quid, mate. Try and make it last. That ain't a goldmine under my bedroom floor you know.'
'Thanks, Mike. I got to give some of this to me mum. Either that, or tell her I lost another job.'
'Not again! Blimey you've had more jobs than a pigs got tits. What did you do this time.'
Paul related the story about mixing the paint to save time and how it had refused to dry. He blamed the
fact that he thought the paint had been bought on the cheap.
'You silly sod!' Michael laughed, 'What will you get up to next?'
'I don't know. I'm really cheesed off lately.' Paul chewed his bottom lip. 'I can see why people top
themselves. Ain't much to look forward to is there. Bet if I saved up for a bike they'd drop the bleedin'
bomb before I got to the shop. As for getting married, who wants to bring kids into a world like this?'
'That's what I keep telling you. Love 'em and leave 'em. Less hassle that way.'

'No, I can't do that. I love Chris. I wouldn't want to hurt her, especially after all that Deiter put her through.'

'You shagging her yet?'

'You know I'm not. I know she's not a virgin, but we agreed to wait until we're married.'

'More fool you then. My governor at work told me, "If you're not, then you can bet someone else is." He reckons birds are worse than blokes, except they keep quiet about it. In my experience I think he's right.' *Ask your mum!*

'Perhaps your right, I just don't know anymore. I'm beginning to think Deiter weren't so unlucky after all. One crash and it's all over.'

'Yes, but he didn't choose to die, did he?' Michael looked down and studied his boots.

'Nor did James Dean, but shit happens.'

Michael shrugged. 'Come on, get on the back. Let's go and find the others. Get your helmet.'

'No, can't be bothered. Let's go,' Paul mumbled, straddling the bike.

Michael kicked the engine into life, and accelerated away. Turning a corner he was confronted by a rope across the road, young girls either side of the road were turning it while a third youngster skipped in the middle. At the sound of his bike they dropped the rope onto the concrete and the girl that had been skipping ran to the kerb. As Michael passed, the girls put fingers into their mouths and pulled faces at him.

'Oi! We're playing!' yelled one.

The gap between the Morris Minor and Michael closed as he amused himself annoying the driver. Inch by inch the bike crept closer. Paul watched and began to sweat. If the man in front panicked and braked he knew they would plough into the back of the car. He tightened his grip and closed his eyes.

With a flick of his wrist, Michael accelerated past the terrified driver and raced down the road. Feeling the bike surge forward, Paul opened his eyes and swallowed. *You silly sod! Bet you scared that bloke shitless!*

The bike came to a halt outside the motorcycle dealer at the end of a line of shops.

'What have we stopped for, Mike? You buying another bike?'

Michael removed his helmet and ran a comb through his hair. 'That look alright?' he asked.

'Yes, but I thought we'd be going to Bentini's or Ma's. We won't find Roy or Tony here.'

'Do you want to bet, look over there, that's their Bantam ain't it?'

'Blimey, you're right! Wonder what they're doing?'

'Let's go and find out. I want to ask this bloke about something for my boss. That's why I came here.'

Inside the shop Paul gazed enviously at the rows of gleaming machines and sniffed. 'I love the smell of them new tyres,' he said, wandering between the rows of motorcycles. 'Oh, there they are, Mike! At the back. Oi! Roy, Tony, what you two up to?'

'Feeding the ducks on the pond! What's it look like we're doing!'

Michael took his eyes off the Royal Enfield he was admiring. 'Yeah! What *are* you doing? Thinking of getting a *real* bike? The Bantam not good enough?'

'No, it goes alright, Mike, but me and Tony are fed up sharing it all the time. It's OK when we go out together but at other times it's a friggin' nuisance.' Roy pulled his shirt collar up. 'We're thinking of getting a better one between us and sharing them. You know, I'll ride the Bantam one week, then it's Tony's turn, or something like that.'

'Sounds good. At least one of you *might* keep up with me. What are you getting?'

'We like the look of this Tiger, what do you think.'

'Can't go wrong with the Hundred and Ten, I tossed up between that and my Rocket. Great bikes, both of them. Yeah, get it if you can afford it.'

'Well, we'll need to *borrow* the deposit,' Roy winked. 'We can manage the payments between us.'

'Whose gonna sign the HP papers?'

'I talked me dad into it. He's not keen on me having it, but …'

Michael shrugged. 'Jammy devil! I had to get me uncle to sign mine. Make out he was me dad.' *As it turned out, he was!*

'Right, mate,' Roy said to Tony, 'Look's like the Triumph it is then.'

'Will you get it in time for our trip to Sheppey?'

'Yeah, we've already asked that. The geezer says if we get the papers back tonight he'll sort it for us. Nice bloke, he is. Anyway, why are you two here? Changing *your* bike, Mike? Or is Paul getting a moped?' Roy laughed and bounced back to avoid the punch thrown by Paul.

'Only a joke, mate! You're on a short fuse, ain't yer!'

'Come on, Mike. Go and sort out what you came for then take me to Bentini's.'

'Yes, your majesty. Of course, your royal highness.' Michael bowed.

Paul turned and stormed out of the shop followed by taunts and whistles.

'Leave it out you two; he's in a bad enough mood already. You coming for a coffee?'

'Might do. We got to get these papers sorted first, going to ride over to me dad's place, get him to sign before he changes his mind.'

'What? At work you mean? Can't you wait for him to come home?'

'If we do we won't get the bike in time, and we ain't going to show up in front of the Chieftains on a Bantam!'

'Good point! OK, might see you later then. Cheers!'

'Yeah. Alright to pick up the dosh at Bentini's? Got to pay the deposit before the bloke will sort out the agreement.'

'I'll pick it up on the way and me and Paul will take the same amount. Oh, that reminds me.' Michael wriggled about, trying to get his hand in his pocket. 'There you go, five quid each, got to keep the books straight.'

'Fair enough. See you there in an hour or so. Cheers, Mike.'

Stopping in front of his house, Michael turned the engine off and stood the bike up on its rest. 'Stay there, Paul. This won't take a tick.'

'Don't forget my money, Mike.'

'Quiet! You want to tell everyone? Silly sod!'

'Sorry, Mike. I didn't think. Sorry.'

For the second time that day Michael pulled back the rug on his bedroom floor. Using his knife he eased the cut floor board free and reached down. Quickly counting out banknotes into three piles he shoved the rest back and replaced the board. With the carpet safely back in place he ran down the stairs. *How that teacher of Paul's managed to get this lot just from selling porn I don't know.*

'That you, Michael?' a slurred voice called from the kitchen.

'Yes, mum.' *Christ! When did you get back?* 'And no, I ain't going near the off licence. See yer!' *You want booze, you get it. I promised dad I wouldn't run your errands anymore.*

The front door was opened and closed before his mother could protest.

'Alright, Mike?'

'Yep, all sorted. Right, hang on; let's get down Benito's place. Get some records on. Wonder if the wop's got any new ones?'

Paul slid back on the seat as Michael accelerated away. Readjusting his balance he sat and enjoyed the thrill of riding with his tarnished hero.

Johnny Ray was busily *'just walking in the rain'* when the pair walked in.

'Here you are, shove that in. We don't want him on, can't see what all the birds see in him. Elvis, yes. He's brilliant. Hope he comes to England soon.' Michael thrust a handful of coins out to Paul. 'Might as well get the coffees while you're there.'

'OK, Mike, I'll see what's new.'

'That's better, good old Jerry Lee! Bet he wears out a few pianos, he's wild! Benito got anything new?'

'A couple, Mike, but nothing I've heard of. I stuck with some of our favourites. *Be Bop a Lula* should be next.' Paul answered.

'Great!'

Michael leant forward and whispered, 'Put your hand under the table, take your money. Don't bother counting it, it's right. Try and make it last.'

'Cheers, Mike,' Paul mouthed.

'Want to play cards while we're waiting for the others?'

'OK, but what? Can't play brag with just two of us.'

'I know that, smart arse. One hundred and one. Finishing with a black jack doubles the other one's score. Tanner a game.'

'Sixpence? No, threepence, you're too good at cards.'

'Scrooge! OK, threepence a game. Cut for deal.'

'Got any fags, Mike. I must have left mine at home. Oh, and while I think of it, can you get me some more from your uncle?'

Michael produced his case and offered it across the table.

'Cheers! Got a light?'

'Bugger me, ain't you got anything? Apart from the cheek of the devil, that is.'

'That reminds me, Mike,' Paul laughed. 'I passed these two blokes standing at the bus stop; they were comparing their silk ties. One had a pin-up girl on his and he was saying, "Neat but not gaudy, as the devil said as he painted his bum blue." I thought that was great! Cheek of the devil and painting his bum, get it?'

'Ha, bloody ha, very funny, I don't think.'

Paul inhaled, then rolling the cigarette between the tips of his thumb and fingers began inspecting it. 'What are these?'

'Turf. Like it?'

'No. I think the name says it all. Smells like me dad's bonfire on washday. Got anything better?'

'Give us it here.'

Paul passed the cigarette back to Michael, then watched in dismay as his friend dunked it into one of the cups. It floated in the froth.

'Why'd you do that!'

'You said it wasn't good enough, so ...'

'But now you can't drink your coffee,' Paul smirked.

'Yes I can,' Michael said, switching the cups around. 'That one's yours now!'

Chapter 21

Leaning against the frame of the office door, oily fingers clutching a miniature cigar, Michael asked, 'Any sign of that bike coming back?' An audible gurgle from his stomach betrayed the fact that he as not as relaxed as he tried to appear.

'Put that out, Mike. It stinks.'

'Sorry. Seem to be smoking more than ever lately. Anyway, any news about the bike, I was looking forward to working on that.'

'Your mate, the copper, he started on it while you were away. But he seemed to think there was something fishy about the brakes. He was right as it happens, but I think it's a storm in a teacup.'

'Oh, I see. Blimey, he keeps on that he's fed up in the police, but once a copper, always a copper I say.' Michael dropped his cigar and stood on it, moving his foot from side to side. 'What do you want me to start on? How about that Rover over there?'

'Yes, that certainly needs your golden touch. Miss-firing something chronic. I thought a gang of cowboys were coming to town when he drove it in!'

Michael touched his quiff and bowed. 'It shall be done, o master!' Hastily avoiding the ball made from rubber bands aimed at his head, Michael walked across to his first job of the day and lifted the bonnet.

'Mike! I forgot to ask you, I need you in on Saturday afternoon, that OK?'

Michael stood up and looked back toward the office.

'Sorry, boss. No can do. Got something important arranged. How about a couple of evenings when I get back? Or ask PC 49, he does Saturdays.'

'He wouldn't be up to it, he's only learning don't forget. The customer's in a hurry and I promised him he'd have it back on Monday.'

'Tell you what; tell the geezer the parts came in wrong and you've had to send them back. Tell him he can still have it Monday, but not till close of play.'

'How's that going to help? There's more than a days work to do.'

'Easy. I'll come in early, do the overtime before the day starts. How's that sound?'

'Suits me, I knew I could rely on you. Thanks, Mike. Make sure you've got your key, I'm not coming in early to open up.'

Outside Roy's house, he and Tony were busy polishing their new acquisition as another bike pulled up. Getting off, Michael and Paul stood admiring the Triumph. Tony lit a cigarette and offered the packet around.

'She's a beauty, Roy. What's she go like?'

'Brilliant, Mike! Bloody brilliant! Can't wait to run her in, then I can open her up.'

Tony ran his hand over the petrol tank, 'We've taken it down the mad mile, handles great. She'll do the ton easy I reckon. We'll have to challenge the Chieftains to a burn up.'

'Hold your horses, mate, one thing at a time. Don't you get into anything with them this weekend.'

'Give us a bit of credit, Mike. This cost too much dosh to bugger up racing those silly sods.'

'Leave them to me. *I'll* sort them out; *and* that bird of theirs if I get half a chance!'

'No change there then!' Tony laughed.

Michael ran a comb through his hair, leaning back, checking his quiff in the reflection of the highly polished bike. 'Shame our girls can't come, if you'll pardon the pun. Never mind, there'll be plenty of talent on Sheppey from what I hear.'

Roy shifted his weight from one foot to the other. 'Kay wouldn't leave her nan, even if she said she could go with us. What with her mum and dad being killed in the Blitz, then her mum's sister dying like that, her nan's the only family she's got now. She thinks a lot of her.'

'Sometimes I think families are not all they're cracked up to be,' Michael said, his cigarette clinging unaided to his lip. *I mean, who'd want a mum like mine? And me dad, he's always on at me. I can't seem to do nothing right. He don't like my clobber, don't like my hair, don't like my music, don't like me mates, don't like my bike. Bloody hell, I didn't ask to brought into this shitty world.*

'Yeah, and look at mine. Dad's done a runner and me mum, well …'

'Nothing wrong with your mum, Paul. She's a laugh. Tony and me think she's great, wish my mum would let her hair down now and again. Her idea of a good night out is a game of Bingo!' Roy slapped his leg and laughed.

'Right then, every one ready? Don't try to keep up with me and Paul; we'll see you at Benito's.' Michael started his bike and revved the engine. Roy did the same with the new Tiger.

A window in a house on the opposite side of the road flew open. 'Oi! You lot! Clear off! I'm listening to the cricket.'

'Bollocks!' Michael yelled and roared off down the street. Paul swivelled on the pillion seat and raised two fingers to the red faced protestor. Roy revved the new bike a few more times, engaged the clutch and shot off after the others. The unique smell of Castrol R oil drifted toward the man shaking his fist as they disappeared from sight.

Michael's bike slewed to a stop amidst a shower of small stones. Taken by surprise, he fought to stop it falling over; Paul thrust a foot down to help. The Chieftains laughed as they lounged around their bikes, drinking coffee. A couple of the leather clad riders were kicking a Carnation milk can back and forth, stirring up dust from the gravel. The neon sign in the window of Bentini's flickered.

'Bike too big for you to handle? Perhaps you should think about getting a Lambretta, might be more you style.' Bad Breath taunted.

'Up yours!' Michael retorted. 'Wait until you're sucking on my exhaust fumes, then we'll see.'

'You're having a laugh, mate. We'll have had a couple of pints and be eating our chips before you two arrive. And where's your mates, chickened out have they?'

'They'll be here. They got a new bike, a Tiger hundred and ten, but they've got to run it in so they won't be racing this time.'

'Any excuse. So it's just you then. Never mind, we'll show you a thing or two.'

'Says who? Just tell us how to get there, then we'll know where to wait for you.'

'Cocky bastard, ain't yer?'

The door of the café opened, a top heavy girl tottered out on stiletto heels. 'We ready then?' she asked, pulling her chrome studded leather jacket down and her skirt up. She made sure Michael caught a glimpse of her underwear as she got up behind Bad Breath.

Titsaleaner! Great! I thought she wasn't here. God, I fancy that!

'Keep your eyes off, mate. She's ours.'

'More's the pity, talent like that's wasted on you lot. Right, here's the other two, we're all here now.'

'OK, that's enough bleedin' chat. Beer's waiting, let's go get it!'

The Chieftains bikes leapt into life and swung off the forecourt before Michael could react.

'Quick, Mike! Don't lose them!'

Spraying gravel, Michael's bike thundered after the Chieftans. 'Hang on, mate, this could get a bit hairy. ain't letting them get away with that stunt.'

Paul gripped on and thrilled to the surge of adrenalin. *I'm going to miss Chris, but it's worth it! I can't wait to get my own bike!*

Two of the Chieftains sat with their feet on the road waiting for the lights to change as Michael charged up behind them. A quick glance left and right then Michael roared past the stationary riders. Ignoring the red light, he accelerated to beat a car advancing from the right. Paul responded to the drivers' horn by raising an index finger as the Chieftains looked on in disbelief. Glancing back Michael saw the lights change and the bikes cross the junction, the race was back on.

He leant the machine over, responding to the curve in the road. Paul leant with the bike, reacting naturally as he had done so many times before. Coming out of the bend Michael spotted the rest of the Chieftains up ahead, riding three abreast with no regard for any other road users.

Accelerating, Michael crouched lower.

Paul leant forward and gripped on firmly. *Go on, Mike! Hammer it!*

As Michael closed with the other bikes one of the riders turned round, saw him and sped forward, indicating to the other Chieftains. Immediately reacting, the bikes fanned out further to occupy both lanes of the road. One rider stayed near the kerb, another rode along the white lines, the third riding against the flow of oncoming traffic, should there be any. Bad Breath grinned and began weaving; both the other bikes copied him.

Bollocks! If that's how you want to play, then so be it!

Paul felt the power increase, closed his eyes and prayed. He sensed how close the bikes were as Michael pushed through two of the riders, but chose not to look. Feeling his friend sit up Paul opened his eyes. The road in front of them was empty. *That's shown 'em, Mike. Bloody brilliant!* Looking back, Paul could see the gap opening up.

Approaching the cantilever bridge separating the island from the mainland Michael crouched down and accelerated. The bridge operator, sitting in a hut wrestling with the crossword in his paper, got out of his chair and opened the door. Leaning out, he was just in time to see the motorbike roar past. Scratching his head he watched the tail light fade into the distance before returning to his puzzle. But as he picked up the paper, licked the end of his pencil and gazed at the ceiling for inspiration he heard the sound of more motorbikes approaching.

'Oh gawd, must be that lot of troublemakers again. I don't know why they come here, charging around on those noisy bloody bikes. Two years National Service would soon sort them out.'

The headlight of Michael's bike penetrated the darkness between the hedges on either side of the narrow lane. Concentrating on the reflections from any remaining cats eyes he sped into and out of bends. Paul hung on, unable to see far ahead, placing trust in his friend. Michael eased the bike over once again but lost contact with the road. Snaking from side to side Michael brought the bike back under control and slowed to a stop.

'Sorry about that, mate,' he gasped. 'Loose bloody stones on the road, hundreds of them.'

'Never mind that, it weren't your fault.' Paul was off the bike and tugging at his zip. 'Gotta take a leak, I'm busting.' Standing at the side of the lane he looked sideways at Michael who had decided to join him. 'At least we beat all the others. Christ, I don't know how you do it sometimes. Thought we was gonners when you rode between them back there.'

'Luck of the draw. I guessed they'd move aside.'

'And if they hadn't?'

'You wouldn't be here asking all these daft questions, would you.'

'Blimey, you could have wiped us all out.'

'Death comes quick, you wouldn't have felt anything. Don't want to live forever do you?'

'No. Anyway, who cares? I don't mind dying, better than losing an arm or a leg. Remember that bloke and his bird on that bike last week, uurgh! And at least it would have been the end of all them nightmares.'

'And started some for your mum instead.'

'And yours!'

'Some hopes. My parents probably wouldn't notice until pay day.'

Paul finished shaking and zipped up his fly. 'That's better! Talk about the relief of Mafeking. Come on let's get going. I can hear bikes. Don't want them to catch us up now we got this near.'

Michael nodded and climbed back on. Racing through the shadowy blanket of evening he was soon testing his vision and reactions to the full. *I see what the geezer with bad breath means, these lanes are great! Be even better if I could see them properly!*

A cerise glow hovered in the darkness, an isolated oasis of light, tingeing the night sky.

Michael slowed the bike and pulled onto a forecourt of cracked concrete, a spider's web of fissures, allowing weeds to thrust through in an attempt to reclaim the land.

'This must be the place. The Pink Flamingo Club, that's what he said. Don't look like much, does it?' Michael stood astride his bike, staring at the single storey building. Peeling paint on the walls did nothing to excite him. Only the garish neon sign, with its animated bird, gave any idea that this was a club.

'Where's all the crumpet? Come to that, where's *any* bugger?'

'Ain't even open. Not flipping Norfolk again! We rode all the way here for this? Roy and Tony *will* be pissed off this time! They …'

The sound of approaching motorbikes interrupted Paul and minutes later the Chieftains swept onto the parking area. Michael waved a hand toward the building, 'It's bloody shut!'

Bad Breath drew back a jacket sleeve and peered at his watch. 'No it's not, you moron. It's too early. Don't open till eight! Follow us; we're going to find somewhere to kip.'

'Hurry up then, my bloody legs are frozen,' Titsaleaner protested, rubbing her thighs vigorously.

Oh! Don't do that! Michael tugged at his crotch and wriggled on the seat of his bike. 'Where we off to then? What about our mates? They're not here yet.'

'We said meet here, didn't we? So, they should be here when we get back. Come on, before some other tykes beat us to it.'

Michael followed the Chieftains closely. Minutes later the bikes ahead braked and swung off the road. *What the …? There's nothing here, what they stopping for?* Then his headlight illuminated a house under construction.

'This is it, mate,' Bad Breath yelled. 'We slept here last time, bloody brilliant. Better than sleeping on the beach this time of year.'

'But it's a building site. We shouldn't be here,' Paul protested.

'Well we are, and we're staying. If you don't like it, find somewhere else!'

'Shut it, Paul, you're like a tit in a trance. It's OK. No one lives here yet.'

Reluctantly Paul followed Michael around the rear of the building, past piles of bricks and sand, dodging scaffolding and planks of wood. Entering a space, that would one day become the back door, the youths stumbled through into the downstairs rooms. A torch flicked on. 'That's better, good job someone's got a brain. Give us it here,' Bad Breath demanded.

The staircase echoed and the smell of bricks filled the air as heavy boots disturbed the dust. 'Same place as last time, right.'

Turning to Paul and Michael, the Chieftain's leader added, 'You two sort yourselves out. And clear some of this rubble for your mates while you're at it. We'll all be pissed as farts when we get back, so better get it done now.'

Outside the club Michael and the others joined the queue of youngsters waiting to be let in. A man with cauliflower ears, re-arranged nose and vacant stare was methodically patting pockets.

'What's that all about?' Michael asked. 'Checking for booze?'

'No, knives. They've had a bit of bother here, the old bill threatened to shut the place.'

Michael pulled a handkerchief from the top pocket of his drape and held it to his nose. Breath from rotting teeth made him retch.

'You OK, mate?'

'Yeah. I'm fine. What time does this place shut?'

'Supposed to be mid-night, but it usually goes on till one.'

Michael took his knife from a side pocket of his drape, wrapped it in the handkerchief and carefully returned the ironed cotton square to its proper place. The youths shuffled slowly toward the doors, the man was taking his time but no one argued. Finally Michael reached him. 'Arms up.' Hands as large as hams forcefully patted Michael's pockets. 'You're clean. Next.'

Michael had studied the man, seen that he only checked from about the waist down. He guessed that the man was carrying out the check as instructed; apparently no one had mentioned top pockets. While the search was in progress girls stood dutifully waiting for their escorts, unmolested by the bouncer. He would have been surprised if he had searched their handbags.

'You were lucky, Mike. How did he miss it?'

'Be quiet, you silly bugger.'

Paul shuffled his feet. 'Sorry, Mike.'

Inside the club teenagers were taking up their traditional places, girls on the seats lining the dance floor, adolescent males leaning against the walls. A mirror faceted ball slowly revolved, sending spots of light around the hall. Photos of Elvis, Buddy Holly, Eddie Cochran and many others had been pinned to the plasterboard walls. On the stage a youth, with his back to the waiting crowd, was busily sorting through piles of records.

As he stood up the record player crackled into life. *'Well it's Saturday night ...'* Elvis began the night's entertainment. The youth bent down and adjusted the volume. Girls got to their feet and began jiving together while the boys stood and watched, swilling beer to summon up Dutch courage.

'What do you reckon, Mike. Fancy any of this lot?'

Michael was staring at the cleavage of a girl across the hall. 'Sorry, Paul. What did you say?'

'I said; do you fancy anything here?'

'Not really, though I might give that one a chance later.'

'The one with the red dress and big tits?'

'No. Her mate. The one with glasses.'

'You're joking! I can see her spots from here.'

'Not her spots I'm after. Listen, mate. If you want an easy shag always go for the ones that look as if they'd be grateful. You don't have to look at the mantle piece while you stoke the fire, know what I mean? Remember the three F's. Find 'em, fu ...'

'Yeah, yeah, I know, and forget 'em! I give up. They really don't mean a thing to you, do they?'

Paul walked away. *Wish Chris was here, I miss her.*

'Wanna dance?'

Michael turned around and was met by the charms of Titsaleaner.

'What? Yeah OK, but what about...'

'It's alright, he's chatting up some blonde bitch, looks like she's on the game. See! She's got a silver chain round her ankle.'

Michael straightened his boot lace tie, pulled himself to his full height, took hold of her hand and led the way. Out on the floor Michael hooked both thumbs through his belt and began dancing.

'Oi! Remember me? I thought you said you wanted to dance.'

'I am!'

'No, I meant with me!'

'Oh, right. Hang on; wait until the next one starts.'

'*Ready, - steady, - go man go!*' Little Richard started a rush for the floor. Pony-tails swished, skirts swirled and crepe soles bounced. Titseleanor grabbed Michael's hand, pulled herself toward him until her breasts touched his chest then stepped back again. 'Come on! Dance!'

Michael swallowed, took her outstretched hand and began to jive.

'That's better!' she said. 'We'll show these locals!'

Michael took hold of both her hands, swung her between his legs and back out again. He spun her roun she ducked beneath his arm, moved in close then away from him again. Her short, pink polka dot skirt whirled, exposing matching pink underwear trimmed with black lace. 'You're good,' she smirked, *accidentally* brushing the front of his tight trousers with her free hand.

Supporting himself with one hand against the wall, Bad Breath was busy chatting up the blonde with traffic light red lips. He turned to see why the dancers were clapping and glared at the exhibition taking place.

Titseleanor was *more* than half the reason for the enthusiastic encouragement, but the dancer's rapport also contributed to the circle forming around them. Michael was lost in a world of his own. He was possessed. Perfume wafted as she closed in, her breasts bouncing. He dropped a hand to his crotch and tri to make himself comfortable. Titseleanor smiled and pulled herself closer, rubbing her body against his.

Pushing the blonde away, Bad Breath snarled, 'Stay here! I gotta sort something out.' Pushing his way through the crowded floor he reached out and grabbed Michael's arm. 'That's enough. I told you before, she's ours.'

'We're only dancing,' Titseleanor protested, breathlessly.

'Bloody well looks like it. Get back to the others. And you, *mate*, keep your hands off or else!'

Michael reached for his knife, thought better of it and walked off to join his friends.

'What was all that about, Mike?'

'Nothing, Paul. He just didn't like me dancing with her, that's all.'

'Not like you to take it like that, you scared of him?'

'Don't be a prat! Cause I'm not, I could take him any day. But there's always another way to cook his goose.'

'What's that mean?'

'You'll see.' Michael looked across the hall. Titseleanor slowly eased her skirt up one leg, revealing a black suspender crossing bare flesh between stocking top and panties. Paul nudged his friend.

'Did you see that! Oh, bugger me!'

Roy joined Paul and Michael, carrying a tray of glasses. 'Here you are; get stuck in, lads. Not a bad plac this, Mike. The music's great, that bloke knows what he's doing. I'm going to talk to him if there's an interval, ask him about some of them records he's played.'

'Cheers, Roy.' Michael lifted one of the pints and gulped at it. 'Blimey! I needed that! Hot work out there.'

'Yeah, we noticed. Pushing your luck, ain't you?'

'She started it,' Michael licked his lips. 'But I'm going to finish it. Anyway that's for later; let's see if m theory still works. Watch and learn.' Clutching his drink he crossed the floor. The girl wearing heavy framed glasses, hands folded demurely on her lap, glanced up as he approached.

'Wanna dance?'

'What? Me? Yes please! Thank you.' She was on her feet instantly.

Michael reached down and placed his pint beneath her chair. Taking her hand he rocked back and forth, sending her spinning. She smiled shyly, revealing braces on her teeth. 'I love Elvis, he's the greatest.'

'Yeah, so do I. See my mate, Roy over there? The guy with his shirt collar pulled up? Well, he knows all his songs, got his own band too. Thinks he *is* Elvis some times!'

Turning beneath Michael's arm she smiled again. 'Will he be singing here?'

'No! He only performs with his own group. And his manager decides where and when.'

'Wow! And he's your friend?'

'Yeah, *and* his manager too.' *That was quick thinking, I even amaze myself at times.*

She looked up into his eyes and squeezed his hand. The record finished and Michael led the way off the floor. 'Would you like a drink?'

'Yes please! I'd like a coke please.'

'Have a Babycham.'

'No thank you. I'm not allowed.'

'OK, keep your eye on my beer, I'll get you one.'

Crossing back to his friends Michael winked, 'Another notch on the bedpost.'

At the serving hatch he pushed a pound note across, 'Double vodka and coke mate. Sorry I haven't got anything smaller.'

'Anything else?

'No. That's it, cheers.'

Taking the tall glass he joined his new dance partner. 'There you go, sweetheart. Get that down you. The evening's young, lot more dancing time yet.'

The girl looked at her wrist watch, 'No, I'm sorry. I haven't got much more time. My dad doesn't let me stay out late.'

'Come on then, drink up. Let's get back out there.'

She took a couple of mouthfuls then sprang to her feet. 'I don't know your name, but I'm having a great time.'

'I'm George. What's yours?'

'Annette, but everyone calls me Anne.'

'That's my favourite name! Come on, Anne, let's rock!'

The girl put a hand to her head and swayed before slumping onto a chair. 'I'll have to go soon, George, my brother will be here on his motorbike to collect me.'

'I've got a bike, we all rode down here on 'em. Didn't take long, goes like a bomb. How do you fancy coming outside to see it?'

'If you like. Ooh, my head's spinning; it must be all that dancing. I'm not used to it; usually I just sit and watch.'

Michael took her arm and led her outside.

'Which one's your bike?' she asked.

'Oh, mine's not here, I put it around the back. Didn't want anyone messing with it. Come on, I'll show you.'

'But it's so dark.'

'You'll be OK. Just hang onto my hand. It's just round here.'

Michael skirted the empty beer crates stacked against the rear of the club dragging his dance partner behind him.

'This will do, come here.' Michael put his arms around her and squeezed. He dropped one hand, lifted her skirt and began to stroke the inside of her thighs.

'What are you doing! Stop it!'

'Relax, I won't hurt you.'

'No! No! Let me go!'

'Is this your first time? Come on, you'll like it, you'll see.'

'No, I don't want to. - No! – No, please stop. Oh! Oh, that's nice. Oh, oh, oh. Go on! You do love me, don't you!'

'Course I do.' Michael closed her mouth with his. Empty beer bottles rattled in the crates.

'There you are; I told you you'd like it.' Michael returned his handkerchief to his pocket and tossed a condom into the bushes.

'You won't tell anyone, George, will you!'

'No, of course I won't. Who do you think I am?'

'Thank you. Will I see you next week? I'd really like to, I think you're smashing.'

'Yes, of course. I'll meet you here, show you a few more moves. You're a good dancer.'

'Lovely! I can't wait. Come on, my brother will be here any minute now. Don't want him wondering where I am.' Her words were becoming slurred.

Too true! He'll know you're pissed, even if you don't! 'Better get yourself tidied up in the Ladies while you've got a chance.' Michael led his latest conquest back toward the light spilling from the club.

The roar of engies filled the lanes as alcohol fuelled riders weaved from side to side.

'Hang back a bit, Roy,' Michael shouted as his friend drew alongside. 'One of these clowns is going to drop their bike if they keep on like this.' Roy nodded, slowed down and pulled in behind Michael.

Reaching the house, Michael parked his bike well away from the Chieftain's; Roy followed his example and stood the new Tiger alongside.

'How's she doing?' Michael asked.

'Great! You wait until she's run in. I reckon she'll give your Rocket a run for your money.'

'Yeah, yeah,' Michael stifled a simulated yawn. 'We'll see.'

'Hang on, Mike. Gotta take a leak.' Paul walked over and began dampening a pile of builder's sand. The other three joined him.

'Can't write your name in it like you can in snow,' Tony laughed, as he lurched forward.

'Steady, mate! I nearly pissed all over you!'

The four friends staggered down the side of the building to the back, pulled themselves through the door opening and stood laughing uncontrollably.

'How we going to get up those bloody stairs?' Tony asked.

'We're not,' Michael replied. 'Paul, there's a pile of empty sacks in the next room. Go and get them, we can all sleep down here.'

Paul felt his way along the wall, through a gap and into what would someday be a front room. Groping around in the gloom, he found the sacks and gathered up an armful.

'Cheers, mate. Don't forget some for yourself. *And* Roy and Tony.' Michael dropped the sacks to the floor and lay down.

'They was for everyone!' Paul protested.

'Do as Mike says, go and get some more. Hang on; I'll give you a hand.'

'OK, thanks, Tony.'

Michael heard noises above. Titsaleaner giggled, and a shower of dust descended. Michael brushed his eyes and concentrated.

'No. Not here. You'll have to wait.' The words were followed by more giggles. Michael lay still, his imagination running wild.

'Get off! I said no, didn't I? Go to sleep, you randy sod!'

Scrabbling noises were followed by more dust falling.

The thunder of boots on the bare stairs woke Michael and the others. He blew on his fingers and winced as he sat up.

'That's got to be the worst night's sleep ever! I ache every bleeding where I can think of and then some. On top of that it's cold enough to freeze the bollocks off a brass monkey.'

'You lot should have pulled some birds,' Bad Breath laughed as he passed through. 'Given you something soft to lie on.'

Titsaleaner swirled her skirt, brushing Michael's face. 'Why didn't you come upstairs?'

'What? And put up with all that farting? Blimey, it was bad enough down here.'

She wrinkled her nose. 'I see what you mean.'

Paul blushed as he stood up, brushing dirt and pieces of sacking off his clothes.

'Am I as bad as you lot?' Michael asked needlessly, as he began shaking his drape.

Bad Breath turned at the entrance of the building. 'We're off to the café for breakfast, you lot coming?'

Michael shook his head. 'No, we're heading back. Got an early start tomorrow, going to earn a bit of extra bunce.'

'Please yerself. So you won't be racing either?'

'Next time, when Roy and Tony have got their bike ready.'

'Thought so, chicken, the lot of you. See you around then.'

'Yeah, see yer.'

Chapter 22

Michael reached out and thumped the alarm clock. Blearily he rubbed his eyes and yawned. *Why did I agree to go in so early, I must be mad.* Hastily getting dressed he crept down to the kitchen and put the kettle on the gas stove.

Brushing toast crumbs from his chin he used his feet to propel the motorbike down the garden path. Reaching the road he started the engine and set off through the estate. The milkman was the first person Michael saw. Slowing his bike, Michael moved across the road, giving the blinkered horse a wide berth. *Poor thing. Fancy having to pull all that milk, those metal crates must weigh a bloody ton.*

As he turned the next corner Michael was surprised to see a woman walking towards him. Clutching a handbag with one hand, she was busily poking pieces of hair back under her headscarf. *Mrs P! What are you doing out at this hour?* Michael braked and moved in to the kerb.

'Wotcha, want a lift?'

'Michael! What on earth are you up to? Have you been out all night?'

Michael grinned, 'Not this time, Mrs P. No, I'm on my way to work. Where are you going?'

'Work, same as you. They're having a special do for all the local big knobs. They asked me to come in early and give the staff a hand to get the place ready. The extra money will be handy.'

'Get on. I'll give you a lift.'

'No, Michael, it's out of your way. Thanks all the same.'

'Don't be silly, I'll have you there in no time. Where exactly is it? - Oh, don't worry, I remember, Paul told me.'

Hitching her coat and dress up, Paul's mother got onto the pillion seat and grasped Michael firmly around the waist. 'Thanks, Michael. This will save my poor old feet, and the bus fare.'

Leaving the open common land behind, Michael entered a road running through woods. Rhododendron bushes and oak trees lined both sides. Suddenly Michael turned off the road and bumped down a footpath.

'What are you doing, Michael? Why have you stopped?'

'Thought you might like something to get the day started.'

'What! I've got to get to work. Turn around and get back on the road.'

'Cost you a kiss.' Michael lowered the foot rest and steadied the bike as Paul's mother got off.

'Hurry up then. I can't afford to get the sack.' She closed her eyes and opened her mouth. Michael pulled her to him.

Standing back, Michael gently took hold of her hands. 'I think about you a lot. You're different somehow.'

'*Yes,* I'm old enough to be your mother for a start!'

'That doesn't matter. I wish I could see more of you.'

She laughed, 'You've seen all there is, and more than once!'

'No, I mean I wish I could take you out, to the pictures or dancing. I wish you weren't married.'

'Well I am; even if he is on the run, thanks to you.'

Michael kicked at the leaf mould. 'I'm sorry, Mrs P. If I could turn back the clock ...'

'But you can't. What's done is done. I'm very fond of you too, Michael. You know I am. But we'll just have to do what we can, when we can. I dread Paul catching us at it; we've got to be careful.'

Michael nodded, 'You're right, Mrs P. Come on, one more kiss and I'll take you to work. Don't know what I'm supposed to do with this though.'

She laughed, 'That's your problem! Can you still ride the bike?'

Michael stopped at the tall wrought iron gates and stared. 'Blimey! This is posh! A private road? We've just had a war yet these houses ain't been scratched. They must be worth a fortune.'

'I expect they are. I work in one down the end, mock tudor they call it. Anyway, thanks for the lift. I'll walk from here thanks.'

'As you wish, m' lady. Can't have you seen with the peasants.' He touched his quiff in salute. 'You'd think with all their dosh they'd have a proper road, all that sandy stuff and stones would do me tyres in.'

'Get off with you or you'll be late. And mind how you go.'

'See you, Mrs P. Bye!'

In the garage, Michael sipped tea from a chipped enamel cup and shuddered. *Condensed milk! I should have bought a pint off the milkman this morning.* Spitting tea leaves out, he leant back over the car's engine. *That mum of Paul's has really got to me. Don't know why, but she has.*

The noise of the corrugated iron door sliding open brought Michael back from his day dreams.

'Morning, Mike. Any of the others here yet?'

'No, only me so far. Want a cuppa? It's just boiled.'

'Why not, four sugars don't forget.'

'We've only got condensed or exasperated milk, which do you prefer?'

'Evaporated, that other one's too sweet.'

I suppose it would be with four sugars! 'Right you are; I'll bring it in to you.'

'Cheers, Mike. How's the motor getting on?'

'Bit of a pig. Might have to get someone to give me a hand later, if that's OK.'

'Anything you say, Mike. Just make sure it's ready by tonight.'

Entering Bentini's, Michael stopped suddenly. Paul bumped into him. 'Suds! And Jimmie! Blimey, who l
you two loose! Oh, wotcha, Roy. Didn't see you there.'
'Where you been? Thought you asked us to meet you here.'
'Sorry, Roy. This twat wanted a beer, but we're here now.'
'Want a coffee, Mike? Me and Jimmie were just going to get them in.'
'Cheers, Suds. Nice one. Here, stick some records on while you're there.' Michael held out some chang

Roy sat drumming his fingers on the formica table top, singing along with, *'Baby let's play house.'*
'Good old Elvis, he's really got it.' Tony tapped his spoon against the side of his glass cup in time to th
music.
'Here you go lads, dig in.' Jimmie put the tray on the table and sat down. Hands reached for the drinks
and a friendly tussle for the sugar dispenser broke out.
'How did you two get here? Bus, then walk? Long way from your stomping grounds ain't it?'
'Leave it out, Mike. We might be crazy but we ain't mad! No, we both got bikes now. You must have
passed them when you came in.'
'Probably. But which ones are they? Come on, mate, give us a clue!'
'Sorry, mine's the A.J.S twin and Jimmies' is the Dominator. Come and take a butchers.'
'Paul, you stay here and keep an eye on the coffees, you know what that wop's like. He'll clear the table
so we have to buy some more if we're not careful.'
'But Mike ...'
'Just for a minute, when I come back in you can go out, OK?'
Paul frowned, but, as usual, did as Michael said.

Michael, Roy and Tony walked around the two bikes, bending down to admire the engines, taking turns
to sit astride the machines, all the time nodding appreciatively.
'Bloody handsome, both of them! How did tearaways like you get bikes like these? Robbed the post
office?'
'You cheeky sod, Mike. Me and Jimmie graft for a living. We don't all sit on our arses doing some
apprenticeship like you.'
'Yeah, Suds is right. I think the question should be; how do YOU find the spondulicks to pay for yours?
Michael grinned and raised his hands above his head. 'It's a fair cop, governor. But I didn't think the
Bank of England would miss a bar or two!'
Laughing, they headed back inside Bentini's.

'All right if I go now?' Paul scowled as the others sat down.
'Can do, but we're taking them out in a minute. You can ride with me or Jimmie if you like.'
'No thanks, I'll ride with Mike.'

'Take it easy,' Michael called across to Suds. 'Roy and Tony can't belt it yet, still running it in.'
'OK, Mike. Anything you say. You set the pace and we'll keep up with you.'
Michael checked the road and roared off the parking area in a cloud of dust and blue smoke. *Pity we
didn't have Titsaleaner to start us off, I know they say 'more than a handful's a waste' but bloody hell!*
The other bikes followed. Drawing alongside Michael, Roy shouted, 'Four bikes! We're a bike gang
now!'
Michael didn't answer but his bike surged forward. Paul guessed what was coming and held on; glancin
back he saw the other riders dropping further behind. The vision of Deiter, dying on the road close to whe
the riders had just passed, flashed through his mind.

Reaching the infamous bridge Paul leant over in unison with Michael as the deep, throaty, sound of the engine bounced off the Victorian brickwork. As Michael brought the bike back up straight Paul heard him shout. 'Oh, bugger!'

He peered over Michael's shoulder and winced as he saw that the roundabout ahead was blocked by a man lying on the road in front of a stationary lorry, the twisted remains of a cycle trapped beneath its front wheels. Paul felt the bike shudder as Michael braked, he closed his eyes but quickly opened them again as the bike leant over once more. Without thinking he leant with it. Michael tore into the roundabout, narrowly missing the rear of the lorry, and exited onto the road on his right.

Braking again, he pulled the bike to the side of the road and stopped. 'Shit! That was close!'

Paul got off and gripped his legs. 'I can't stop shaking. Christ, Mike, how did you do it?'

'Don't ask me, it all happened so bloody quick!'

'Suppose something came round the roundabout, with us going round the wrong way!'

'Well, nothing did. I've told you before; the devil looks after his own. Get back on, I need a coffee.'

'Oi! Mike! Hang on! You two alright?' The other riders ran toward Michael as he turned his bike back toward Bentini's.

'Sod me, mate,' Roy said breathlessly. 'We thought you'd bought it back there. The bloke on the pushbike has, he's brown bread. Dead as a door nail. We had to park up, weren't going to copy you!'

'That was something else, Mike. I've heard of blokes doing that for a dare, but ...'

'Never had a choice, Suds. Road was blocked, going too fast to stop, it was shit or glory. Anyway, we're going back for a coffee, coming?'

Without waiting for an answer, Michael accelerated away, Paul clinging on tighter than before.

Paul brought the drinks to the table, the cups rattling in the saucers. Over in the corner the jukebox clicked and whirred, selecting Paul's choice.

'I thought we were all going to keep together, Mike. Why did you tear off like that? Before we got to the roundabout, I mean.'

'I don't know. Just don't like dawdling.' *Something came over me, made me shiver. I lost control somehow. I could have sworn I saw Deiter.*

Michael picked up his drink, ran a finger through the froth and licked it off. A record dropped into place, Elvis began singing.

'I know it's a bit slow, but I love this one. He's brilliant,' Paul said pushing his chair back, balancing it on two legs.

'Yeah, and those jackets he wears, real crumpet pullers.'

'Trust you! You've got a one track mind you have!'

As Paul got off Michael's bike the front door opened and Mrs Parker came out. 'Hello, my darling. Have you and Michael had a good time?'

If you think that nearly shitting yourself on the back of a bike is having a good time, then yes I have. 'Not too bad, mum. What's for tea?'

'Spam and watercress sandwiches. Run in and put the kettle on, there's a sweetie. I just want to see if next door's cat has been messing in the garden again. As soon as I start to prepare the ground for my bulbs he thinks it's for his convenience.' Putting a hand to her mouth, she laughed. 'Didn't mean that! But it's right all the same.'

She waited until Paul was out of sight. 'I've got a day off tomorrow, Michael. You could come around if you like. Paul will be at work,'

Work! I don't think so! More likely he'll be hanging about on the common. Michael smiled. 'Tell you what, better than that, I'll go to work and tell the boss I'm not feeling too good. You walk through to the bus stop and I'll pick you up there about half eight, take you out for the day. How's that sound?'

'There's no gas, mum. Have you got a shilling for the meter?'

'Yes, darling, just a minute. There's some on the mantelpiece, I forgot to put them in again. You can do it, there's a good boy.' Turning back to Michael she nodded and said in a low voice. 'I'd like that, I'll see you there. Bye.'

Michael waved to Paul and pulled away from the kerb.

Chapter 24

'You're late, Mike. Problems?'
Michael stood holding the side of his face. 'Bloody toothache, boss. Been up all night. Then me bike wouldn't start so I've had to walk here. If it's OK with you I'll take the day off and go to the dentist. I can't concentrate and I wouldn't want to bugger anything up.'
'Yes, of course, that's alright. You shoot off and get it sorted. See you tomorrow?'
'Thanks. Yes, I should be OK. I'll sort me hours out later.' Michael clutched his cheek and winced. 'See yer.'
'Oh, Mike. I forgot. The police want to speak to you.'
'Me? Why?'
'Don't worry, it's just about that bike they took away. I said I'd call them when I'd seen you. How about Friday? You take the time off and get it sorted and I'll add the hours you miss to that German bloke's bill. After all, he started all this.'
Michael nodded. *Now what do the bluebottles want?*
Leaving the garage he strode down the road, turned the corner, mounted his bike and rode off toward the bus stop where his date was patiently waiting.

Entering the park gates Michael slowed down and parked his bike in the shade of a large tree.
'This is great Mrs P, our first date.'
'Cheeky! How can we date? I'm married don't forget.'
Michael took her hand. *Good job you forget sometimes!* 'Don't spoil the day, Mrs P.'
'You can stop calling Mrs P whenever we're alone. Call me Pauline.'
'Pauline? Is that why Paul is …'
'Yes, it was his dad's idea.'
'OK, Pauline it is then. Thanks. Have you been here before?'
'No. I suppose I could have, but it would mean catching two buses. Why have you brought me?'
'It's somewhere the gang don't come to, so we're not likely to meet anyone we know. We can enjoy ourselves without any worries. And there's a lake if you fancy taking a boat out.'
'Sounds lovely. Let's do it! My husband never took me anywhere.'

'Get in, Pauline. You sit at the back and leave me room to row. But mind your skirt, there's a bit of water in the bottom.'
After waiting for her to get settled the attendant pushed the small boat away from the mooring platform. Michael stuck the oars into the water; the sun sparkling on the ripples as the boat cut through the surface. Pauline released her grip on the side to adjust her headscarf.
'This is so nice, Michael. It's cool out here on the lake.'
'Not too cold are you? That breeze is a bit fresh.'
'No, I'm fine. Just keep rowing, I'm enjoying this.'

The boat bumped gently against the island and Michael jumped out.
'Sit still, Pauline. Wait until I tie this rope. Won't be a tick.' With the boat secured, Michael held out his hand and helped her ashore. While regal swans surveyed the newcomers, noisy ducks left the bank and paddled away.

'Now what, Michael? Are we going to play at being the Swiss family Robinson? Or is this Treasure Island?'

'It's my treasure island, now I'm alone with you.' Michael took her in his arms and pecked her cheek. She blushed. 'Oh, I see. That's why you brought me out here, is it? I wondered how long it would be before you tried your luck.'

'It's not like that. That's not the reason at all.'

'Oh, I don't mind. But it'll have to be somewhere private.'

'No. You don't understand. I just want to be with you. I know we can't start courting properly, but I want to think of you as my girl.'

'Michael! What are you talking about? Courting? Your girl? I thought I was just another one on your list I'm not silly enough to think there's any future in it, me being that much older than you.' She put a hand to her hair. 'But I've got needs, same as you, and if we help each other now and then that's fine with me.'

He put his arms around her and squeezed. Their lips found each other and he closed his eyes. The two stood locked together as only lovers can. He breathed her scent, ran his fingers down her neck, felt her compliant body pushing against his. Reluctantly breaking away, he held her at arms length.

'I love you, Pauline, I really do. Please don't tell me you don't feel the same. You can get a divorce and then I can marry you.'

'Divorce! Marry! What are you saying? You're not trying to get into some young girl's knickers now you know! I've already said you can have me, just find a secluded spot that's all I ask.'

Michael shook his head. 'I can't make you realize, can I? I love sex with you, but it's not enough. I want you all to myself, every day and every night. I want to set up house with you, come home from work and find you waiting for me.'

'It won't work, Michael. Don't be silly. Let's enjoy ourselves by all means, but you'll find a girl your own age one day. Then's the time for you to think about getting married. Even if I agreed, which I don't, there are too many obstacles. What would your parents think? And the neighbours, they …'

'Sod the neighbours. And sod my parents! As if they'd care. It's you I want and I mean to get you. Bugger anybody else.'

'That's the first time I've heard you swear, Michael! Calm down and give me a cuddle, you silly thing.'

Michael became lost in the warmth of her body and the scent of her hair.

'I love you, I love you,' he whispered, gently biting the lobe of her ear. Standing back from their embrace he bent down and spread his jacket, inside out, on the grass. 'Sorry about the swearing, Pauline. It won't happen again, promise. Come on, sit down.'

Kicking off her shoes she pulled up her dress slightly before joining him.

'Hope we don't crease your coat too much.' She smiled and snuggled against him, his manly smell sending a shudder through her body.

'Are you getting chilly?' Michael asked.

'No, Michael. It's lovely. I'm glad you thought of bringing me here. Look at the lake, look how peaceful it is. We'll have to do this again sometime.'

'I'd like that. This can be "our place," our secret place, away from all our troubles.'

'What troubles have you got? A good looking young man with your life ahead of you, you shouldn't have troubles.'

But I have! More than you could ever imagine. I'd love to tell you, get them off my chest, but that would mean telling you about Paul. Then you'd have nothing more to do with me, and I couldn't bear that!

'I only meant keeping up the payments on the bike, things like that.'

She kissed him. 'After living through the Blitz you learn to get things in proportion. Trust me, I know.'

'I expect you're right. All that rationing me mum had to cope with, coupons for this, coupons for that. Don't know how she managed. Still, it's a pity you don't have to have coupons for booze.' *That would stop her little games.*

'Why?'

'Oh, I don't know. Don't even know why I said that. Come on, I'll row us back. We can get a cup of tea and some lunch, there's a café where you can sit inside or out.' Michael struggled to his feet and helped her up.

As she looked at him, a small frown creased her forehead. 'Why do you wear your trousers so tight?'

'Because it annoys me dad, that's why.'

She stroked the front and tweaked the top of his zip. 'Those can't be comfortable.'

'They were, before you did that!'

'But how can you dance in them? Paul gets a rash where they make him sweat.'

'Dance? - Mmm, it's difficult, there's not much ballroom!' Michael laughed and ran toward the boat.

'Sorry about that, couldn't resist it.'

She swung her handbag, but he was out of reach.

Chapter 25

After tapping his pipe out on the top of his garden spade, the man blew through the stem. Satisfied, he fille it from a soft leather tobacco pouch and struck a match. He took a few more puffs before pushing his cap back and scratching the side of his head. A bright eyed robin, perching on the fence, watched as the man dug into the earth.

'Your dad's always digging. What's he up to this time? That's horse shit he's shovelling, ain't it?' James peered out of the kitchen window.
'I don't know, getting the ground ready for something I suppose.'
'Don't you ever give him a hand, Suds? Poor old bugger looks knackered to me.'
'What! Me? Work in the garden? No thanks, looks like hard work to me.'
'Yeah, you're right. Bung that kettle on again. I couldn't spit a sixpence.'
Suds got up from the battle scarred kitchen table, the dents and knife cuts in the wood witness to its years of service. The four chairs gathered around it had suffered likewise, white paint knocked off, bare wood starting to appear.
'Where's your mum?' James flicked his lighter without success.
'In the front room, listening to the wireless. The Archers, probably.' Suds poured the hot water into a teapot and sat down.
James began shovelling sugar into the milk in his cup while they waited for the tea to brew. 'Good to be back with Mike and the others ain't it, I missed hanging about with them.'
'Yeah, but it don't seem the same somehow. Roy and Tony are still up for a laugh but Mike and Paul seem to have changed. They're alright some times, then one or the other of them gets a bit arsey, don't you think?'
'Well they both got problems don't forget. Paul's dad's done a runner and Roy told me Mike's mum's got a drink problem. Don't say anything though, he told me never to mention it.'
'Well that's nothing new! I've got a drink problem too, I can't afford it!'
'Silly sod. It ain't funny, Suds. Roy said Mike's mum's been scraped up off the pavement more times than you can count. Pissed as a newt.'
'Oh. I can see why Mike don't want to talk about it then.' Suds removed the tea cosy and poured the tea. 'Thinking about Mike and the others, remember when we all used to get into the old manor house up near the allotments? All those missing floorboards, you had to balance across a plank from room to room?'
'Yeah, and that bloody barn owl. I nearly fell off when that flew out,' James smiled. 'The good old days, eh?'
'That must have been some place before the fire. Bells to call the servants. And that lift thing we tried to get going.'
'Yeah! And all them statues in the gardens. I remember the first time I saw one. It was dark and we were creeping through the trees. I thought it was a ghost, nearly shit myself.'
'I remember that! How about the time Paul got us chucked out the Odeon? That must have been the world's biggest fart!' Suds spooned more sugar into his drink. 'Bugger me, he couldn't have timed it better just as that blonde bird, what's her name? Anyway, just as the music died down and she was kissing that geezer. Remember?'
'Cause I do. Tony was telling me nothing's changed. They chucked him out of a caravan for nearly gassing them.'
Suds put his cup down. 'Come on, Jimmie. I can't finish this, I'm awash with bloody tea. Let's take the bikes out and burn some rubber.'
'Sounds good to me. Mad mile first then we can try that café by the common. Mike says they do smashing cheese rolls there.'
'OK, but no more tea!'

James opened the garden gate and waved Suds through. Kicking their bikes into life, the noise bounced off the prefabricated, single story, flat top boxes that had replaced the 1930s buildings destroyed in the Blitz. These temporary dwellings had earned the accolade 'Little Palaces,' for their fitted kitchens, complete with hot and cold running water, virtually unknown refrigerators and a copper tub for washing clothes. Bedrooms boasted built in wardrobes.

Suds pointed across the road at huge heaps of rubble. 'They were good days too!'

'What, the war you mean?'

'No, you silly bugger. Playing in the dirt over there.'

Opposite the homes, the remaining area of a bomb site was a magnet to the younger children of the estate. Heaped high with the detritus of war, piles of earth, bricks and broken tiles were criss-crossed by tracks through the weeds growing on the slopes.

'Oh, yeah. I remember. You had a bigger trolley than me. Where'd you borrow them pram wheels from? Nicked 'em I bet!' James paused. 'Sometimes I used to pretend mine was part of a Wild West wagon train being chased by Indians. Or a roman chariot; or one of them racing cars I saw on Pathé news. Funny to see kids still playing there.'

'I didn't nick the wheels, smart arse. I swopped my shrapnel collection for 'em. The other thing I used to do was to race my sister on our scooters. But me mum put a stop to it the day she went home with her legs all grazed and bleeding. The scabs lasted for ages.'

Suds revved the bike's engine and began to pull away, narrowly missing a man riding a tricycle with a large box fixed between the front two wheels.

'Oops! Sorry mate, my fault. Didn't see you there.'

'Don't knock the ice cream man over, the kids round here will lynch you!' James laughed.

'You're the bloke what comes round selling brushes aren't you?' Suds asked.

'Yes, son. You can't sell ice lollies in the winter. I used to be a skilled toolmaker; that is until Jerry shot up our crate over Dresden. Now my nerves are too bad to go back to my old trade, so I have to do what I can to make ends meet. Knocking on doors trying to get people to buy a brush is worse than this lark, at least with this I get to put a smile on faces.'

'Here, treat yerself, mate.' Suds thrust a ten shilling note into the man's hand. 'You bomber crew have earned it. And I'll get me mum to buy some brushes.' Speeding away he headed for the mad mile with James in close pursuit.

Folding the note the man put into the leather bag hanging around his neck. *These teddyboys aren't as bad as the papers make out. Some of them anyway.* Ringing the bell on the handlebars of his tricycle he called out. 'Lollies! Get your lovely ice lollies! Always licked but never beaten!'

Children appeared from the bomb site and out of the prefabs. Wafting on the air, the smell of the coconut ice lolly being held aloft, attracted them like bees to honey.

Chapter 26

Michael lay in his bed watching another smoke ring heading for the ceiling. Stubbing out the remains of h cigarette he glanced at the life size poster of a pouting Brigitte Bardot pinned to his bedroom door. He ble the nubile sex kitten a kiss. Taking care not to knock his shins on the utility wardrobe he swung his legs free of the blankets, stood up and stretched.

Bending over, he selected one of his few records stored in a chrome wire rack. Wedged between the foc of his bed and the bedroom wall was his pride and joy, a Dansette record player. Switching it on, he place the records over the spindle of the deck, then using his handkerchief he began wiping the dust from the tw front supporting legs, giving their brass ferrules resting on the bare floorboards an extra rub.

The silence was broken by the hum of valves warming up. Michael selected the speed and moved the control to auto. Elvis extolled the virtues of being a *'Poor Boy,'* while Michael swivelled his legs and ran comb through his hair. 'Good film, that. Shame he gets shot at the end. But we all gotta go sometime.'

Lifting the mattress he extracted his trousers, having carefully placed them there the night before. A qui examination of the creases was followed by the ritual of pulling them on over socks. A fluorescent yellow pair were his choice this morning.

Taking a bright red shirt from the wardrobe he held it at arms length and admired his handiwork.

'Not bad, even if I say so myself. Still, when I marry Pauline I'll be able to give this lark up. Women lo ironing.'

Buttoning it up, he threaded gold coloured links through the cuffs, red glass stones glinting in the light from the window as he turned his wrists.

He swung the wardrobe door open to use the mirror. It took three attempts before he was satisfied with the knitted tie, the horizontal black and yellow bars always presented a challenge. Michael wanted a black knot. A scimitar shaped, gold colour tie clip with red stones set into its handle, secured the neckwear to hi shirt.

Picking up his clothes brush, a black duck housed in a dual tone grey body with orange feet, he remove the dust from the velvet collar and slipped his drape jacket on. A final check in the mirror and he was satisfied. Picking up the money and door key from the top of a wooden crate, that had once held oranges but now served as his bedside table, he made his way downstairs.

As he approached the front door he glanced into the front room. The curtains were still closed, but in the glow from the wireless tuning panel his mother's face took on a strange pallor. She was slumped in a chai dressing gown wrapped around her, slippers on her feet. One arm hung limply down, a saucer beside her piled high with cigarette ends. Her mouth resembled that of a clown.

Stepping into the room, Michael bent down to retrieve the empty gin bottle lying on his mother's lap. H picked it up carefully, avoiding the bottle neck ringed by lipstick. He was still disgusted by his mother's drinking, but had lost the moral high ground now.

Lifting the lid of the galvanised dustbin, Michael added the bottle to the others nestling amongst potato peelings and cabbage leaves. His father did his best, but meals in Michael's home were poor at best and boring by repetition.

I need to get away from all this. Marry Pauline and settle down in our own home together. A nice little council house on a different estate. Or even one of the prefabs like where Jimmie and Suds live, that'd do.

Michael walked aimlessly through the streets, his mind working overtime. The sound of a tennis ball as bounced off the road distracted him from his thoughts. Catching it, he took aim and threw the ball at the ti can in the middle of the road. A direct hit sent the two pieces of crossed firewood into the air.

'Oi, mister! That's our game, that is!' The small girl stood with arms on her hips, glaring at Michael.

'Sorry! Good shot though, weren't it!'

The children balanced the sticks on the can and the game resumed.

A small boy cuffed his snotty nose. 'Bloody teddybears, my dad says they ought to be in the army.'

Michael grinned. *Wish I was their age again. Even school weren't that bad, apart from the dinners that*
s.

Roy and Tony stood looking at a new bike parked outside Bentini's. 'Ain't seen one of them before.
What is it?' Tony walked around it. 'Here, take a look at this! It's got a tyre pump clipped on it. That could
come in handy.'
'MV Augusta, a bleedin' wop bike. What's the matter with a decent British one? We kick their arse in the
war but before you know it people are buying their gear.'
'Yeah, and we're buying coffee from Benito,' Tony laughed. 'Come on, let's get inside.'

'About time he got some new records, these ones will play the same track on both sides soon.'
'Well he's got *Volare*. I might have guessed he'd get that,' Roy snorted.
'Oh, Dean Martin's not bad, I like him in films.'
'Yeah, suppose so. But it ain't rock 'n roll is it.'
Tony sprinkled more sugar, scooped froth from his coffee and sucked it off the spoon. 'Handsome!'
Roy looked past his friend, recognising a girl sitting with her back to them by her shoulder length hair
and studded leather jacket.
'That's Titsaleaner! Look Tony, over there.'
'Oh yeah, does look like her. But where's the Chieftains? If it is her she can't be on her own. This is our
place.'
'Well they can't all be in the bog, there's only room for one at a time.'
'Go and chat her up. Never know; you might get lucky.'
'Bollocks. You try it. I got more respect for mine.' Roy cupped his hand over his crotch.

Tony looked up from his drink at the sound of the door opening. 'Here's Mike. Bet he'll chance his arm.'
'What? All of it!'
'Silly sod. You know what I mean.'
Michael swaggered over. 'Wotcha you two, no Paul?'
'We knocked for him, told him we was coming here, but he said he was sorting out the aerial for his
mum's wireless. Where's yer bike?'
'Back at home. Want another coffee?'
'Might as well. And bung some different music on. That's the third time Benito's played that sodding
one. We're supposed to choose what we want to listen to.'
'Leave it to me, soon have this place rocking.'
'While you're at it, take a butcher's at the bird over there. Roy's sure it's Titsaleaner.'
'Got to be! Look at the way she's hunched forward. Them tits of hers must weigh a bleedin' ton! It must
be her. What's she doing here though?' Michael ran a comb through his hair.
'Go and ask; that's *if* it is her. Go on, I dare you! You always said you fancied her.'

'Thought it was you, how's it going? You on yer own?' Michael leaned onto the table, supporting himself
on his knuckles he dropped his eyes a fraction. The unzipped jacket moved open as breasts swelled. She
smiled up at him.
'Yep. Just me, all on my lonesome. Ain't no law against it is there?'
'No, of course not. But where's your gang though?'
'How should I know? Get me a coffee then sit your arse down. Unless of course you prefer your mates, I
saw them come in about half an hour ago.'
'No, it's OK. I'll join you. Hang on while I get the drinks.'

'There you go, won't be a tick. Just take this tray to the lads.'

She raised the coffee cup. 'Cheers.'

Michael strutted back to Roy and Tony. 'I think I've pulled. And don't dribble in your coffee, it ain't hygienic.'

Michael tugged at his trousers, hitching them up before sitting. 'Now, what are you doing this far from home? And how did you get here?'

'I got the bus then walked if you must know. And I came to see you; we never finished our dance on the Isle of Sheppy, did we.'

Michael shifted on his chair and grinned. 'No, and I won't be sleeping downstairs next time either.'

Opening his cigarette case he offered it across the table. Taking a cigarette she held it lightly between her lips, moving it back and forth, suggestively.

'You going to light it?'

Michael swallowed and leant forward with his lighter.

'Thanks, ain't you smoking?'

'Oh, yeah. Just wasn't thinking.' *I was, but not about fags!*

She leant forward. 'I'm glad you turned up. I took a chance coming here. If the others saw me the shit would really hit the fan.'

'So why did you come?'

'I told you, I'd like to finish what you started. Come on; take me for a ride on your bike.'

'Can't! I did the same as you, caught a bus then walked. Oh, bugger.'

She tipped her head back, thrusting her attributes toward him, and blew smoke up at the ceiling. 'Who's silly boy then?'

Michael leapt to his feet and rushed over to his friends.

'Quick, Roy. Lend me your bike, she's up for it!'

'Sod off, Mike. It ain't even run in yet. You'd tear the guts out of it, I know you.'

'*Please!* Come on, I'll treat it with kid gloves, I promise.'

'What do you think, Tony? It's half yours, mate. Do you think we can trust this randy blighter?'

'Hurry up; she might change her mind in a minute. I'll put in a good word for you two; mind you I'm a hard act to follow.' Michael laughed at his own joke.

'Don't bother. She ain't worth getting carved up for. They're a crazy bunch of bastards, them Chieftains. You saw 'em that night at the pub, coshes, razors, knives and chains. No thanks!'

'Let him have it, Roy. It's his funeral.'

'Cheers, lads. I knew you wouldn't let me down.'

They watched out the window as she wriggled up onto the pillion, her skirt hitched up high enough to ac as a belt.

Roy licked his lips. 'Her bloody legs'll get frozen.'

'Don't worry about that, Mike'll soon rub 'em better! Lucky bugger.'

As the bike disappeared from sight the boys sat down to wait for Michael's return.

'Not sure that was a good idea, mate,' Tony sighed.

'You're right, it wasn't! Look who's just arrived! Some of the bloody Chieftains!'

'Oh, bloody hell. If they're here when he gets back there's gonna be bother with a capital B.'

'Trust him. He had to push his luck, didn't he. Now we stand a chance of paying for his pleasure. Prat!'

'Wotcha. Just you two? Where's yer mates? And where you hid that bike of yours?'

'Wotcha. We came on the bus, bike's in for a service. That's right ain't it, Roy?'

'Yeah. Don't know where Mike and Paul are. Must be down the pub or up the rec.'

'Well we ain't stopping. Quick coffee and a slash, then we're going to bomb up and down for a bit.'
'Right. Well we're just going over our list of songs. Got a gig this Saturday.'
Bad Breath nodded. His friends found an empty table and called him over.
'See yer then, bring that bike of yours next time. You can try to keep up with us.'

Tony lowered his voice, 'How long before Mike gets back do you reckon?'
'Not long, she was gagging for it. Not as though he's got to waste time chatting her up. And, knowing Mike, he won't hang about.'
'Tell you what, you keep an eye on that lot and I'll stand outside. Try and stop him coming in.'
'Brilliant! Off you go then; I'll sit here and watch.'

Tony paced up and down, anxiously watching and listening. Behind him the door opened and Bad Breath came out. *Oh cheers, Roy. Nice of you to let me know they're on the move!*
Tony watched as he walked over to his bike, turned, flicked the remains of his cigarette into the air and lit another. He began to walk toward Tony, changed his mind and turned back to the café.
You going back in or what? Tony walked to the edge of the road. Before long the sound of a bike approaching set his heart racing. *That sounds like ours, must be Mike!* As he glanced back at the door it opened and Roy appeared.
'Stay there, Roy! Stay in the doorway, he's coming!'
Bad Breath looked at Roy then slowly turned to face Tony.

Michael slowed the bike as he approached Bentini's, his pillion passenger snuggling contentedly against him. *What you waving your arms about for, Tony? Get out the way, you silly sod.*
'Watch out! See the bikes! Oh shit! They're here!' Fingers dug into his sides. 'Keep going,' she screamed. 'Don't stop!'
The bike surged forward and Tony was treated to the rear view of plump buttocks disappearing down the mad mile.

Turning left at the roundabout Michael pulled into the kerb.
'Christ, that was close! You didn't say they were coming. Lucky Tony warned me!'
'I didn't know, did I. You think I'd have been there if I did?' She tossed her hair and sniffed.
'No. I suppose not. What do you want to do now? We can't keep cruising up and down till they bugger off, they're bound to see us.'
'Take me to where I live, it won't take long. Then you can get back to your mates.'
'OK. Where to then?'
'Head toward Woolwich, then I'll tell you where.'

Half an hour later, Michael swung off the road and parked. Roy and Tony rushed out to meet him.
'Where you been? God, that was close. They've only just finished racing up and down. It's a wonder you didn't run into them.'
'Yeah, I saw 'em, Roy. They were heading back toward Woolwich while I was on my way here. Not sure if they saw me though.'
'Was it worth it?'
'Oh yeah!'
'I bet. Hope the bike's not as knackered as you.'
'It's OK. I kept the speed down just for you. And because I didn't want me supper getting cold, did I? Anyway, I can cross her off me list now.'
'What?' Roy frowned, 'You ain't going to see her again?'

'For what? I've had me wicked way with her, she ain't nothing special.'
Tony shook his head. 'Paul's right, you don't give a toss for women do you.'
'Why should I? Easy come, easy go. There'll be plenty more before I settle down.'
'And who do you think would be daft enough to marry you?' retorted Roy.
'I've got my eye on someone, don't you worry. Someone very special.'
'Who?'
'That's for me to know and you to find out.'

Chapter 27

Roy and Tony exchanged glances as they sat on the new furniture, grey vinyl upholstery with blue moquette cushions. Wall lights, their conical shades of etched glass sprouting from gold coloured metal, lit the room. A television combined with a record player, wireless and cocktail cabinet took pride of place along on one wall. Michael's 'uncle' liked his creature comforts.

'Here you are, boys. Be careful, Jim only just got these for me.' Putting the large tray down, she took off the plates, cups and saucers and placed them on the low coffee table. 'Sorry about the beer mats, Jim's getting me proper coasters and things when he can.'

'Cheers, Nell. Don't forget the cakes; you know what this lot are like.'

'Give us a chance, Jim. I've only got one pair of hands.'

Roy began to get to his feet. 'Can I help?'

'No, it's OK. I can manage. You just carry on talking. Leave the teapot on the tray; it's too hot for the table. There's milk and sugar so help yourselves. Won't be a minute.'

Tony poured the tea and carefully sat back in his chair. 'I like these,' he said, holding up a cup.

'Yeah, they're smart. I've seen 'em in Woolworth's,' Roy studied the motifs covering his plate. 'Me mum's saving up for some I think.'

'Oh, they're only until Dodgy gets his hands on some decent gear,' Jim said. 'Nell's got her eye on some with French pictures in colour. I like these black and white ones meself, but got to look after the little woman.' He leaned forward and added more sugar to his tea. 'What do you reckon on the new television?'

'Ain't seen nothing like it. Must have cost a bomb.'

'You're not far wrong, Roy. Go over and drop the flap next to the screen.' Jim pointed with his teaspoon.

Roy walked across and gave the door a gentle pull.

'Harder than that, it's still a bit stiff.'

The door dropped down at Roy's next attempt, revealing glasses, a lemon squeezer, cocktail sticks and bottles. A small strip light bathed the contents in a creamy glow. Inside, the cabinet was lined with mirrors, one across the back, a second acting as a shelf and third on the door itself, all decorated with gold outlines of cocktail glasses and bottles.

Roy stepped back. 'Wow. That must keep the electric meter busy. We have to switch lights off indoors when we're not using them.'

Jim laughed. 'Close the door, Roy. Watch the light.'

Roy lifted the flap back. 'Yeah, what?'

'No. You were too quick. Open it again, but this time close it *slowly* and keep your eye on the light.'

Roy leaned forward, squinting as the gap closed. The light went out just before the door closed. 'That's clever. How does it do that?'

'There's a switch. The door pushes it and turns the light off. Clever, ain't it?'

'You don't do bad for a bread delivery man do you. My old man slogs his guts out at the factory but he can't afford things like this.'

'Ain't what you know, it's who you know that counts in this life.' Jim patted the side of his nose with a finger. 'Anyway, you called to see about the bookings for the band. Well, I've tried the bloke down the caves again but he says they're concentrating on jazz bands. You can't play jazz can you?'

Tony choked on a dough nut.

'No, I didn't think so. So that one's out the window. There's no rock n roll concerts for a while at the Gaumont, but when there is I think I might be able to get you booked.'

'Not looking good then?'

'No, Roy. I'm doing my best but it's bloody hard work. Too many bands, not enough venues. Every one wants to get on the bandwagon.' Jim laughed. 'That was a good one, didn't mean it but ...'

'So what are you saying, Jim? You want to call it a day? We're all keen as mustard but if you've had enough just say so. We can find another manager, or go it alone.'

Jim lit another cigarette and nodded. 'I'm sorry lads. I just don't think I'm any good to you. I don't understand your music and I'm probably not trying all the right places. You'd be better off with someone else, someone a bit younger perhaps.'

Tony picked up a cream horn. 'Fair enough; and you're right about too many of us chasing rainbows. But that's how it is. We've just got to prove we're better than them. Perhaps Mike will take a shot at it.'

'Ah, that reminds me,' Jim got out of his chair and picked up a box from behind the curtain. 'Do us a favour, give this to Mike. Tell him to try and flog it, Dodgy says there's more if we want.'

Roy took the box and shook it. 'What is it?'

'Open it, take a look. It won't bite yer.'

'Packets of loose tobacco and … What are these?'

'Rolling machines. You use them to roll your own fags. Ain't you seen 'em before? Only thing missing i the cigarette papers, otherwise I'd show you how to make them.'

Roy shook his head, 'OK. I'll take it for you, let Mike sort it out.'

'Cheers. Right, come on lads, get stuck in. Don't want all these cakes going stale.'

Chapter 28

Michael turned over in bed and opened one eye. 'Nine o'clock! Bugger, I'm late.' Throwing back the sheets and blankets he leapt out of bed and grabbed his jeans. 'Hang on. It's Friday, I've got to go down the cop shop, see about Deiter's bloody bike. Well they can wait; I'm having another half hour.' He flopped back on the bed and pulled the blanket up over his head.

Parking his bike outside the jewellers opposite, Michael looked across at the police station. *Well, I never noticed that before. An air raid siren stuck up on the roof. Wonder if it still works?* Crossing the road he stopped and looked at the glass fronted notice board just inside the low brick wall. A poster with a colour picture caught his attention. *Colarado beetle...report at once...threatening potato crop...Blimey, sounds like a nasty bit of work. Bung a load of DDT on the fields; that should sort the little buggers out.*
As he approached the entrance he lit a cigarette and threw the empty packet into the bow fronted iron basket fixed to the wall, a reminder of the horse that had been replaced with bicycles.

'I've been told you want to see me, about a bike, a motorbike.'
'You've been in here before, son, haven't you.' The desk sergeant stared at Michael. 'Yes, I remember; that under age girl.'
'That's right, but it weren't me. Remember?'
'Wait there.' The man behind the counter left Michael reading the notices pinned to a board on the wall.
'Stolen. Black BSA three speed bicycle. Reward.' Michael dropped his cigarette butt to the floor and stood on it. 'Lost. Brown and white mongrel dog, answers to the name of Bengie.' *Is that it? Ain't exactly work for Sherlock Holmes.*

'Right you are, son. Come on through.'
Michael walked through the flap in the counter being held up for him.
'Second door on the left, and don't forget to knock.'
'Yeah, yeah, I know.'

'Enter.'
Michael opened the office door. The room was made smaller by a row of filing cabinets. Light from the metal framed window was aided by a single bulb inside a white and green, enamelled shade. The man behind the desk ignored his visitor and continued writing. An ink bottle vied for space amongst books, papers and a sandwich leaning against a large mug of tea.
Michael tried to read the note that lay in the 'IN' tray. *Who wrote that? A doctor? It's worse than my writing and that's saying something.* The 'OUT' tray contained a packet of Players cigarettes and a Hank Janson paperback.
Michael coughed. The man put his pen down and looked up.
'You're here about the motorcycle.'
'That's right, my boss told me to come here.'
'It's in the yard out back, follow me.'

'Here it is. Try the brakes, careful though, it's heavy.'
'I know. I've got one like it.' Michael began the pretence of checking the bike. 'What am I supposed to be looking at? The back brake needs tightening, front seems OK. Needs a lot of work doing on it.'

'You were with him that day. Witnesses said there was a gang of hooligans racing but by the time the ambulance and police officers arrived they had all left the scene. Don't suppose you knew any of them?'

'No. It was only me and Deiter that day. We weren't racing, just riding our bikes for something to do. H came off and I called 999.'

'Did you see anyone interfere with this bike? Did the deceased do anything to it?'

'Deiter wouldn't, he always got me to do any work that needed doing.'

'So, did you work on it just before the accident?'

'No. Who says I did? They're lying, I never touched it.'

'And I never said anybody did. Are you sure you've got nothing to hide?'

Michael put a finger down his shirt collar and swallowed.

'Nothing. I told you, I never touched it.'

'Then how do you explain the brakes?'

'Why ask me? They could have worked loose. But he wasn't all that popular, he made enemies easily. Perhaps some one had it in for him. I don't know.'

'Did you like him?'

Michael lit a cigarette. 'Sometimes. He didn't really fit in. Always wanted to "go back to the Fatherland," as he put it. It was his dad who got him sent over from Germany. I think he would have bee better off staying there.'

'Do you know any one who would have wanted him …'

'Well, he was in all the trouble up Notting Hill, but I don't think any of them blacks knew where he was from.'

'Yes. I heard about that. But it was one of them that got him off. Him and a woman gave each other alibis. No charges were made, but he had to report here. You must already know that.'

'Yes.'

'Anyone else?'

'Not really. We all get into bother with you lot now and then. Deiter enjoyed a good punch up but that was all. Although thinking about it, Pat might have had it done.'

'Who's she? What did she have against him?'

'No! Pat's not a woman. He's a bloke. Well almost.'

'Almost? What's that supposed to mean?'

'Pat's a shirt lifter. A nancy boy, queer, a bum bandit. You know what I mean. Deiter stabbed him and put him in hospital.'

'Was Deiter a homosexual then?'

'Good job he can't hear you say that. No, he hated them.'

'Well I'm not satisfied. We've had people look at this machine and the general opinion is that somebody deliberately tampered with it. That's murder. And according to you, you were the only other person there that day.'

Lighting a cigarette from the end of another Michael frowned. 'So, are you accusing me?'

'Not yet. Not enough evidence. We need to track down the rest of the hooligans that were there that day. See if they know anything.'

'So, can I go now? I'm supposed to be working.'

'Yes. You're free to leave. I may be contacting you again if we get more to go on.'

'What about the bike? We're supposed to be fixing it for Deiter's brother.'

'No chance. That's evidence. It stays here until we sort this out.'

Michael sat on his bike, hands trembling. *Why don't they leave things alone? What do they hope to prove?* His thoughts were interrupted by a clattering sound and turning he saw a rusty cycle being pushed along the pavement by a man of indeterminate age with a bulbous purple nose and a bushy unkempt beard. Bicycle wheels, minus tyres, grated. Tin cans and a kettle clanked against the rusting frame. A hole, where the saddle should have been, now held a bunch of wilting flowers.

Michael sniffed the air. 'Bugger me, if it ain't Smokey Joe. Thought you was dead and buried. See you ain't found the soap shop yet!'

The tramp blinked his watery eyes but ignored Michael as he walked past, pushing his worldly possessions alongside him.

You don't give a fig either, do you mate. Michael looked him up and down as he passed. A moth eaten bowler hat as dirty as the face beneath, a patched overcoat and protruding woollen scarf. Grubby trousers with frayed bottoms bunched over shoes that relied on yards of string to keep their soles on.

Michael lit a cigarette. *Just you and that old bike. But perhaps you've got it right. You've got your problems but they can't stack up against mine. At least they don't hang you for being a tramp.*

Michael took his clock card from the rack and knocked on the office door. Without waiting for an answer he stepped in. 'Morning, boss. Reporting for duty, here's my card for you to sign. Been down to see the cops like you said.'

'How'd it go? What did they have to say?'

'Oh, you know. Nothing really, but they're keeping hold of the bike.'

'Why?'

'How should I know? Coppers are all the same, suspicious bunch of b's.'

'Well that suits you, Mike. You never wanted to work on it in the first place, did you.'

'What's the point? It's knackered. Be cheaper for Alfred to buy a second hand one if he wants a bike.' Handing back the clock card, Michael's boss smiled, 'And I suppose you know where there's a bargain.'

'Glad you mentioned bargains, you interested in rolling tobacco? Could do you a good deal.'

'No thanks. But if you get your hands on some cigars …'

'OK, I'll ask around. Now, what do you want me to work on next?'

'Check that moped the new bloke fixed. Then I'll sort something else out. There's one coming in after lunch I bet you'd like to get your hands on, a Daimler.'

'Great! Thanks, boss. And don't forget to bill Alfred for my time, not our fault we can't finish his perishing bike.'

Michael sat and studied the races in the paper while he ate his sandwiches. He ticked the greyhounds he fancied, tore the page out and pinned it on the wall behind his work bench.

'Check those tomorrow, see how much I would have won.' Screwing up the remainder of the paper, Michael threw it in the general direction of the waste bin and strolled toward the office. The grating noise of the corrugated doors opening, accompanied by a flood of sunlight across the workshop floor, announced the new arrival.

Michael whistled appreciatively, and walked over to the saloon car. 'Tasty. *Very tasty.* That cost a few bob, I bet.'

'There you go, Mike. It's all yours. Make sure you handle it with kid gloves; the chauffeur's already having kittens. Anyone would think it's his.'

'What's the problem? What needs fixing?'

'Complete service, bumper to bumper. Anything needs doing, do it. The owner can afford it.' Michael's boss gave him an exaggerated wink.

'Got yer, boss. I can't wait to get started.'

'Anything you need that's not in the store room, let me know. I'll phone around and you can nip out on your bike and get it. The bloke in the peak cap is coming back for the car tonight.'

'Leave it to me. There's bound to be lots of things need replacing.' Michael grinned.

'That's what I like to hear. Go on then, time's wasting, you've got about four or five hours, tops.'

'By the way, boss. I checked out that moped like you said. Good job too, that new blokes made a right mess of it. And I spent ages explaining what to do. A simple job like that and now I've got to do it myself. I'd get rid of him, I would. Waste of space he is.'

'Fair enough, Mike. I said if he was no good I'd give him the elbow.'

Michael turned away and smiled. *Good! That's one less copper to worry about!*

Driving the car into the workshop and parking it over the inspection pit, Michael sat admiring the luxury of the interior. After running his hand over the gleaming dashboard he glanced over his shoulder. *Hello. What's that headscarf doing there? Looks like it's caught between the door and the seat.*

Getting out, he released the door and retrieved it. *I've seen this before, it's Pauline's! The one she wore the park. She must have lost it getting a lift home. I'll take it to her.*

Michael was about to close the door when he noticed something else. Bending down he pulled the article from beneath the front seat.

Knickers! Pauline's knickers! Crossing to his jacket, hanging from a nail in the wall, he stuffed the item into a pocket. *I can't believe it. Why? She must be a flaming nympho!* Storming back to the front of the car he released the bonnet and began yanking off the spark plug leads.

'There you go, boss. Couldn't do much more without telling the geezer his car was a write off!'

'Cheers, Mike. Well done. You can get away now if you like. I'll sign your card, you deserve it. I'll see you in the morning.'

'Thanks, I've had enough today and I got things I need to sort out.'

Mrs Parker opened her front door, 'Hello, Michael. You're off work early, aren't you? Paul's not home yet.'

'I came to return these.'

She took the headscarf and smiled. 'Where did you find it? I thought it was lost for good.'

As she turned the scarf between her fingers the underwear dropped onto the front step. She blushed as she bent to pick them up.

'And who do these belong to?' she demanded.

'You, of course.'

'No they most certainly don't! How dare you!'

'Well, I found them with your scarf. They must be yours.'

'Come in. I don't want all the neighbours hearing.'

Michael stepped into the hall and closed the door.

'Right. Now where did you find my scarf and … and these?' She held out the garment between thumb and finger.

'In that posh car you get a lift in. I had to work on it today and both of them were in the back.'

The dirty sod! So much for his, 'my wife doesn't understand me,' sob stories. That's the last time I let him park on the common. 'So that's where my scarf went. But these knickers aren't mine. They're too small for a start. How did you think I could get into them?' She hooked her thumbs into the waist band and pulled. 'Do you still believe they're mine? But I think I know who they belong to, that children's nanny. She's always looking at Bert with cow eyes, but I'm shocked all the same.'

'I'm sorry, Pauline. I just put two and two together.'

'Yes, and came up with five. You've upset me; I think you'd better go. And take these with you.' She held the underwear out at arms length.

Michael stuffed them back in his pocket. 'Can't I stay for a while? Have a cup of tea, talk about our future plans.'

'No. I want you to leave. And we haven't got any future plans. I thought I'd made that plain in the park the other day.'

'But I want to marry you. I love you.'

'Don't be so daft.' She opened the door. 'Go on, Paul will be home soon. I don't want him to find you here when he does. He might, "put two and two together," like you.'

'OK. I'm really sorry, Pauline. You will come out with me again, won't you?'

'I'll think about it. No promises though.'

Michael glanced out of the door, and then turning back kissed her gently on the cheek.

Chapter 29

Miles away, a similar confrontation was in full swing. The man in the 'pie and mash' van lit his pipe and watched.

'I'm telling you, it weren't me!'

'And I'm telling you, I'd know those tits of yours anywhere. It *was* you on the back of that bike. I ain't blind.'

Titsaleaner thrust out her breasts, 'Prove it.'

'I can't, but I know it was you. Who was the geezer?'

'How do I know? You were there, not me.'

'You liar. You had that short skirt on, I saw your arse.'

'Well, why don't you hold an identity parade, like they do in them films. Get half a dozen girls in a line with no drawers on; see if your mates can pick me out from the back.'

'Course they could, most of them have had you.'

'Yeah, and all of them are bigger and better than you!'

'You bitch! Get on the bike. I'll show you. And when I catch that other bloke I'll show him too!'

Titsaleaner smiled. *That's it. Get nice and angry, gets your blood pumping. Shame about your breath, apart from that you're my favourite shag. Although that Michael knew what he was doing alright!*

'Come on then, let's go somewhere and bury the hatchet,' she said, thrusting her hips toward him.

As Bad Breath kicked the bike into life the girl climbed on the back, reached around and squeezed his crotch.

Reaching the junction with the high street, Bad Breath stopped the engine and planted both feet on the ground. Titsaleaner got off. She watched as a man, dressed in black and wearing a top hat, walked down the road leading a funeral procession. Behind him a highly polished hearse crept along. On the roof of the car floral tributes accompanied the deceased on the last journey. Strangers on both sides of the road stood in silence as the cortege passed, men removed their hats in respect.

A throng of mourners followed the coffin, black armbands worn by the men, black lace veils covering the faces of the women, children holding the hands of their parents. Titsaleaner clamped her lips shut as she saw a small boy almost jerked from his feet by a young woman as he began kicking the pile of horse manure that had been carefully avoided by the adults.

On the pavement, alongside Titsaleaner, a plump woman whispered to her companion. 'I heard it was T.B. My friend, Flo, told me that. She heard it from a friend of hers that lives in the same street.'

The other woman raised a hand to her mouth.

As the last of the people bringing up the rear passed by, Titsaleaner hitched up her skirt and remounted. Bad Breath swung the bike out into the high street, heading for Woolwich common.

Chapter 30

'There he is. Be a love and go and get me some.'

Paul turned the page of his Eagle comic and ignored his mother.

'Hurry up; you'll miss him in a minute. Go and get your mum some winkles. You should try them, they're lovely.'

'I don't like winkles, or shrimps.'

'You've never even tasted them. Go on, here's the money, you can keep the change.'

Paul jumped up and rushed out to the van parked a few doors down the street and joined the queue. He stood behind a stout woman, watching the sweat run down her neck soaking into her summer dress. Putting a thumb and finger to his nose he squeezed. *Blimey, what a stink, them shrimps don't half whiff. How can mum say she likes 'em? Uurgh!*

'I've cut you some bread, there's dripping in the tray in the oven and home made goosegog jam. But you don't know what you're missing.' She broke the head off a shrimp and picked up another.

Paul went to the tall kitchen cupboard, slid open the frosted glass door and took out a jar. Taking off the greaseproof paper lid, secured by an elastic band, he stood licking the stickiness off his fingers. Gooseberry, summer '57, the handwritten label stated.

'Darling, bring me a pin please. There's some in my pincushion, on the side.'

'Yes, mum,' Paul sighed.

'How are you getting on at work? You don't say much about it.' She dug the pin into a winkle and eased it from its shell.

Paul looked away. 'It's OK,' he lied. 'No worse than any of the other jobs I've had.'

'You must be very good at it. None of your clothes have got a speck of paint on them.'

'Mr Smith's got overalls; that's why. He takes 'em to the laundry.' Paul spread margarine on another slice and dipped his knife in the jam.

'What a nice man! And fancy him sending you home with that tea and sugar. I don't get anything from my lot, and they're loaded with money.' A jet of water squirted from a prawn as she broke it open.

'Mum! All down my shirt!' Paul jumped up and ran from the room.

'Sorry, dear,' she called after him, 'Put it in the dirty washing basket. There's a clean one in your wardrobe.'

Returning to the table Paul glared at his mother. 'That's the last time I get those for you. Bloomin' stinky things.'

'Yes, dear. More tea?'

'No. I'm fed up with tea. And I'm fed up with home made jam. Why can't we have Spam?'

'I forgot to buy some, that's why.'

Paul slid his legs beneath the table and slouched down in his chair. 'Yeah, but you didn't forget the shrimp and winkle man comes today, did you.'

'You can ...' A knock at the door interrupted her. 'See who that is, darling.'

'Why can't you go?'

'Because I'm your mother. Now go and answer the door.'

Sliding his chair back across the lino covered floor Paul slouched out of the kitchen.

'Oh, it's you, Mike. What do *you* want?'

'Sorry, who was you expecting? The Queen? I'm going down the boozer, thought I'd give you a lift.'
'No. Don't fancy it.'
'How about the youth club?'
'No. I'm staying in tonight. Can't be bothered.'
'Huh. Please yourself. See you then.' Michael strode back up the garden path. *Miserable little git.*

'Who was it?' She added another winkle shell to the growing collection on the plate in front of her.
'No one.'
'Don't be silly, it must have been some one.'
'Mike.'
'Why didn't you ask him in then?'
'What for? He's going for a coffee or something.'
'You could have gone. I've got a couple of shillings in my purse.'
'Don't want to. Leave me alone. You're always on at me, you are. I'm going to bed.' Snatching up a pile of comics Paul stormed out the room, stamping feet marking his progress up the stairs.
'I'll bring you up some cocoa later, shall I?'
Paul scowled. *Save it for your fancy man, that's if chauffeurs drink cocoa.*

Propping himself up in bed, he began reading. Wondering how Dan Dare would get out of trouble once again, he turned the pages to find the Riders of the Range.
Stampede! Paul reached out for the packet of Rowntree's fruit gums on the table beside his bed and became absorbed in the story. The last picture showed the cattle racing toward a sheer drop while Jeff Arnold, riding hard and whirling a lasso over his head, raced to turn the herd away from destruction.
At the bottom of the page Paul became engrossed in an extra picture strip of Jeff showing how to prepare a lasso. After flicking through the rest of the pages, he dropped the Eagle comic to the floor, sorted through the pile on his bed and settled for a well thumbed copy of Superman. *Wish I could get a job drawing cartoons, bet I would be really good at it.*

Chapter 31

The youth shook the jam jar and held out his hand, 'Sixpence please.'

Roy dug deep in his pocket. 'There you go, mate, two bob. That's us four paid up. Make sure you buy Elvis' latest one. And don't forget to mark our names, we ain't paying twice.'

Tony raised a thumb. 'Cheers, mate. I keep forgetting he collects money for the records. I'll get the next round of teas.'

Kay smiled. 'Yes, thanks, Roy. Mind you, he should get you to get the records for him. Be a lot cheaper.'

'Do you know what, I understood most of that. I must be getting tuned in.'

'It's not my fault you lot don't talk properly. You should come to Cheshire, see if they understand you.'

Elaine opened her handbag and took out her powder compact. 'Take no notice, Kay. He's winding you up. Next time we're down the pub ask him if he wants a drink. Bet he'll understand you then,' she laughed.

The youth left their table and replaced the stack of records. Waiting until the first one dropped and began to play, he returned to his thankless task.

'Come on, Roy. Dance with me.'

'OK. Good one this.' She began singing. 'R-O-C-K Rock!'

Taking her hand, Roy sang as he led Elaine onto the dance area.

'Why don't you play this?'

'What, with just drums and guitars? What about the saxophone and double bass?'

'I see what you mean. Wouldn't be the same, would it?'

Michael paid the entrance fee and sauntered into the club. *No new crumpet then. Oh well, have to see who's with who. Must be some spare talent.*

'Over here, Mike!' Tony waved both arms in the air.

'Hi, gang. How's it going?'

'Great, Mike. Much easier now we've got the other bike.'

Kay gave Tony a reproachful look.

'So I take it Roy's got the Bantam tonight.'

'Yep! The Tiger's a real beast. Goes like a bomb.'

'I prefer the other one, or better still, the bus.' Kay sipped her tea.

'If you're going to be one of us, you'd better get used to bikes.'

'I know, Mike. But you don't wear a skirt.'

Tony grinned, 'He don't like girls wearing them either. Always trying to get them to take 'em off.'

Kay dug him in the ribs. 'Trust you. One track minds, all of you.'

'What's the matter with that? Natural ain't it? How do you think you came into the world? Stork bring you? Is that how they do it in Cheshire?'

'Don't be daft. It's alright for you boys, but us girls have our reputations to think about. Right, Elaine?'

'Yes. It's one rule for one and another rule for others.'

Michael shook his head. 'Did you bring the violin, Roy?'

'No, mate. But I think I'm going to cry.'

'Men, who'd have them! Come on Elaine, let's dance.'

'What she on about? Her reputation? You're shagging her you said. Who's telling porkies?'

'She is, but don't you say nothing to her. She told me not to tell anyone.'

Michael drew thumb and finger across his mouth. 'There you go. Mouth zipped. According to them, every girl's a virgin. I *don't* think.'

'You should know. You seem to be the tester.' Roy dunked his biscuit, 'Anyone got any snout?'

Michael took out his case and offered it around.

'*Pall Mall*, where'd these come from?'

'Where do you think?'

'Your uncle.'

'Got it in one. And he got some rolling baccy, next time we go up the field I'll bring some. It don't sell quickly as proper fags.'

'My dad'll probably buy some, he rolls his own. Even puts cork tips in them. Clever.'

'OK. Tell him I can get it cheaper than he's paying for it. How about a machine? Has he got one of them?'

'Never seen him use one, but I'll ask.'

'What are you lot plotting now?' Elaine licked her lips. 'Bit dry in here tonight, what do you reckon, Kay?'

'Nothing. Man's talk. Roy, get the girls a drink, and get me one too.'

'Yes, boss. At once, boss. Lick your boots, boss?'

'Stop messing about, Roy. We're thirsty.' She began to sit down as another record began to play, change her mind and took her friend's hand. 'Oh, come on, Elaine, I love this one. Let's dance.'

Michael swivelled in his chair at the sound of a stick tapping across the floor. 'Blimey, look what the cat's dragged in. What's he doing here?'

'Hello, Michael. Hello, Roy. Hello, Tony. How are you?' The German accent caused a few heads to turn and stare.

'Wotcha, Alfred. Ain't seen you for a while. Didn't know you were a member.'

'I am not. I have come to see why my brother came to this club. The man at the table said this place is for teenagers but still he let me in.'

Michael waved a hand at an empty chair. 'Tony, get Alfred a tea.'

'Thank you. Do they sell coffee? I prefer coffee.'

'You heard the man. Go with him, Roy. Here's ten bob, get us all some biscuits as well.'

'But ...'

A scowl silenced Roy and the two wandered over to the hatch. Moments later they were laughing with the woman volunteer.

Michael took a quick glance at the girls jiving. 'Right. Quick, Alfred, before they get back. Why are you really here? You chasing me about Deiter's bike? The law's got it; they won't let us get on with the repairs.'

'No, Michael. I know about the motor cycle, the authorities informed my father. I came to see the club.'

'But you can't dance. Oops, sorry. I mean ...'

'Do not apologise, Michael. Krieg ist, pardon, war is war. There are many men who can not dance, women too.'

'Deiter told us about your mother, and your other brother. That was a bummer, but my dad lost five of his relatives in an air raid shelter. Anyway, it's all over now.' Michael drained the last of his tea and held out chrome case.

'I will tell you another reason I came here.' Alfred accepted a cigarette. 'The motorcycle has caused much trouble. I can not stay in the house every evening, always they argue. My step mother is angry with me for trying to restore it and she is angry at my father for keeping it.'

I wish he hadn't kept the bloody thing too. And I wish you'd left it alone, the coppers had finished with it, now you've stirred up a hornets nest. 'So you came here to get out of the way. I don't blame you. My house is no barrel of fun either.'

'Barrel of fun? What is ...'

'Leave it, Alfred. It would take too long. Anyway, here come the drinks.'

'There you go. Five teas and one coffee. Custard cream or a diggy gee, Alfred? Help yourself.'

'Thank you. What means ...'

'Digestive, digestive biscuit. Try one.' Roy pushed the plate across the table.

'Where's my change?'

Tony put his hand in his pocket. 'Sorry, Mike. I forgot. Hang on, I'll dig it out.'

'Don't bother, we'll want some more before long. Hold onto it. You can be tea wallah.' Michael grinned at Alfred. 'Don't even ask!'

'So, what brings you here, Alfred?'

'I've been all through that. Leave him be. He's pissed off at home, wants to see what we all get up to.' Turning to Alfred he said, 'Tell you what. Why don't you come down the pub, er, beer hall to you? I'll pick you up on my bike. It's a bit far to walk from where you live.'

'Thank you. I would like that.' Alfred stretched out a leg and massaged it with both hands.

Michael grinned. *Good. And I can keep tabs on what the police tell your old man.* 'That's settled then. Alright if I dance with Kay, Tony?'

'Ask her. But don't go chatting her up. I know you.'

Michael held his hands up, palms facing Tony, a look of shock on his face. 'What me gov? You must be mixing me up with some one else.'

'Get out of it. Go on, before I change me mind.'

Michael strutted onto the dance floor and split the two girls apart.

Elaine walked back and joined the others. 'Hello, Alfred. Nice to see you here.' She tucked her skirt under her and sat down. 'That was great, I was really enjoying that. He plays some cool records, worth sixpence a week.'

'Your tea's getting cold.' Roy helped himself to another biscuit.

'Now look who's arrived, it's Suds and Jimmie!' Tony stood up and putting two fingers in his mouth whistled. The newcomers headed toward him.

'Who let you in? Standards must be slipping.'

Suds got two chairs from an adjacent table and sat down. 'Yeah, Tony. That's why we're here; they asked us along to raise them again after you lot joined.'

'Cheeky bast … bar steward.' Roy looked at Elaine; she pretended not to have heard.

'Just like old times, mate. All the gang back together. Where'd you get the drinks from?'

'Get Suds and Jimmie a drink, Tony. And more biscuits too.'

'Thanks, Mike. I'll have tea with two.'

'Jimmie? What do you want?'

'Same again, not too much milk though.'

'So. What's happening?' Suds passed his cigarettes around.

'Not a lot. How about you two?'

'Got a party lined up if you're interested. Bring your own booze.'

'Sounds great, when? Where?' Michael blew a smoke ring across the table, Roy batted it away.

'My mum and dad have been asked to a wedding, they'll be away for the night. So, it's my place on Saturday, coming?'

'Count me in.'

Roy and Tony nodded in agreement with Michael.

'How about you, girls. You up for it?'

'If Roy's going, I will.'

'Kay?'

'Why not? I enjoy a good party. But I can't stop out too late on account of my Nan.'

'That's that then. Ask Paul and Christine when you see them. Where is he anyway?'

Michael tapped cigarette ash onto the floor beside him. 'He's got the miseries. Didn't want to come out tonight. He looked like he'd found ten bob and lost a pound when I called around his place.'

'Sounds like he needs a party then.'

'Is it possible I could come to the party also?' Alfred asked.

'Who's he?' asked Suds. 'Friend of yours? Thought we'd seen the back of the likes of him.'

'It's OK. He's Deiter's brother. But they're as different as chalk and cheese.'

Turning to Alfred, Michael said, 'I don't think it's your sort of thing. Mostly we'll be dancing and ...'

'Thank you, Michael. I understand. But the invitation to visit the beer hall?'

'No problem, I'll pick you up and take you like I said.'

'I will leave now. See you later, alligator.'

Alfred made his way to the door, stopped to say something to the man signing youngsters in, then left.

'What was he on about? Beer hall? See you later, alligator. Is he a nutter like his brother?'

'Leave him alone, Suds, mate. He's just trying to be one of us.'

'If you say so. But if *he* tries to start running things, we're off.'

'You bet. And quicker than a rat up a drainpipe. I don't know why they let all these blinking foreigners in.' Jimmie stubbed out his cigarette. 'First they bomb the shit, oops, sorry girls. First they bomb us, then they're all lovey dovey. Send 'em all back home, that's what I say.'

'Well you'll have to wait until you rule the world. Our government don't seem to mind who they let in. They say we need people to make up for those killed in the war.' Michael leant back in his chair and reached for his cigarette case.

'Don't make sense. We fight to stop an invasion, get ourselves killed, then they let all the foreigners in to make up the numbers again. What's the difference?'

'We get to keep speaking English for one. I had enough trouble at school learning French, let alone German.' Michael frowned at the thought of 'Chalky' White, his disillusioned language teacher.

'If you lot have finished, how about a dance? I came here to enjoy myself.'

'Sorry Elaine, come on then.' Roy tugged his shirt collar erect and bounced out onto the floor. A few timid teenagers moved out of his way. Elaine took his hand and began to jive.

'*When. When you smile. When you smile at me. Then ...*'

'That's nice, keep singing.' She spun around, swirling her red and white gingham dress, exposing pristine white underwear. 'I didn't know you liked the Kalin Twins.'

'Yeah, I do.' Roy held his arm aloft; she ducked under and leant back. 'I think this is their first record.'

The quiet of the suburban street was broken by loud goodbyes and the sound of motorbike engines revving.

'See you lot on Saturday then.'

'You bet, Suds. See you, Jimmie.' Michael kicked his machine into life as he watched the other two ride away. *Not a bad night, that. Pity there was no crumpet. Still, roll on Saturday.*

Chapter 32

The music issuing through open windows left no one in any doubt that this was the right place for the party. Teenage boys leant against the wall of the prefab, smoking and swilling drink from bottles. Two of them had climbed up onto the corrugated low pitched roof and sat with their legs hanging over the side of the building. Inside, girls were dancing around their handbags. Michael stood and watched.

As Jimmie passed, Michael grabbed his arm. 'I forgot to bring any beer. Where's the nearest place?'

'You can go to the King's Arms or there's an off licence next to the shoe shop, just down the road. It's about the same distance which ever one you go to.'

'Cheers.'

'You off, Mike? You ain't been here long, what's up?'

'Nothing, Roy. Forgot the beer, that's all. I'm just nipping out to get some. Be back in a minute.'

'I'll come with you. I've finished most mine already.' Roy looked around the room. 'Oi! Tony! We're going out for some more supplies, coming?'

'OK. Let's go out the back door though. There's too many idiots blocking the front.'

Stepping out into the garden Michael stopped. 'A wheel barrow! Just the thing, come on.'

'Do what? What do we need that for?' Tony kicked the wheel.

'Carry more booze. Get in, Roy, I'll push you there.'

'You're having a laugh. Get me whistle all dirty, you can sod off.'

'How about you, Tony? Chuck that sack in, it'll be a laugh.'

Reluctantly Tony shook the sack, lined the barrow and eased himself down into it.

'Keep your feet away from the wheel and hang on!'

Michael managed to steer around the side of the building and down the front path. Out on the pavement he began to run.

'Not so fast, you'll tip it over,' Tony protested. Michael began to zig zag, narrowly missing garden fences until a water access cover, raised slightly above the pavement, caused him to loose control. The barrow lurched to one side, tipping Tony out.

'Ow! You silly bugger, Mike. That bloody hurt. And look! I nearly fell in that dog shit! It's all right for you to laugh.'

'Get back in, you pansie. We're nearly there.'

'Not flipping likely, you get in. I'll push.'

'Oh, leave it out. Come on, race you to the offie.'

'Hang about, mate. You got enough? Hope you ain't bent me dad's barrow. He uses that for his manure.' Suds stared at the strange load it was carrying.

'I thought it ponged! You knew that, Mike, I bet,' Tony exclaimed.

'No, I didn't. I thought it was you. Anyway, let's get these bottles inside; we're missing the party by the sound of it.'

'The geezer next door's been round already, complaining about the noise. Cheek! That's good music that is.'

'So, is he going to give us bother, Suds?' Roy asked.

'No, I bunged him four bottles of brown ale, don't know who brought them, but it did the trick.'

'Nice one, what about the other side?'

'He's OK. He lives on his own, bit mutton and geoff, probably can't hear it.'

'Right, that's that sorted then. Now, where's all the talent?' Michael pulled at his crotch and grinned.

'Thought you was in love?' Tony frowned.

'I never said that, anyway she ain't here. Besides I like to keep the old chap happy. And sexercise is good for you.'

'Yeah, but not so loud. We've brought Kay and Elaine along don't forget.'

'That's you two knackered then. All the more for me!'

'What about Paul and Christine? They coming?'

'He said they were, Roy. But you know how he changes his mind. It's up to him, he knows where we are.'

Even with the metal framed windows wide open it was beginning to become very warm inside the prefab.

'Oi, Jimmie! Where can we dump our jackets?' one of the teenagers yelled across the room.

'Use the bedroom, but don't make a mess. Me mum keeps it spick and span.'

Soon the bed disappeared under a pile of zip jackets, drapes and cardigans. Tony unbuttoned his shirt as he danced; Kay copied him and undid the top buttons of her blouse.

'Want another drink,' he asked. 'I've got a mouth like the bottom of a budgie's cage.'

'Yes please, Tony. Babycham, if there's any left.'

'OK, leave it to yours truly. Be back in a shake.'

Michael loosened his bootlace tie, sliding the skull halfway down toward the silver ends. He moved closer to the window and lit another cigarette. *Blimey, it's like an oven in here. It's no good; the jacket's got to go.*

Tony fought his way back from the kitchen. 'The Babycham's all gone, I'll nip down the road before the offie shuts, get some more.'

Kay shook her head. 'Don't worry, I'll try something else. What is there?'

'No, it won't take long. Keep your eye on my beer, I've lost two already.'

Before Kay could protest, Tony pushed through the dancers and wobbled down the front path.

Michael took off his drape and headed for the bedroom. 'Where you off to Mike, had enough?'

'Not likely, Suds, this is a great party. I'm just going to dump me jacket. Stick that *Splish Splash* one on again, good job you got it by Bobby Darin, that Charlie Drake bloke's taking the piss.'

Michael stepped into the small bedroom, someone had closed the curtain.

Kay threw her cardigan on the bed and smiled. 'Hello, Mike. It's hot isn't it. Alright for you boys, you can undo your shirts.'

Michael used a crepe sole to push the door shut behind him as he reached out and pulled her toward him, nuzzling her neck. She pushed him away.

'Ooh, your sideburns tickle. Wait! What are you doing, Michael? - No, don't!'

'I'm only undoing your blouse. Thought you said you were hot?' Michael slid his hand inside her bra and caressed her breasts.

'Stop it, Mike. I'm with Tony.'

'So?' He tweaked her nipples. 'Come on, you know you want to.'

'What? In here, you must be joking.'

'Does this look like I'm joking?'

'Oh - my - god!'

Michael pushed her back onto the pile of clothes, lifted her skirt and fumbled with her underwear.

'No, Mike. Please don't. What about Tony?'

'Nobody misses a slice from a cut cake I always say. And anyway, how's he going to know? I won't tell him.'

'Promise?'

'Of course, now help me with these knickers of yours. Bleedin' suspender belts, always in the way.'

'Oh! I felt that! You shouldn't have! I might get pregnant.'
'You didn't expect me to stop on the vinegar stroke did you?' Michael grinned.
'But Tony always wears something.'
'Yeah, well, these things happen. Look on the bright side, if you get in the pudding club he'll have to marry you.'
'You sod. You'd do that to your mate? I'll tell him.'
'Be my guest, it's your word against mine. Now, get yourself sorted out, someone might come in. They might start a queue.'
'You, you, bloody sod. Get out, I hate you.' She beat her fists against his chest.
'Didn't feel like that just now. Seemed to me you were loving it.' He opened the door and left her sitting on the bed, dabbing her eyes with her skirt.

'Alright, Mike. Good here ain't it.'
'Brilliant, Jimmie. Is Tony about?'
'Ain't seen him. Might be taking a leak in the garden, there's always some tart in the bog.'
'Right. I'll get another beer then. See you later.'
'Alligator!'
'Don't you start all that crap,' Michael grinned.

The sound of motorbikes drowned the music. Looking out the window, Roy groaned. *Oh no, not you!*
The youths stood aside as Titsaleaner entered followed by her escort. Not many of them noticed the colour of her hair or saw the black and white check skirt brushing the tops of her stockings. She grabbed one of the goggle eyed boys and began dancing. He tried to concentrate but her breasts had the effect of a hypnotist's hands.
'Where's the beer?' Bad Breath grunted.
'In the kitchen,' Roy said, 'but it's a bring your own party.'
'Says who?'
Roy shrugged his shoulders and pulled at his shirt collar.

Michael came back into the front room with a pint glass in one hand and a cigarette in the other. He pushed his way through to the newcomer.
'Wotcha, mate. Who invited you?'
'No one; didn't know there was a party. Heard the music as we rode past, thought I'd invite meself.'
'Alright if I dance with your bird?'
'Why not? Everyone else does. I'm just here for the booze. - Hang on a minute! – It was you on that bike, you had her on the back.' He pointed at Titseleaner.
'What are you on about? What bike?'
'I don't know *whose* bike you were riding, it wasn't yours. But it *was* you alright.' Grabbing hold of Michael's shirt he twisted the material and pulled him forward. 'I've told you before! She's ours. I'll teach you to mess with her.' Bad Breath pulled back his other arm and swung a punch. Michael's head rocked back and he spat blood.
Pulling himself free he caught hold of the lapels of the leather jacket and jerked his head forward, catching Bad Breath full in the face.
'Have a dandruff sandwich!' Michael grunted.
'Bastard!' I'll have you! I'll cut you so's your own mother won't know you.'
Michael caught hold of his wrist as the youth reached for his knife. 'Not today, mate.'
A fist to the stomach caused Bad Breath to double over in pain. Michael pulled his fist back again but was attacked from behind. Blows from a stiletto heel rained down on him. Turning to face this new threat

Michael saw Kay's face distorted by fury. He put his hands up to defend himself but she continued to lash out with her shoe.

'Leave it out, Kay! That bloody well hurts.'

'Good!' She tried to kick him but missed her target and stubbed her toes on his shin. 'Bugger! That hurt.' She broke off her assault and hopped around holding her foot. Michael seized his chance and ran for the door. Roy's outstretched foot tripped Bad Breath, giving his friend time to get out. The sound of the Road Rocket racing off signalled an end to the fight.

Bad Breath picked an embroidered antimacassar off the back of a chair and wiped at the blood from his nose.

'Good riddance to bad rubbish. I'll 'ave 'im later.'

'Get me a drink, will you.' Titsaleaner grasped Bad Breath's arm.

'Get it yourself.' He wiped his mouth with the sleeve of his jacket. 'If that crazy bird hadn't interfered I'd have had him. It *was* him I saw with you, wasn't it.'

'Told you before, you imagined it. I don't go with no one that don't belong to the gang.'

'Liar. Get me a beer while you're out there.' He reached down and smacked her backside.

Chapter 33

'Pass your father the gravy, Alfred. And don't spill it; I've just washed this tablecloth.'

Alfred glared, but obeyed his stepmother. For the sake of his father, Alfred was trying to refrain from causing any further rows. Sunday dinner time had become one of the only times the three of them shared a meal at the table.

'I am pleased to hear you are going out in the evenings. Have you found new comrades?'

'No, father. I have been to the club where the young people go to. Deiter's friends are there, I know many of them. The music is strange but very much alive.'

'I would have thought that you would find more suitable friends, considering that if it were not for them your brother would still be alive.' A potato waving on the end of a fork emphasised his stepmothers' words.

'What do you mean?'

'Well, it is very obvious, Alfred. If your brother hadn't become mixed up with them he wouldn't have bought that awful machine.'

'That may be as you say, but my brother had no fear. A motorcycle is exciting. If I remember correctly, he had one before Michael.'

'That's right, argue with me again. You are always against me. Speak to him, Ernst.'

'How is Michael?' his father asked.

Placing his knife and fork on the plate, Alfred picked up a glass of water and sipped.

'He is quite well, father. Although he did look very tired when I saw him. His eyes – there was something about his eyes. He reminded me of the Russkie prisoners before we shot them.'

'Don't start on about all that again. Your father has asked you before. He does not wish the war to be mentioned, especially at the dinner table.'

'Sorry, father. But that was how Michael looked.'

'I understand. If you have finished eating I am sure your mother will excuse you from the table.'

She nodded.

'Thank you. I will leave you two to finish your meal in peace.' Alfred wiped his mouth with a napkin and stood up.

His father held up a hand. 'While we are talking about Michael and your brother, you must tell me if there is any news from the police.'

'That is the reason I have begun to associate with him. I need to know the truth.'

'What do you mean; the truth?'

'The authorities have not released his motorcycle to be repaired. Why is that? It was an accident, was it not?'

'I do not know, my son. I do not know. We must wait for information.'

Chapter 34

'This is nice, boys. I love playing cards; I'll make the tea after this hand.'

'Cheers, Mum. Got any more custard creams? Come on, Mike. It's your bet.'

Michael peeled his cards from the kitchen table and checked them once again. 'I'll raise it to tuppence.' As he tossed the coins onto the pile he straightened his leg and felt his foot contact Paul's mother's slippe

'Tuppence! That's it, I'm out.' Paul threw his cards down in disgust. His mother added two pennies to t pot. Michael felt her foot rubbing up and down his leg.

'Two more, Mrs P. I think you're bluffing.'

Her foot found his crotch beneath the table and caressed it. Michael suddenly became uncomfortable an shifted position.

'You know me too well, Michael. What have you got? I'll see you.'

What have I got? I've got a stomping great hard on, thanks to you. 'Ace high.'

'Is that all? Pair of fours, I win.' She spread the cards out and scooped the coins toward her. 'I'll make t tea now. Would you put the kettle on please, Michael. You're nearest.'

Michael winced. 'No, it's alright. I don't want tea, thanks.'

She laughed. 'Well I do. Paul, be a love, put the kettle on.'

'Oh, mum. Why me? Can't you do it?'

'Do as you're told. Then you can have my biscuit.'

Taking advantage of Paul while his back was turned to fill the kettle, Michael mouthed. *'Will you marry me?'* Immediately another nudge added to his discomfort.

'Ow!'

Paul turned around, 'What's up, Mike? You OK?'

'Banged me knee against the table, that's all. And I've changed me mind, get me a tea.'

'Please,' Paul's mother said. 'And the answer's no.'

'Do what mum? Do you want the kettle on or not?'

'I was just reminding Michael to watch his Ps and Qs.'

'Oh.' Paul rubbed the side of his head. *What's she on about now?*

A knock at the door sent him from the sink to answer it, wiping his wet hand down his trousers as he went.

'Hello, Chris. What are you doing here?'

'As you seem to have forgotten me lately I thought I'd come around and see what the problem is,' she pouted.

'Problem? What are you on about?'

'We're supposed to be going out together aren't we?'

'Yes, of course.'

'Then where have you been? I haven't seen you for ages. You asked me to go to a party with you and then you never called for me. Have you found someone else?'

'No, Chris! You know I haven't. It's just that I've not been well lately. Come in and ask Mike, he'll tell you. We're playing cards. Me mum's feeling a bit lonely, I told her I would stay in for a change. Come in for a little while, and then we can go down the pub if you like.'

'Huh! Michael would say anything. He's always been the one looking out for you, ever since you joined his gang.'

'No he wouldn't. What do you mean, looking out for me? I can look out for myself. I don't need him!'

'And it seems you don't need me either. Go and play your silly games, mummy's boy.'

'What's the matter, Chris? Why are you upset? Don't you want to go to the pub?'

Christine turned away and marched up the garden path. 'No, I don't,' she shouted. 'And I don't want to see you again, ever!'

Paul tried to swallow the lump in his throat. Wiping his eyes he went back to the kitchen.

'Are you crying, my darling? What's happened? Who was that at the door?'

Paul turned, ran back to the hall and up the stairs. A door slammed.

'Oh dear. Why is he so upset, Michael? Do you know?'

Michael put two cigarettes between his lips, lit them and passed one across the table.

'No, Mrs P. He's getting a bit moody lately, but don't we all at times?'

She stood and picked up Paul's cup. 'I'll have to go up to him. I don't like to see him like this. I'll take him his tea.'

Michael nodded, 'Shall I leave?'

'It's your choice, but perhaps it would be better. We can play cards again another time.'

Watching her swaying hips he followed her through to the staircase in the hall. As his arms reached forward to grasp her from behind a handkerchief dropped from her apron pocket. Michael stooped and retrieved it. Scrunching it in the palm of his hand he let himself out of the front door. Once in the safety of the garden he opened his fist and inhaled the scent from his trophy before folding it carefully and placing it in the top pocket of his jacket.

A knock on the bedroom door brought no response. She knocked again.

'Go away! Leave me alone.'

Opening the door she stared at Paul. He lay curled on the bed clutching a pillow around his head, sobbing.

'Oh, Paul, my darling. Whatever is the matter? Who *was* that at the door?'

He turned over. 'No one.'

'Don't be silly. I heard you talking to somebody. I'm your mum, surely you can tell me who it was.'

'Christine.'

'So why the tears?'

'She's chucked me.'

'Oh. Why?'

'I don't know. Ask *her*.'

'Here, drink your tea. Let's hear all about it.' She sat on the bed and patted him. He ignored her, so after a minute or two she decided to leave him alone.

Later that evening Michael sat up in bed tracing the monogram 'P' with his finger. He inhaled the fragrance it held time and again before placing it reverentially beneath his pillow.

Chapter 35

Suds stopped at the traffic lights and waited. He was on his way to call for Jimmie; it was their night to pl
snooker. Looking to his left he recognised Bad Breath walking toward him.

'Oi! Want a lift?' he shouted.

The leather jacketed youth ran up to him. 'Cheers, mate. Can you drop us off at Bentini's? The others ar
there; I can get a lift back to Woolwich.'

'No problem, bit out of my way but that's OK.'

'Good man.' Bad Breath climbed onto the rear of the bike.

'Ready? Hold on!' As the lights changed colour Suds sped across the junction and through the urban
sprawl.

'How fast we going?' the pillion passenger shouted into the wind.

'Sixty!'

'What's up? Stuck in third?'

In place of an answer Suds accelerated. The bike tore around bends, down narrow streets, until he reache
the mad mile. *Now I'll show you!*

His eyes flicked continually from the road to the speedometer and back again. Timing was everything. H
slowed for the bridge, leaning the bike further and further over. Then it was time to brake hard as the
roundabout loomed ahead. Suds leaned the bike once again, circled the roundabout and accelerated once
again. Clear of the bridge he leant forward and urged the machine on even faster.

'Ninety five!' he shouted. 'But we're out of road.'

The brakes slowed the machine and Suds stopped opposite Bentini's on the other side of the dual
carriageway.

'There you go. Pity we didn't hit the ton. Might be the speedo, probably was a hundred.'

'Cheers, mate. Want a coffee?' Bad Breath asked.

'No. It's OK thanks, I'm calling for someone. We're off to play snooker. Why were you walking?
Where's your bike?'

'Hit the back of a parked car, didn't I. Had to push me bike back home, I've done the bloody front wheel
in. Now I got to get a new one from somewhere. Don't know where I can get bits for a Norton do you?'

'No. Your best bet is to ask Mike. He'll know.'

'That bastard! No thanks. Me and him have got a score to settle.'

'Oh yeah, the party. I forgot.'

Suds scratched his nose. 'Hang on. - I just remembered. I know where there's a Norton you could get
bits off. Wouldn't cost you nothing.'

'You pulling my pisser? Free? Where?'

'Aah, that's the dodgy bit. It's in the yard at the back of the cop shop over near where Mike lives.'

'And how am I meant to get a wheel off it, go and ask the bluebottles I suppose.'

Suds laughed, 'Well, you could try that! But it's only a brick wall with a bit of rusty barbed wire on top.
You and your mates could do it easily and there must be lots of things you could nick off it. But if you're
chicken…'

'Chicken! You cheeky bleeder. We done lots of jobs, nicking bits from a law shop's nothing. Tell me
where it is.'

After making sure Bad Breath knew where the motorcycle was being kept, Suds rode off to meet Jimmie

Five youths walked down the high street, keeping in the shadows, stopping to check if any one else was
about at this late hour. Reaching the police station they walked slowly past and stopped outside the shop
next door.

'All clear?' Bad Breath asked in a low voice.

'Yeah, come on, let's get on with it.'

Keeping to the side of the shop wall the gang cautiously advanced. At the end of the alley they stood in darkness in front of a gate and stared up at the barbed wire. Bad Breath tugged at the handle, it wouldn't budge.

'Right, you two, bend down.' Bad Breath hissed.

Placing hands against the gate a couple of the gang complied. Bad Breath took off his leather jacket and climbed onto the youth's backs. Throwing his jacket across the wire he pulled himself onto the top of the gate and manoeuvred into position. Gripping the wire through the leather protection he took a deep breath and dropped down. Swiftly he drew back the bolts and opened the gate.

'Right, get my jacket down you two, and don't rip it. We'll start looking for the bike.'

By the dim light of the stars overhead the remaining three began the search.

In the gloom a plaintiff whine attracted Bad Breath's attention. 'What was that?' he whispered.

'It's over here, it's a dog. The rozzers have locked it in a cage.'

'What for? Oh, never mind, just find this bike.'

'Here it is! Under this tarpaulin!' came an excited cry.

'Shut it you wanker!' Bad Breath snarled. 'You want everyone to hear? Shut yer mouth and listen.'

The youths waited in silence. 'OK, it's all clear, let's take a gander at the bike.' Bad Breath crossed the small yard as the cover was pulled further back.

'Well slap me down with a wet kipper! That bloke Suds was right on the money. It's a Norton alright. And it don't look in bad nick, either.'

'We gonna have the front wheel off then?'

'Don't be so bloody daft, we'll take the whole thing. Look a bit strange bowling a wheel along wouldn't it? If we nick the bike we can say it broke down if anyone stops us.'

'Then what?'

'I'll strip it down for spares and dump the rest.'

At the end of the alley, Bad Breath looked left then right. 'Come on you lot, let's get it out of here.'

Two of the youths walked on either side while the others pushed from behind.

'Christ! This is sodding hard work,' one of the complained.

'Just keep it moving. Turn into the road where we left the bikes and van.'

'We'll bloody well have to; we can't push this all the way to Woolwich.'

'Just shut it. Keep pushing, we're nearly there.'

A few days later, following an embarrassing and fruitless search, a telephone call informed the garage that the motorcycle would not be returned for repair. No explanation was offered.

Chapter 36

Ernst opened the door to Michael. 'Good evening.'

'Is Alfred in? I've called to take him out.'

'One moment. I will tell him you are arrived.'

'Cheers.'

Michael lit a cigarette while he waited. After a while, Alfred appeared wearing a shirt that was obviously too large.

'Wotcha, Alfred. All ready for the pub? Neat shirt, where'd you get it?'

'It belongs to my brother.'

'Oh.' Launching his cigarette in the direction of the next door garden, Michael sauntered back to his bike. He waited patiently as Alfred struggled to mount.

'You on? Don't drop your stick, and keep it out of the wheel.'

'I'll do what you tell me. Thank you.'

'There you go, Alfred? Lager, no lime.'

'Thank you. Prost!'

'Bottoms up. Have you any news about Deiter's bike? We still haven't seen it since the coppers took it away.'

'Do you not know? It has been stolen. The authorities came to see my father.'

Bugger me! So that's why we won't be getting it back! 'Do what? Stolen? From a cop shop?'

'What means cop shop?'

'Sorry. Police station. Where the police sit around drinking tea.'

'How strange.'

'So what happened, did they tell you?'

'My father tells me some people steal the motorcycle in the night. The authorities have made a search but can not find it.'

So that explains that business at the garage the other day. Bet they think I nicked it. Wonder who did? Whoever it was did me a favour, that's for sure.

'How is your father? Still giving you grief? You know, is he still arguing with you all the time?'

'Not so much my father. My stepmother, she is the one. Always she finds fault with what I do.' Alfred moved his leg and knocked his stick to the floor. Michael reached down and retrieved it.

'Thank you.'

'Bit of a bugger that leg of yours. Does it hurt?'

'Winter is the bad time, the cold adds to the pain. The winter of forty seven was terrible for me.'

'It weren't too clever for anyone, mate. Bloody great icicles hanging off the roofs, snow everywhere, and freezing indoors as well as out. My fingers used to go white and hurt like buggery when I warmed them in front of the fire.' Michael shivered at the thought. 'My mum knitted me a balaclava, you know, a hat made of wool.'

Alfred nodded.

'Anyway, it kept my ears from dropping off but my breath made the wool wet and I ended up with a chapped chin.' Michael drained his drink. 'Coal was like gold dust. I remember one day the coalman's horse slipped on the ice and everyone rushed to help.' He laughed. 'Help themselves I mean. While the poor bloke spread horse feed onto the ice to give the animal some grip, people were nicking coal from his cart.'

'That is terrible. In Germany they would have been shot.' Alfred thrust his hand into his pocket. 'Another beer?'

'Cheers. Give us the dosh; I'll go, save you getting up.'

'Thank you.'

While Michael stood at the bar, the street door opened.

'Wotcha, Alfred! What you doing here?'

'Hello Roy, hello everybody. I come with Michael.'

'Oh yeah, I see him now. Oi, Mike, get 'em in!'

Michael turned round and grinned. 'Trust you, what you all want? The usual?'

'Cheers, Mike. Don't forget the girls.'

As if I ever forget girls! Michael used two fingers to reply then ordered the drinks.

'Babycham, please, Mike,' Elaine called across the pub.

'Me too!' Christine echoed before turning to speak to Alfred.

'Do you like it here?' she asked.

'Yes.' He lowered his voice. 'But some people look at me. I think I would not come without Michael.'

Tony flicked his lighter and lit a cigarette. 'It's that accent of yours. A lot of people ain't got much time for Germans.'

Alfred sighed. 'I know. My stepmother for example.'

'But, she married your father, surely ...'

'Love is blind. But she does not love me. It is time for me to leave home, find some friends that are my own age.'

'We don't think of you as being old. Well, not that old anyway.'

'I will be twenty four years in October.'

Christine smiled. 'That's funny. My birthday is in October, October the tenth. I'll be seventeen.' She shuffled her chair closer and placed her hand over Alfred's. 'We should share a birthday party.'

'I would like that.' Alfred raised his glass and finished his drink as Michael returned.

'Where's Paul, Chris?'

'I'm not seeing him anymore, Mike. He's gone all sulky lately, says one thing then does something else. I've had enough.'

'That's a shame. Still I don't blame you, last time I was round his place he was like a pregnant duck in a thunderstorm.' Michael passed his cigarette case around. 'And what about Kay, Tony? She washing her hair or something?'

'Still upset about the trouble at the party the other night. Don't know what's got into her.'

'Oh, she'll get over it. She gave me a right hammering, don't know her own strength.' Michael felt the lumps on the back of his head.

'Yeah, strange that. She really had it in for you, didn't she.'

You can say that again, and in more ways than one. 'Yeah. Fancy her helping that Chieftain bloke instead of me. I can't make heads or tails of it. Still, she is from up north, what else can you expect? Foreigners, I ask you.' Taking the cigarette case back from Tony he returned it to his jacket pocket. Alfred looked down at the floor. 'Oh, sorry, I didn't mean you, mate. Come on, drink up. It's Tony's round next.'

Chapter 37

'I'm bored. It's time we did something.'

'Yeah, like what, Roy? It's OK for you, you got your band. Why don't you get out and play more?'

'That's easy for you to say, Mike. But your uncle's dumped us and you don't want to take his place. How are we supposed to get gigs?'

'I dunno. There must be someone who'd be your agent.'

'Like who?'

'Why not try Pat again? He's out of hospital now and he's the one with all the contacts.'

'Oh yeah! You think he wants anything to do with us, after Deiter nearly killed him.'

Michael choked on his cigarette, 'I see what you mean,' he spluttered. 'Oh well, that's put the kybosh on that then. What about Alfred? He wants to get out of his house more. Why not ask him?'

'You're having a laugh. Another bloody German? He'd be a great help, I don't think.'

Tony pushed himself off the wire fence dividing the field from the allotments. 'Why don't we go down to Margate again? That was great.'

'No, I don't fancy it. How about Southend instead? The Kurzel. Supposed to be just like Dreamland in Margate, but with knobs on.' Roy brushed cigarette ash off his waistcoat.

'Now you're whistling Dixie,' Tony said excitedly. 'Take the girls on our bikes; give us a chance to show them what they can do. What about you, Mike? Gonna bring this secret love of your life you keep on about? Who is she?'

'Mind yer own. I'll still come with you though, bound to be plenty of crumpet going spare.'

'You can take Paul then,' Roy said. 'That's if you can winkle him out of his shell.'

'I'll ask him, but … No, hang about, I've changed me mind. You lot go, I'm not really in the mood. I'll still ask Paul though.'

Roy looked puzzled. 'And how's he going to get there? Shanks's pony?'

'Leave it to me; I'll call round at Jimmie's place, see if him and Suds fancy it. One of them could take Paul.'

'Sounds good to me boss, be great to go down there mob handed. But you should come, all the old gang together.'

'No, Roy. I just don't feel like it. Think I might be going down with something. My get up and go seems to have got up and buggered off.'

'Oh well, if you change your mind before Saturday just let us know.'

Outside Bentini's the noise of the bikes filled the air. Suds, with Paul riding pillion, circled the gravel forecourt, followed closely by Jimmie. A few teenagers sat on the low wall and watched in envy. Roy and Tony, restrained by the girls, sat on their bikes revving the engines needlessly. Roy was eager to set off; Michael had lent him his Road Rocket in exchange for the Bantam.

'Oi! You two!' he shouted above the din, 'Come on, let's go!'

The bikes swung onto the dual carriage way and began the race to be first to arrive in Southend.

Michael washed the dirt from his hands, scooped up the grimy water and splashed his face. After winning a short battle with the roller towel he clocked out and locked the garage doors behind him.

'Another day, another dollar. I don't like working all day on a Saturday though,' he said to himself as he sat on the Bantam. 'Right, now, let's see if she's home. I expect she's been lonely without Paul.'

Chapter 38

A hesitant knock at the door was answered by the waft of Eau de Toilette, the scent of roses complimenting the floral pattern of her skirt, a skirt that filled the doorway thanks to her starched petticoats. Christine smiled, turned and called out.

'Bye, mum. We won't be late.'

'You be home by ten o'clock, my girl. Do you hear me?'

'Oh, mum. We're going to the pictures, be in by eleven. OK?' Without waiting for a reply she stepped out of the house and closed the door.

'Hello, Christine. You look beautiful.'

'Thank you, Alfred.' She touched her lacquered hair. 'Come on then, it's a bit of a walk to the bus stop. Especially with my leg.'

'I have the same. We are a matched pair.' Alfred smiled as he tapped his leg with his stick.

'Sorry, Alfred. I forgot. Does it often play you up?'

'It is not so bad. Some days are better than others.'

Alfred held Christine's hand and stared up at the posters above the entrance to the cinema, poster paints proclaimed the titles of films on offer today. The main feature was 'They Were Not Divided,' and the 'B' supporting film starred Roy Rogers.

'Do you know these movies?' he asked.

'No, but I do know Roy Rogers is a cowboy and the other one sounds like a love story.'

The doors were opened and the queue began to file in.

'Will you pay for the seats please? I give you the money, sometimes I am not understood.' Alfred passed Christine a ten shilling note. 'Buy some chocolate also if they have any.'

'No, Alfred. I can pay for myself, thank you.'

He looked down at his feet. 'I am sorry. I did not mean to offend you.'

'Don't be silly, it's just that I always paid my way when Paul took me out.'

'I understand. - Which seats are the best?'

Christine giggled. 'There's not much to choose between them. The bughutch is too small to make much difference. How about the back row? At least we won't have peoples knees jammed into the back of our seats.'

'The back row is fine. Please let me pay. I have looked forward to this evening.'

'OK, if it makes you happy. Thank you. But I'll pay for the ice creams in the interval.'

The cinema owners' wife, shining her torch, led the way to the rear of the cinema. Christine stood aside to allow Alfred to pass. 'You get in first, go to the far end, then we won't have to keep getting up and down when people arrive late.'

Alfred shuffled along the row of seats, leant his stick against the side wall and made himself comfortable.

'This is a good idea. I like it here in the corner.'

The lady with the torch tugged at the curtains while ignoring advice offered by the waiting audience. Finally the silver screen was ready.

Throughout the Pearl and Dean adverts people chatted on, clouds of cigarette smoke curling up toward the ceiling. Roy Rogers was greeted by cheers as the light from the projection box sliced through the blue haze. Christine continually dipped into her box of chocolates as the hero battled against the bad men in black hats.

As the film credits rolled, an irregular shaped hole appeared in the image, growing rapidly. The projector stopped and the house lights came on. Minutes passed and the audience began stamping their feet. The lights were extinguished and the projector whirled again, this time a crowing cockerel introduced the newsreel. People began moving about, changing seats, going out to the foyer for sweets. The trouble in Cyprus meant nothing to most of them and they cared even less for General De Gaulle.

'Roy Rogers was a good film.' Alfred lit another cigarette. 'When he was tied to a chair I could not see how he would escape.'

Christine snuggled up against him. 'Yes, but Trigger always come to his rescue. He's a very clever horse. Would you like an ice cream?'

'No. No, thank you. Would you?'

'I don't think I'll bother, I'm full of chocolates! I hope the next film is as exciting as that one was.' She squeezed his hand. 'I'm glad you asked me out.'

The audience began pushing and shoving as the National Anthem began to play. Sheepishly, those unable to get out in time stood up until it finished.

Outside, Christine turned to her escort. 'I'm sorry about that, Alfred. I didn't know it was a *war* film. I'm so sorry.'

Alfred put his arm around her shoulders and gently pulled her against him. 'It was not your fault. But it made me feel sad, the two who died at the end of the film, they could have been my brother and I.'

'Let's forget about it, shall we? - I know; you can buy me a bag of chips if the shop's still open.'

'Another good idea. Come on, I will race you! And next time we come to the cinema we will make sure we know about the film.'

Chapter 39

Michael checked his bootlace tie, ran well scrubbed fingers down his sideburns then knocked at the door.

Mrs Parker stood with a red and white headscarf tied on top of her head, a pinafore tied around her waist and pink slippers on her feet. A cigarette, clinging to her lip, began to bob up and down as she spoke.

'Hello, Michael. What are you doing here? Paul's gone to Southend; I thought you'd gone with them.'

'No, I wanted to, but I had to work. Can I come in?'

She leant out of the door, looking up and down the road.

'Oh, alright then. The kettle's on, we can have a cuppa. I've had enough of ironing anyway.'

Michael stepped in, closed the door behind him and followed her through to the kitchen. The sight of a loaf and bread knife on the table brought an audible rumble from his stomach.

'Was that you? Are you hungry?'

'Sorry. I haven't had time for dinner. I was in a hurry to come round to see you.'

'Silly boy. Cut yourself some bread. There's dripping, jam, or a bit of mousetrap, but you might have to scrape it a bit.'

'Dripping sounds good to me, with lashings of salt.' Michael ran his tongue around his lips.

'Go on then, help yourself; this isn't a café you know. I'll make the tea.'

Scooping small globules of cream, along with a couple of tea leaves from the top of his tea, Michael tapped them into the saucer.

'What time do you expect Paul back?' he asked.

'I told him mid-night at the latest, the others wanted him to stay out all night but I put my foot down.'

That's a pity. Never mind, it's still early. There's plenty of time yet. 'I think they were winding you up, no one said anything to me about making it an all nighter,' Michael grinned as he sawed at the loaf.

'Oh, leave that, Michael! You're making a right pigs' ear out of it. That bread's got to last until the baker opens again on Monday and Paul likes to mop up the gravy from his Sunday roast. If you keep cutting doorsteps like that there'll be none left!'

Michael sat down and watched. The gentle swaying of her buttocks as she cut a thin slice ensured that his tea wasn't the only thing to be stirred.

Paul's mother turned round and handed the plate to Michael. 'Help yourself to the dripping; it's in the tray at the bottom of the oven.'

As he stood up she smiled. 'I've never seen dripping have that effect before! Perhaps you should have had the jam!'

'I don't think that would have made any difference. You can't keep a good man down, they say,' Michael smiled. 'How about a game of cards? We've got a couple of hours before they get back.'

'Yes, cards would be nice. What shall we play?'

'Strip poker!'

'Now, now. Anyway, I don't know the rules to poker.'

'Don't worry about it. We couldn't play anyway, there's only the two of us. Tell you what, we'll play rummy. Each hand you lose, something comes off. Fair enough?'

'Go on then, I could do with a bit of fun. Paul walks round like a wet week all the time. Let's cut for deal.'

Michael sat stripped to the waist, a St. Christopher medallion nestling in the hairs on his chest. 'Have you fixed these cards?' he asked.

'How could I? You're shuffling them hard enough to wear the spots off.'

'Huh! Ain't doing me any good though, is it? I haven't won a hand yet.'

Mrs Parker leant back in her chair and lit another cigarette. 'Good. I'm enjoying this! Hurry up and deal, I want those trousers off next.'

'Well, that's a start, I'm glad I stuck with collecting aces,' Michael said as he unbuttoned her blouse. She used the opportunity to rub her hands up and down the front of his trousers.

'Don't do that! It's bad enough already. I'll never last the game out at this rate,' he protested.

She smiled and tugged at his zip.

'Right, that's it. You've asked for this.' Michael pulled her to her feet and began kissing her feverishly. A quick fumble behind her back and a white brassiere fell to the floor. Michael kissed her breasts and tore at her panties while she wrestled with his obstinate trousers

The kitchen table groaned under the unusual activity. A pile of carefully ironed garments were pushed aside and joined the clothes scattered on the kitchen floor.

'Why won't you marry me,' Michael panted. 'I want this to go on for ever.'

'We've been over all that before,' she sighed. 'You know it's impossible.'

'No it's not. All we've got to do – Hang about! That's a bike outside! They're back early!'

Michael helped his partner in crime off the table then began scrabbling through the tangled mess on the floor for his clothes. Clutching them to his naked body he blew her a kiss and he rushed out the back door. 'See you, I love you.' She dressed hastily while laughing at the sight of Michael's snowy white buttocks disappearing into the gloom.

The cool night air colliding with his hot sweaty body made him shiver. He held the bundle of clothes tightly and ran down the garden path. The concrete finished at the vegetable garden and Michael bit his lip as he found a large stone with the sole of his bare foot. Gooseberry bushes scratched his flesh as he ploughed between them in the darkness.

A cat, tight rope walking the back fence, turned and glared at him as he scrambled over and dropped down into the fields behind the houses.

'Shit, shit, and double shit! Bloody fence, bloody splinters! Still, never mind, it was worth it. Oh, Pauline why won't you change your mind? I need you so much.'

Michael began hopping around with one leg in his trousers, gave up the battle and lay down on the cold grass. Once the stubborn garment had been tamed he stood up again and began to finish dressing.

'Bugger, where's me other sock?' He searched the area without success then pulled himself up the fence to peer over. The garden was a mass of shadows, only the area outside the house was visible by the light from the kitchen window. *I can't see it. Christ, I hope it's not on the floor in there.* He ducked involuntarily as he saw Paul's mother embrace her son in the kitchen. Dropping back down to the grass, he put the remaining shoe onto his foot and tied the lace.

Keeping low he followed the line of fences to the end then began to hurry down the road. He chose to walk the long way round to avoid passing Paul's house. Before long a blister caused him to stop and line the sock-less shoe with his handkerchief.

'That's better, bleedin' sock. Where the devil did I drop it? If Paul finds it, he'll know it's mine. He's seen them often enough.'

'You're back early, my darling. Did you have a good time?'

'Yes, it was great. But it didn't feel right without Christine.'

'Never mind, my love, I expect you'll be back together again soon.' Mrs Parker began to sort out the hastily scooped up clothes that lay in a heap on the table. She began to smooth the creases and stack them neatly.

'Huh, I don't think so,' he sighed. 'Leave that, mum, I'll do it. You can make some cocoa.'

'That would be nice, sweetheart. Try to straighten them out if you can. I'd just finished ironing them when they toppled over and fell onto the floor.' She took a bottle of milk out of the larder, sniffed it, poured some into a small saucepan and lit the gas.

'What's this?' Paul held up a sock, 'It looks like one of Michael's, what's it doing here? And where's the other one?'

She blushed. 'Oh, he left them here for me to mend; you know his mother can't do it.'

'But there's nothing wrong with it, there aren't any holes at all.'

'It must have been the other one.'

'So, where is it then?' Paul held the sock to his nose. 'Blimey, he could have washed them before he brought them round.'

'I thought I had. The other one must still be in the water in the copper or perhaps it's on the washing line. I'll have to look for it in the morning. Come on, my darling, drink your cocoa. It's way past your bedtime.'

Chapter 40

Perry Como was advising anyone listening to, *'Catch a falling star,'* while the girls at the table nearest the jukebox swayed in unison to the song. Bentini did his best to sing along as he dispensed their coffees; his Italian accent would perhaps have added a little something to the lyrics, if he had been able to sing.

'That's enough of that slush. Got any dosh?'

'Here you go, Suds. Do us a favour; get us some more drinks while you're at it.'

The door opened and Michael swaggered in.

'Wotcha! What are you two layabouts doing up this early. I thought you'd be laying in after your trip yesterday.'

'Hiya, Mike. No, we come back early. Hang on, I'm just going to feed the jukebox and get some coffee. Want one?'

'Cheers, Suds. Hurry up, get your arse into gear, I want to hear how it went at Southend.'

Duane Eddy's *Rebel Rouser* got fingers tapping as Suds returned with the drinks.

'Nice one, mate. Roy really rates this, it's something different. Anyway, how did it go?'

'It was alright. Loads of Teds, and plenty of crumpet. Paul was a pain though, walked around all day looking like he'd shit himself. He was a right misery. We dumped him in the end, told him where to meet us and went off to enjoy ourselves.'

'Suds is right. Us two, and Roy, Tony and their birds, we all had a laugh. And you should have seen the Wall of Death geezer, you'd have loved that. How he gets that motorbike to do that beats me.'

Michael stretched and yawned. 'It's easy, Jimmie. All you gotta do is get the speed right. If I'd been there I'd have asked him if I could have a go. Bet I could have shown him a thing or two.'

'Well, next time we go, you can,' James said, offering his cigarettes around.

Michael lit one, leaned back and blew smoke into the air. 'What about the talent? Did you have any luck?'

Suds smirked. 'We did and we didn't. Jimmie and me picked up two cracking birds, all tits and legs. Just like the ones in them magazines.'

'Yeah, but they got the last laugh, didn't they? All me and you got was a handful of tit and a grope under the pier.'

'Ah, but next time we see them ...'

'You must be joking, mate. I'm not going all that way for that. They were leading us by the nose, or our cocks more like. Think of all the cash we splashed, and for what?'

Michael laughed. 'Sounds like you needed the maestro with you, to show you how it's done. I could give you lessons if you like, half a crown an hour, how's that sound.'

'The proof of the pudding is in the eating. Where's this love of your life, why don't you bring her with you. Does she need a license to be out in daylight, or don't they make paper bags her size!' Suds laughed, rocked back on his chair, lost his balance and crashed to the floor.

'Out! All of you! Get out!' Bentini jumped up and down. 'You are banned. Get out!'

'Shut it, Benito,' Michael answered. 'We'll be back when you learn how to make a decent cup of coffee.'

Bentini's spluttering rivalled that of his coffee machine as the three of them left.

Roy and Tony sat with their legs dangling over the low wall outside the King's Arms, a packet of Kensitas cigarettes and two pints of lager separating them. Roy swung his feet, making the back of the heels of his crepe soled shoes bounce off the wall. Cigarette ends littered the pavement.

Tony jumped off the wall and massaged his buttocks. 'Boring ain't it. And that sodding wall is hard. Why don't we go inside, sit comfortably.'

'Yeah, OK, mate. Oh, hang on, Tony, I forgot to tell you. Bet you'll never guess who I got a letter from, came in the second post.' Roy reached inside his jacket and pulled out an envelope.

'I know! Her Majesty's Prison, they've got a cell ready for you.'

'Idiot! No, mate. It's from Pat.' He held it out triumphantly.

'What's he want? Apart from young boys, that is?' Tony asked sarcastically.

'A band's let him down and he wants to know if we can help out.'

'Bollocks to that! He bats for the other team, makes me shudder just to think about him. Greasy bastard.'

'He wants us to play *for* him, not *with* him. The money's good and besides we ain't done much lately have we? Never know; he might be interested in taking us on again. He did get us some good gigs, remember?'

'Well, as long as we don't end up as a *backing* group. - You'll have to deal with him though; I'll keep out of it. I'd only end up telling him what I think about queers.'

'It's OK. I've already 'phoned him. It's all sorted. Next Saturday he said, about sevenish. And I've spoken to me brother, Billy, he's keen. If I know Billy I reckon he's driving me mum and dad mad with those drums of his right now.'

'Pity Mike dumped that motor, would've been just the job to cart our gear in.'

'That's sorted too. Pat's sending an estate car to pick us and our instruments up. And he said his man will bring us back again if we hang about after the party's over. You can't odds that can you.'

Tony frowned. 'No, I suppose not. I take it you've told Billy about Pat, you know, told him he's as bent as a nine bob note.'

'Of course I have, but he didn't have a clue what I was telling him though. Don't you worry; I can look out for my kid brother.'

'And where is this party?'

'Not far, somewhere out near Sidcup I think he said. I'm not too sure, didn't really ask. Anyway, if he's having us picked up it don't matter, does it.'

'What about the girls? Are they included?'

'Yes, and anyone else we want to bring. But there won't be room for *all* of us in the motor; they'll have to get there under their own steam.'

'I know,' Tony said. 'We could get Jimmie and Suds to take Elaine and Kay on their bikes and follow the car.' He looked up and down the road. 'Saying that, the girls should be here by now.'

Roy slapped Tony on his back, 'You're right, they'll be late for their own funerals, them two. Anyway Saturday should be a good night. And who knows, it could be the start of something good.'

'If you say so. Come on, I'll take the drinks, you bring my fags.'

'There's only a couple left. Never mind, we can use the empty packet to make notes. You know, start sorting out what to play on Saturday.'

'Good idea, Roy. And I've got another one. Why don't we start smoking your fags for a change!' Tony laughed. As he tried to avoid the push from his friend, lager shot out of the glasses and splashed at his feet.

'Oi! Watch it, mate! It's for drinking, not taking a bath. You must have wasted at least two good swigs.'

Chapter 41

Standing on the doorstep, Paul pulled a fluorescent sock from his jacket pocket. 'Here you go, Mike. Mum says she's sorry, but she seems to have lost the one that wanted darning.'
'What? What are you on about? - Oh, hang on, I forgot. – Er, tell her not to worry; I've bought another pair now.' Michael tossed the errant sock onto the stairs behind him. 'I'll keep that in case I get a hole in the new ones.'
'I saw Tony earlier, he was going to meet Roy, then go down the pub,' Paul said.
'Sounds good. You coming down the boozer?'
'Might as well, not much else to do is there?'
'That's what I like to hear, real enthusiasm. It's being so cheerful that keeps you going. Real ray of sunshine you are.'
Paul looked puzzled. 'You taking the piss?'
'Not so you'd notice it, mate. Come on, I'll take you on me bike. We'll see if the others are still there.'

Michael parked his Road Rocket while Paul pushed open the door to the Public Bar and stepped inside. An Alsatian dog, lying beneath a table, growled a warning. Paul retreated.
'Get in, you big girl's blouse. It won't hurt you. And hurry up, I need a drink.'
Paul held the door open for Michael, and then followed him into the fug. Roy spotted them and called out.
'Over here, Mike. Just in time, it's your round. I'll have a pint and the same for Tony. Good man.'
'Yes, mate, that's right. Two pints,' Tony laughed, in reply to Michael's two raised fingers.

'Cheers, Mike, nice one. How's it going?'
'Cheers, Tony. Paul says Kay's not the ticket. What's up with her, women's trouble?'
Tony sipped his drink before replying. 'No, at least I don't think so. I've called for her a couple of times this week and her Nan said she was feeling off colour. I don't think it can be much, probably a bug she's picked up somewhere.'
'Or something she's eaten don't agree with her,' Paul chipped in. 'Anyone got a fag to spare?'
Michael produced his case and handed around, eager hands dived in.
Roy lit one and threw a box of matches onto the table. 'You know we was talking about how we ain't got a manager now that your uncle's dumped us. Well ...'
'Hang on, he didn't dump you. You all agreed to split, that's what he told me,' Michael interrupted.
'OK. Fair enough, anyway Pat's got in touch with us. We're doing a gig for him on Saturday.'
'And we're allowed to bring who we like,' Tony added. 'Do you two fancy it? Should be a laugh.'
'I'll come.' Paul's answer surprised them all. 'Will you give me a lift, Mike?'
'I dunno. That Pat's a prat.' Michael grinned. 'Blimey, I'm a poet, and didn't know it!'
Roy laughed and tugged at his shirt collar. 'You'll be writing songs for us if you keep that up. Come on, Mike. You don't have to speak to Pat. And there's bound to be free booze and spare crumpet.'
'I didn't fancy it myself at first, but what the hell. You only live once.' Tony put a hand over his mouth and belched.
'Oh, go on then. How do we get there?'
'We're not sure. But a car's picking us up and our gear, so you could follow us.'
'And we're going to ask Suds and Jimmie when we see them. The more the merrier.' Tony tipped his glass back and drained it. 'Keep up, you lot. I'll get these.' He stood up, banged into the table and sat back down. 'Bugger it! Me legs have gone on strike. You'll have to get 'em in, Roy.'

'No, I've had a skin full. I'm going to call it a day. Tell you what, let's go and get some chips, soak up all this beer.'

The colour drained from Tony's face at the thought.

Chapter 42

Michael and Paul walked down the garden path to Michael's motorcycle.

'Get on, Paul. We're late and I don't know where this gig of Roy's is. If we miss meeting that motor we're buggered.'

'It's not my fault, me mum kept nagging me. First it was, "You can't wear that, or those," Then, "Not too late and no drinking. If there are girls there make sure you don't get into trouble." On and on, she wer Does your mum keep on at you?'

'No. But only because she's too pissed most of the time. Me dad makes up for it though, nothing I do is right. He thinks I should be like him! Can you imagine it? Fair Isle cardigan, baggy trousers and a pipe, listening to cricket on the wireless? Bollocks to all that. Bikes, birds and rock 'n roll, that's the only way t live!'

Michael kicked his bike into life and tore away from Paul's house. Behind the curtains, Mrs Parker smiled as she watched them go.

Al Capone would not have looked out of place inside the shiny, black, Buick car. People passing by stopped to stare at the youths on motorcycles preening themselves, bathing in the reflected glory the car bestowed. Suds, with Elaine on the back, balanced his bike next to James. Kay had made her excuses, so h rode alone.

Michael's Road Rocket could be heard long before it was seen by the waiting riders. Finally it swept int view and slowed as it approached. Suds moved up alongside the car and raised a thumb to the driver.

'That's it, mate. We're all here now.'

The Buick purred away from the kerbside followed by the trio of motorcycles.

Two stone lions, hunched over coats of arms, looked down from columns each side of the gates. For as long as anyone could remember they had guarded the driveway leading up to the ornate house.

A man, with a neck size that was outside of most shirt manufacturers range, stood to one side on the gras and waited for the visitors to enter. Once the car and bikes had passed he closed the gates. Resuming his position, with arms hanging down and fingers curled into his palms, he was someone who would have bee of interest to Charles Darwin in years gone by.

'Hello, lads.' Pat's honey tongue sent Michael's skin crawling. 'You'll have to lump your gear I'm afrai We can't run the car across the lawn.'

Roy laid his guitar case on the grass and helped Tony with the amplifier. 'Don't worry, Pat. We can manage; it's only this amp that's really heavy. Where are we playing?'

Pat pointed to a large summer house standing next to an oblong pond. Stone slabs formed a walkway around the perimeter. Water lilies covered most of its surface except where the constant cascade from the ornate fountain kept them at bay.

'Over there lads. There's lights inside and power points, but don't use the one marked "lawn mower." It's knackered. All the others are OK though. Any problems, give me a shout.'

'Sounds good to me,' Roy said. 'Billy, you bring the microphone and its stand, me and Tony will carry this. Then we'll all come back and give Mike and Paul a hand with the drums, OK?'

Pat opened a gold case and held it out. 'Just one thing. This is the gig you should have played a while back, around about the time of that unfortunate incident. Remember? Anyway, it was cancelled for some reason. Bit of luck for you really.' He flicked a matching lighter and lit the cigarettes. 'Anyway, a guy whose high up in the Columbia record company is coming. Make sure you are at your very best, and I'll do the rest.' He winked, then walked toward the house where the host, a middle aged man dressed in a pink jacket and white shoes embraced him.

'Oh my god. Watch yer backs, and don't go picking up anything you find. A pound note could make yer eyes water,' Michael grinned.

'Why?' Billy asked.

'Just trust me. There's some funny people here. Don't go mincing about on your own. Better still, don't mince anywhere. Stick with your brother; he'll keep an eye on you.'

'Right lads, that's you sorted then,' Michael said. 'You sound OK to me, keep the sound levels like that. I'm off to see what the talent's like here. See you later.'

'OK. Cheers, Mike.' Roy gave a military salute.

Paul stepped off the raised wooden floor. 'I'll come with you, Mike.'

'Oh, no, you won't! I couldn't pick up iron filings with a magnet with you in tow. Stay with the others, I don't want you with me.' *I certainly don't. I've got a date to keep, and two's company but three's trouble.*

Michael strode off, leaving Paul to kick the summer house and the band to run through their opening number.

The missing link held up his paw and forced Michael to stop in front of the gates.

'You leaving?' he grunted.

No, mate, just riding round for the bloody fun of it! 'Yes, the band's left an electric lead behind; I've got to pick it up for them. Get them gates open quick, I ain't got much time as it is.'

Reluctantly, the man complied with Michael's wishes and narrowly missed being struck by the Road Rocket as Michael opened the throttle.

'That was quick, Michael. How did you manage to get away? Is Paul alright? How will he get home, you're not going back are you?'

Michael closed the door behind him and took Mrs Parker in his arms.

'Blimey, what's this? Twenty questions? I told you I'd fix it didn't I? And Paul will be OK, one of the others will drop him off.' Michael led the way into the front room and closed the curtains.

'Put the wireless on, Pauline. See if you can find Radio Luxembourg, might be some decent music on. Then come and sit next to me.' He patted the settee and grinned. 'We've got plenty of time to talk.'

'About what? Motorbikes I suppose, or the top ten records perhaps.'

'No need to be sarky. I want to talk about us getting married, having our own place, maybe even kids.'

'You must be off your rocker, Mike! Marriage and more kids? Don't you think I've done my bit. Paul's more than enough of a handful for me to cope with.'

'Any news about your daughter, she's been gone for months now.'

Mrs Parker didn't answer. She took a compact from her handbag, checked her face in its mirror and dabbed at her cheeks with the powder puff. 'I'll just put the kettle on, I won't be a tick.'

Michael lit a cigarette and put his feet up on the pouffe. *Well that went down like a lead balloon! Bugger!*

When she came back in with the tea tray got to his feet and took it from her. 'Sorry,' he said. 'I didn't mean to upset you. Come on, give us a kiss.'

'I'm not upset Michael, but it's not easy bringing up children without a man.'

'So, marry me, you know it's what I want. Paul and his sister will be old enough to leave home in a few years, then it'll be just you and me. Be brilliant!'

'I wish it was that simple, and I wish you were older. There's too big an age gap. Besides, I'm already married, remember? I thought Ben beating you up might have given you a clue.'

Subconsciously, Michael felt his crotch. 'Yeah, but he's done a runner. If the old bill catch him he'll go down again. This time it'll be for GBH at least. He might as well give you a divorce and be done with it. He can't come home that's for sure, can he.'

Michael put his arm around her and snuggled up close. Her cheap perfume sent his senses spinning; he slid a hand into her blouse and under her brassiere. She responded by nibbling his ear lobe.

'Let's go upstairs,' she whispered. 'I've put fresh sheets on the bed.'

'No, not yet. I want to talk to you, we don't get the chance to be alone like this very often.'

She moved away from him and frowned. 'Go on then, get it off your chest.'

'I love you, Pauline. You must know that by now, I keep telling you. I've never had feelings like this before. I think about you all the time.'

Mrs Parker smiled and placed a hand on his knee. 'You're sweet, Michael. But I don't think you know what love is yet. When I was your age I was always falling in love, it's part of growing up.'

'But I do know!' Michael protested. 'I've had loads of girls, but none of them ever made me feel like this.'

She moved closer. 'I'll tell you what; let's wait until you're twenty one. If you still feel the same then I'l say yes. How's that?'

'Twenty one! That's over two years away! I can't wait that long, I want you now.'

'Then come upstairs.'

'Yeah, OK. But I've got to get you to change your mind.'

She stood up and began unbuttoning her blouse as she walked to the door.

'Hang on, Pauline. There's something else I wanted to ask you about. I tried talking to me dad but it only ended in another row. I'm thinking of packing my apprenticeship in at the garage and getting a job at Shawn Signs. What do you think?'

Mrs Parker undid the side zip and let her skirt drop to the floor. 'Why? Why would you want to do that? thought you loved your job.'

'I do, but I can always mend bikes as a sideline. Suds and Jimmie both work there and the money's good It's piecework, the harder you graft the more you earn.' *And the cash in my bedroom won't last for ever.* 'I I save really hard I can get the deposit for a house.'

'Buy a house? What's wrong with council houses? Getting a bit posh, aren't you?'

'No, it's not like that. I just need to be different to my old man. He's stuck in a rut but I'm not like that. I want to get on in life, make something of myself.'

'I think you should give it a bit more thought, Michael. If you stick it out where you are you'll get your papers, you'll be qualified.'

'You're right. But, if I stick it out here instead, what are you going to do.'

She ran out the door and up the stairs. 'Come with me and I'll show you.'

The 21st birthday party was in full swing, cloth banners with messages of congratulations fluttered in the evening breeze. Guests, clutching drinks, wandered from the house into the grounds and back again. A crowd of teenagers had congregated around the summer house and were dancing to Roy's band. After a couple of slow songs a few of the dancers drifted into the shadows to continue their close contact.

'Right, time to speed things up,' Roy said, clutching the microphone. 'Here we go, one, two, three.' He stamped out the countdown with his cowboy boots. *'It's Saturday night and I just got paid ...'*

James took hold of Elaine's hand and pushed his way through to the dancers. Roy winked at them as they spun round in front of him and the band.

The man in the grey pinstripe suit lit a cigar and offered the case to his companion.

'You were right, Pat, my friend. They *are* good. I think with a bit of polishing we could market them. Look at those kids dancing; they're really enjoying everything your band's playing.'

'I've always had confidence in them. They just need exposure. With you behind them I'm sure we could make a lot of money.' Pat accepted a light and inhaled appreciatively. 'Cuban?'

'Only the best, my friend. Only the best.' He returned the leather cigar case to the inside pocket of his jacket. 'Right, I've heard enough, get in touch next week sometime. Speak to my secretary, arrange a sound test. Now, let's get back to the champagne shall we.'

The two men chatted as they strolled back toward the house.

Paul wandered around aimlessly, without the gang he was lost. He had tried the punch, drunk gin and lime, then settled for brown ale. The world around him was changing, things wouldn't stay still. Narrowly skirting the pond, he staggered into a couple lost in each other's arms. The splash caught the attention of people standing nearby; swiftly someone reached out to assist the shocked girl. Her escort grabbed Paul by his lapels and punched him. Paul swung a fist back at his assailant but missed. The man hit out again and blood poured from Paul's nose.

'You stupid little bastard! Why don't you watch where you're going? There! In you go!'

As the girl scrambled out, Paul entered the pond backwards.

'Oi! You lot! Stop messing about! Those fish cost a lot of money!' the man in the pink jacket screamed from the verandah of the house.

Spitting water and weed, Paul gained his feet and winced in pain as he wiped blood from his nose with the back of his hand. Standing up to his knees in water he began searching the pockets of his suit jacket. Then, bending down, he began groping around in the mud beneath his feet.

'Give us your hand, mate, get outta there,' Suds said. 'What the bloody hell are you up to?'

'I've lost my brass knuckles.' Paul slurred. 'Must 'ave fell out when that git pushed me in.'

'Leave it, you'll never find anything in that lot. Come on, get out.' Suds offered his hand.

Paul ignored the offer of help and continued his search. 'I'll 'ave 'im, I'll bloody 'ave 'im.'

Suds leaned out and grabbed Paul and pulled him to the edge. 'No, let us be having you.' He hauled him from the pond and laughed as his friend stood like a drowned rat, water mixed with blood dripping from his chin.

'It ain't bloody funny. Lend me yer knife.' Paul took two steps forward, then one back. Suds grabbed his jacket to prevent him falling back in.

'Leave it out, mate. You ain't fit to fight the butcher's dog for a pound of sausages.' Holding Paul's arm he led him away from the water and toward a tree on the lawn. 'Sit down. I'll see what I can do. Don't go anywhere or I'll never find you in the dark. Just stay here, I won't be long.'

Paul said something barely audible, tipped his head back and held a wet handkerchief to his nose. Suds disappeared in the gloom.

'Here you go, mate. Get up and try this on. I found it hanging in the hallway.' Suds pulled Paul to his feet and pushed him back against the tree. 'Let's have this wet coat off, and the waistcoat.' Suds supported his friend with one hand while trying to undo buttons and remove wet garments with the other. 'Well, try and help me for Christ's sake.'

Paul's knees buckled and he slid down the tree. 'Leave me alone,' he slurred.

'Alright you win. Here, get your arms in the sleeves, this'll keep you warm.' Slowly, Suds managed to get the cashmere overcoat on Paul despite his protests. 'That's it, fits you like a glove, pity it's a coat,' Suds chuckled. 'Come on, let's go, you're shaking like Elvis. You'll have to show Roy how you do that!' Suds began steering Paul back to where the bikes were parked, the camel coloured coat flapping around his friend's knees as he stumbled along.

'Try and hang on, you drunken sod. If you fall off there ain't much I can do about it.' Suds glared at the sorry sight standing beside his bike.

'I'll be ... Oh, shit.' Paul dropped to his knees and parted company with the free drinks. Suds stepped nimbly aside. 'That's it, mate. Chuck it up, you'll feel better.'

Suds gripped Paul's arm. 'Are you OK now? Ready to roll?' he asked.

Paul shivered. His nose had stopped bleeding but not before it had ruined the front of his recently acquired coat.

'Yeah. I think so. Let's go, I'm bloody freezing.'

The bedroom had lost all resemblance to the tidy haven it had been a short time before. A candlewick bedspread, sheets and blankets lay half on and half off the bed. Hastily discarded clothing littered the bare floor boards. Michael and Mrs Parker lay naked, staring at the ceiling. Cigarette smoke, the incense of lovers, infused the air.

'That was *ace*, Pauline. You really know how.'

'You're no novice yourself. No wonder you have so many girls chasing you.'

'I've had my share. But that's all over now. I only want you, you know that.'

She stubbed out her cigarette and rolled back toward him.

'Well, have me then. That's if you've got any strength left!'

'Cheeky so and so. I'll show you. Come here!'

The utility furniture headboard resumed banging against the wall.

'What's that!' Michael supported himself on his hands and listened intently. 'It's a bike and it's stopped outside!'

After a minute or two, subdued voices in the street ceased and a motorcycle moved off. Michael sank back down. 'They've gone; whoever it was.'

'They haven't! Get off, that's Paul!' Mrs Parker pushed her lover away.

'It can't be. It's too early.'

But the sound of a key searching for the lock soon changed Michael's mind.

'Shit! It is! What's he doing here!'

Mrs Parker was busily searching through the tangle of clothes while Michael lay on the bed fighting his trousers. The bedroom door opened.

'Hello, Mum. I'm ...' Paul stopped and shook his head as if to clear the vision from his brain. He turned and ran from the scene.

'Stop your crying, sweetheart. He's gone now.' She held Paul close to her, rocked him in her arms and patted his hair. 'There, there. I'm sorry, my love. Please don't be so upset.'

Paul tore himself free from the maternal embrace. 'Go away! I hate you! I hate you! You're a bleedin' slag.' Tears trickled down his cheek. 'Why do you keep doing it? You're too old. It's disgusting. Get out of my room! Leave me alone, I never want to see you again.' He threw himself onto his bed and sobbed.

Chapter 43

Mrs Parker put the upright Hoover away and gazed out through the kitchen window at the squirrels frolicking in the grass beneath the Oak tree searching for acorns. Dappled sunlight played on lichen encrusted classical statues.

Must be lovely to live in a house like this, she thought.

Taking her tea, and a chocolate covered biscuit purloined from the kitchen, she stepped out onto the patio to enjoy a fifteen minute morning break from her domestic duties. Sinking into the cushions covering the large wooden reclining chair she breathed in the fresh air. A squirrel stopped scrabbling and scampered across the lawn. The sight of the cute little animal sitting up and begging brought a smile to her face. 'Hello, are you back again? You certainly know a soft touch when you see one, don't you. Here you are, now hop it.'

Mrs Parker lay back and closed her eyes as the squirrel made off with the piece of biscuit.

The sound of someone approaching disturbed her rest.

'Morning, Mrs Parker. How are you today? I thought I'd see if you'd like a lift today.' The chauffer smiled down at her.

'Oh, it's you, Bert. Shouldn't you be polishing the car or something?' She sat up and straightened her dress.

'Done it all. Just clicking my heels until his nibs decides whether or not he needs me. If you like, I'll tell him I need to get petrol and take you to the … I mean, take you home.'

'I know just what you mean, Bert. And you can forget it. I've got more than enough trouble to last me a lifetime.'

'What's up with you all of a sudden? Don't cry. You behind with the rent or something? I can always lend you a few bob if you like.'

'No, it's nothing like that. Just leave me in peace. There's nothing anyone can do, it's a right mess.'

Bert squatted down beside her and placed his hand on hers. 'Come on, you can tell me. A trouble shared is a trouble halved, as they say. If it's not money, what is it? I'll help if I can, but first you've got to tell me what the problem is.'

'I can't.' She rummaged in the apron pocket and pulled out her handkerchief. 'It's something I have to sort out for myself.'

'Oh, well. Please yourself. Don't say I didn't offer.' He stood up. 'Let me know if you change your mind about the lift.'

Waiting until Bert was out of sight; she swung her legs off the chair and returned to the housework.

Chapter 44

Inside the youth club, young dancers were lost in the music of Bill Haley. Bouffant hair and flared skirts partnered Brylcreemed quiffs, drape jackets and crepe soled shoes. A repetitive beat and the sense of rebellion against an older generation's way of life stimulated the teenagers. Girls spun around, boys rocked back on their heels, each couple eager to outdo the rest.

'I'm sorry I can not dance with you.' Alfred frowned.

'I know, Alfred. I just wanted to come and listen to the music. Great isn't it.'

'It is different, that I have to admit. Chris, if you wish to dance, I am sure somebody would be pleased to have the honour.'

'That's sweet of you. If the others turn up perhaps I will.'

The record finished and the next one in the stack dropped and began to play. The Everly Brothers singing '*All I have to do is dream,*' lowered the tempo.

'We could walk around to this one. Shall we?' Alfred asked.

'Why not? Come on, before it ends.'

Paul paid his entrance money then dragging his feet he made his way into the hall. Heading for the refreshment hatch he asked for a coffee.

Turning away to avoid being seen, he drank part of the lukewarm drink before tipping the remainder of a half bottle of brandy into his cup. Returning the empty bottle to his jacket pocket he took another mouthful. *That's better!*

Taking one or two unsteady steps he slumped down at the nearest empty table. The hall was fast becoming a kaleidoscope of colours and noise. Closing his eyes he put his hands over his ears and lowered his head to the table. He groaned. The loud music and alcohol were failing to blot out the picture of his friend with his mother.

Sitting up, he drained the coffee and licked his lips. Then, blinking rapidly, he tried to focus on the teenagers dancing. Connie Francis asking, '*Who's sorry now?*' had many of them singing along. Alfred and Christine ambled past in an embrace, gazing into each other's eyes, oblivious of all around them. They didn't see Paul get to his feet, didn't hear him swear as his feet became entangled in the legs of a chair, didn't see him stagger out of the church hall.

Outside, Paul collapsed down onto the grass, beating it with his fists, and sobbed.

Chapter 45

Michael sat alone. He had half heartedly been trying to avoid the gang since the incident with Paul and Mrs Parker. His coffee cup was empty and cold to the touch, despite Bentini repeatedly wiping the Formica table top in front of him. A gangly youth fed a coin into the jukebox and smiled at the girl standing beside him. Together they returned to their table.

The machined whirred and mechanically selected a record, Perry Como singing *'Magic Moments.'* Michael sang along with the words in his head and lit another cigarette. The couple's second choice dropped into place and the coffee bar echoed to the, *'Swingin' Shepherd Blues.'*

Michael tapped ash from the cigarette into his saucer, ignoring the ashtray. *What a shitty world. I'm pissed off. Me dad don't want me to chuck me apprenticeship, and Pauline don't either. Paul's got the raving hump and now I can't see Pauline. Is it all worth it? I could always do a James Dean I suppose, take me bike up past the ton and smack into something.*

Vic Damone interrupted Michael's dark thoughts.

Bollocks! Yes, that's what I'll do! I'll go round her place and see how the land lays. Cheers, mate! Michael hurried toward the door while the record, *'On the street where you live,'* came to an end.

Revving the engine, as he waited for the traffic lights to change, Michael glanced at the Morris Minor that had drawn up alongside. The amber light glowed and Michael accelerated away. Bending low, he revelled in the air rushing past at an ever increasing rate. Sixty, seventy, eighty miles an hour, the motorcycle responded to his love of speed. Ninety, ninety five. Ahead the bridge that had claimed so many lives before loomed up out of the fading light. Michael knew from experience that it was all a matter of timing. One mistake would be his last.

An inquisitive crowd stood gawping at the ambulance and police car, for these two vehicles usually spelt trouble for someone. Hushed voices discussed the unexpected excitement, as a stretcher, piled high with blankets, was taken from the ambulance. Sombre faces hid any emotion felt by the ambulance crew as they entered the house while four policemen did their best to control the onlookers as the stretcher was carried past them.

'Perhaps her old man has come back and lumped her one again.'

'Might be her fancy man. You know; the one who drives that posh car for some toff. They probably had a row and one of them's done the other one in.'

These and various other suggestions were offered and discounted as to why the police were there.

Michael tore through the estate, adrenalin surging through his body, his senses heightened by the close escape. The noise of his Road Rocket bouncing back from the brickwork as it hurtled beneath the bridge had thrilled him beyond the normal pleasure of riding fast.

He slowed his bike down at the sight of the police car outside Paul's house, and then saw the ambulance.

'Oh shit! What the hell's happened? Why are the rozzers here, and what's the ambulance for?' He parked the Road Rocket and ran toward the commotion. Forcing his way through the crowd, he came up against a agitated police officer blocking the way.

'I'm sorry, sir. You can't go in there.' He held Michael back at arms length.

Michael pushed forward. 'What's up? Who's been hurt? Let me through!'

'I can't do that, sir.'

'But I'm family, let me in!' Michael side stepped, dodged the arm reaching out for him and raced toward the open door.

The sight that met his eyes stopped him as surely as if he had run into a brick wall. A violent shudder began in his chest and finished in his boots.

Mrs Parker was hysterical. On her hands and knees, bent over the lifeless body of her son, she tipped her head back and howled like a wild animal. Her face, distorted in grief, made it difficult for Michael to accep that it really was her. One of the ambulance men gently, but firmly, was trying to ease her off Paul.

'Come on, love. There's nothing you can do for him now. Leave it to us.'

'No! No! He hasn't gone! He can't have! He's too young!' Mrs Parker used her fists to beat the man trying to cover the body.

'I'm sorry, but we've tried everything. It's no use I'm afraid. He's dead.'

The finality of the man's statement hit Mrs Parker like a sledgehammer. She prostrated herself on the hal lino, digging her nails into its cold surface.

'Why! Why did you do it! Paul, my darling, don't go! Please don't go! I've made you a bread and butter pudding.' Her pleas dissolved into huge sobs.

Michael's knees sagged and he leant against the door frame for support.

Fighting for breath he gasped, 'How? I don't understand. How did he die?'

The ambulance man pointed up the stairs. A length of washing line rope dangled from the top of the banister.

'Hung himself, poor devil.'

Michael leant against the wall. 'Oh, fuck.'

A blackness closed around him, his forehead erupting with beads of sweat. Automatically, he put his hands out to save himself as he descended into a pit of swirling dots of light.

'You alright, son? You went down like a ton of bricks. How many fingers am I holding up?'

'Three. What happened. Did I faint?'

'Yes. You hit your head on the wall as you went down, you might have concussion. Sit still, I need to check you out.'

Michael put his hand to the side of his face.

'I'm OK. Where's Pauline? And Paul?'

'If you mean his mother, she's in the ambulance with him. You look fine, so I'd better join them. Are you related to the deceased?'

'No. We're, - sorry. I mean, we were mates. That's all.'

'Do you mind waiting around, I think the police have more to do. They probably have questions to ask.'

'That's OK. I ain't going nowhere. How will Pauline, er, Mrs Parker get back home?'

'I expect the police will see to it. Just make sure the house is locked when they've finished. She's got enough troubles without being burgled. You sure you're alright to leave?'

'Yeah. Get on, I'll be fine.'

Licking the end of his pencil, the police officer said, 'Who did you say you were, sir? Family, I think you told my man outside.'

'Well, almost. I spend a lot of time here. Paul, that's the bloke who killed himself, he was my mate. I sort of looked out for him.'

The man wrote on his pad then asked, 'Any idea why he would do this? A girl perhaps?'

From the top of the stairs another man called down. 'Up here, sir! I've found a book and there's a note. It's been pinned to the banister.'

Following his interrogator, Michael began to mount the stairs, stairs that in the past had led to ecstasy and pain. This time it was to more pain.

On the landing a constable held out a school book. ART NOTES : MR. ATTWOOD. A page from an Eagle comic, protruded from inside the cover. Jeff Arnold's illustrated instructions on how to tie a lasso.

After a quick glance at the illustrated article the sergeant sighed. 'It must have been a long, painful death. A hangman's knot would have been so much quicker, poor little so and so. What's the note say?'

Michael's heart began to beat faster.

Coughing to clear his throat, the constable read the message. 'There's nothing worth living for anymore. My girl friend don't want me. You're a prossie. Me mate's shit on me. I hate him and you.' He held out the note. 'It looks like a page torn from an exercise book.'

'Sound's like he certainly had problems. Not very nice though, calling his own mother a prostitute.'

The colour rushing to his cheeks, Michael turned and started back down the stairs.

The sergeant flicked through the school art book. Sketches and comments, with marks out of ten. Then a message scrawled across a page. FORGIVE ME. PLEASE FORGIVE ME.

'That's odd. That's very odd. What does it mean, I wonder?' He scratched the side of his head. Michael put his hand on the door lock and glanced back up the stairs.

'Where are you going, son? My men are outside, you won't get far. We may need to ask you some more questions so why don't you put the kettle on? I'm sure we could all use a nice cuppa.' The sergeant began descending the stairs.

Michael seized his chance. Running through to the kitchen he threw open the door and sprinted to the back garden fence. Quickly scrabbling over, he ran away from the houses, heading across the fields.

'Strange. Oh, well, we can always pick him up if we need to. But it's a straight forward suicide, why did he run?' The sergeant sat at the kitchen table and waited for his colleague to make the tea.

Michael tentatively knocked at the door. As he stood holding his breath he could hear slippers shuffling across the lino. The door opened an inch or two, part of a haggard face peered through the gap. Puffy eyes, ashen skin, no make up.

'What the hell are you doing round here! Bugger off! I hate you!'

'Please, Pauline. Don't be like that. I didn't know he'd catch us, did I? Open the door, we need to talk.' Michael tried to wedge his shoe in the door.

Mrs Parker reacted and slammed it shut. Her voice, slightly muffled, screamed at him. 'I never want to see you again, let alone talk. Sling your hook and don't *ever* come back. Do you hear me? *Ever!*'

Michael raised his hand to knock again but the sound of Mrs Parker sobbing behind the door changed his mind. Reluctantly, he walked away.

Pauline, my sweetheart, please, don't do this to me. I love you. I'll always love you, darling. You're everything to me.

Chapter 49

Elaine gripped the chains of the swing as Roy put his hands in the middle of her back and pushed. Her shadow, driven by the setting sun, lengthened and shortened as she swung back and forth.

Tony and Kay sat out of earshot on a bench beneath the horse chestnut tree, deep in conversation.

Christine grabbed Alfred's arm as he tripped on a tree root exposed by constant use of the footpath down through the woods.

'Thank you,' he frowned. 'I should look where I am going.'

'Yes, slow down. There's no rush to break bad news.' Her voice was strained, subdued and fraught with emotion. Red rimmed watery eyes and the handkerchief screwed up in her hand told the story.

'You are correct, my love. I will do as you say.' His voice, harsh from grief, accentuated his guttural accent.

She put her arms around him, sank her face into his jacket and wept. He bit his lip then cuddled her close stroking the back of her neck, making comforting noises in her ear. She squeezed him tightly, acknowledging their shared distress.

They broke apart and moved on, arm in arm, down through the trees toward the recreation ground, hoping to find members of the gang. Christine left traces of face powder and a damp patch on Alfred's jacket.

'Hello, you two love birds!' Elaine called out cheerfully.

Alfred raised a hand in reply. Christine stuffed a handkerchief into her mouth. Slowly, they walked toward the swings.

'You two had words?' Roy asked, seeing Christine's distressed state.

'No,' she said softly. 'You tell them. Please, Alfred.' Christine turned away from Roy and lowered her chin onto her breast. Hearing the sound of crying, Elaine stopped the swing with her feet and jumped off. Rushing to her friend she put her arm around her and asked. 'What on earth's happened? I've never seen you like this. Come on, tell me.'

Christine sobbed out loud and clung to Elaine. 'I...I can't. It's too terrible.'

Alfred hesitated. Staring down at the autumn leaves lying on the grass, finally he spoke. 'It's Paul. He is dead.'

Roy grabbed the lapels of Alfred's jacket. 'Do what! What do you mean, dead? He can't be!'

Alfred gently removed Roy's clenched fists and nodded. 'Yes, it is so. Mrs Parker sent a message to Christine.'

Elaine moved nearer as if she couldn't believe what she was hearing. 'But how? When? Was he with Mike on that bike of his? Did they crash?'

'We were told that Michael got there soon after it happened. We have not seen him, so we do not know the details.'

'What details! Tell us what happened, you bloody idiot!' Roy shouted.

'I am sorry. I tell you what we know. Paul took his own life. He hanged himself at his home.'

'Get out of it! Why would he do that?'

'I do not know. Perhaps Michael will tell us. I am sorry to give you the news.'

Elaine, Roy and Christine huddled together while Alfred limped over to Tony and Kay. They had seen the commotion and were halfway toward the swings as Alfred approached.

'Wotcha, Alfred. How's it going? What's up with Roy and the others?'

'I have something bad to tell you. Paul is dead.'

Tony tried to catch Kay as she buckled at the knees. Clutching her stomach she sank onto the grass.

'You stupid kraut! Now look what you've done! That's not funny. I always knew you lot had no sense of humour but I gave you credit for having more sense than to joke like that.'

Alfred gave a deep sigh. 'I wish it was a joke. But it isn't. He has hung himself.'

'Bollocks! I don't believe you.'

Tony comforted Kay.

'As you will. But it is the truth. I am sorry.' Alfred turned to walk back to the others.

'Hang on, Alfred. I'm sorry about what I called you. I didn't mean that. It's the shock. I still can't really believe what you've just told us.'

Resting on his stick, Alfred turned back to face Tony and Kay. 'I understand, Tony. I wish there had been another way to tell you both.'

'Why'd the silly bugger do it, Tony?' Roy asked, as the gang stood in stunned silence.

'Search me. I know he's been pissed off lately, but ...Oh, I don't know.'

Christine swallowed. 'Do you think it was my fault? You know; him and me breaking up?'

Tony frowned. 'No. Of course not. It's nothing to do with you. Who knows why he'd top himself? Could be he was cheesed off with lying to his mum all the time about having a job when he hadn't.'

Elaine spoke up. 'It's not doing any good trying to make sense of it. He's done it and there's nothing anyone can do to change it.'

'You're right,' Roy agreed. 'I don't know about you lot, but I need a stiff drink. Coming?'

'OK,' Tony said. 'Let's go.'

Kay winced and got hold of Tony's arm. 'I don't feel too good. Will you take me home please, Tony? I don't want to go to the pub.'

'Of course I will. But what's up?'

'I don't know. I just feel queer, that's all.'

Slapping Tony on the back, Roy said. 'Good man. Hope you feel better soon, Kay,' then added, 'Anyone else not coming?'

'Me and Alfred will come, won't we.' Christine answered. Alfred opened his mouth, but changed his mind.

'Right then, just the four of us. Let's go and get as drunk as skunks.'

The church bell chimed as the group walked in silence, their pace dictated by the slow gait of Alfred. Elaine shivered as the air temperature began to drop. Tall hedges each side of the footpath added to the gloom, dark shapes flitted above them in the fading light.

'Bats!' Christine cried out. She grabbed Alfred and hung on.

'Are they?' Roy asked. 'I don't think so. Don't they wait till it's really dark?'

Elaine put her hands up in an attempt to cover her hair. 'It's like that film we saw last week!'

'Perhaps we should go the long way round. The grave yard will be really spooky!' Christine said.

Roy laughed derisively. 'You two can, me and Elaine are going to cut through, aren't we.'

'If you say so, Roy. But I'm going to shut my eyes. You'll have to lead me.'

'OK. We'll see you two in the King's Arms then. Come on, Elaine, let's get a move on.'

'Evening. On your own tonight? Where's all the others?' Brian wiped his hands on a small piece of towelling. 'What are you having?'

'A pint of lager and a Cherry B. Alfred and Chris are on their way so keep the change to pay for their drinks.' Roy handed the barman a ten shilling note.

'Well, you sound like you've got all the troubles of the world on your shoulders. Not like you, Roy. What's up?'

'Paul's dead. Killed himself.'

'What! You're having me on!'

'No, it's kosher. He hung himself with his mum's washing line.'

'How on earth did he manage that?'

'He meant to. He tied it to the banister. His mum found him when she got back from the shops.'

'Oh! I'm so sorry, Roy. What a terrible thing to happen. I can't really believe it. He was just a bit of a kid. Why did he do it?' Brian passed the money back. 'Keep it, this round's on the house.'

The door to the public bar opened and Christine held it back for Alfred.

'It's OK,' Roy called out. 'I've just told Brian.'

'Yes, but I can't take it in. Paul, of all people.' The barman avoided eye contact. Dipping pint glasses into soapy water he asked. 'What'll you two have? It's on the house and I think I'll join you. What a shock for his poor mother.'

Christine carried the drinks while Alfred joined the others at their table. Roy passed his cigarettes around and the friends sat looking at each other, acutely aware of the strained atmosphere. Alfred fiddled with a stack of beer mats. Christine tried once again to fix her eye shadow. Elaine sniffed disconsolately.

'I'll get a pack of cards off Brian. We can't sit like this all night.' Roy sighed. 'Wonder where Michael's got to? Anyone seen him?'

Once again Michael sat alone, the bacon sandwich and mug of tea ignored. He stared blankly into space as uncomfortable memories invaded his thoughts. Memories of his friend, staring in disgust at the scene in the bedroom. Memories of his friend lying on the hall floor, a red raw wound to his neck. Memories of the woman he loved, being torn apart by the death of her son. Guilty memories. *That's two people's deaths I'm responsible for, and neither of them deserved to die. Why am I still alive and they're not?*

'Wotcha, Mike. Your sarnie's getting cold by the look of it. Don't you want it?' Without waiting for an answer, Suds picked it up and took a bite, brown sauce oozed out and ran down his chin. 'Bloody lovely. How could you leave that?'

James reached the top of the stairs clutching two steaming mugs. 'Ma says the rolls will be up in a minute. Her old man's just cooking the sausages,' he said, putting the drinks down. 'Oh, wotcha, Mike. Didn't see you in the corner. How's it going?'

Michael took a mouthful of his luke warm tea. 'Haven't you heard?'

'Heard? Heard what?'

'About Paul.'

'Now what's the little twat done? Lasted more than a week in one job?' Suds laughed.

'Prat! No, he's brown bread. Hung his bleedin' self, ain't he.'

James thumped Suds on the back as the sandwich lodged in his friend's throat. 'Cough it up, mate!'

Suds spat the chewed bread out and took a mouthful of coffee. 'Dead! Hung himself? What are you bleedin' on about?'

'He wrote a suicide note, then used his mum's washing line. I saw him after they'd cut him down. He looked bleeding horrible.'

'But why'd he do it? I mean, we all get brassed off, but hanging yourself? That's pretty drastic. Was it over that bird of his, that Christine?'

'Partly, but he never really got over his teacher being murdered.'

'So what's that got to do with the price of fish? That bloody German killed him; didn't he? At least, that's what we heard.'

Michael lit a cigarette. 'Well, that's what the old bill said, so he must of.'

Suds held out his hand, 'Give us one, mate. I've got to get some.' Lighting it, he blew smoke down his nose. 'Are you saying Deiter didn't do it? If he didn't, who did?'

'I didn't say that. All I meant was that Paul felt guilty. If he hadn't told us about all that money it wouldn't have happened. But don't forget the bloke was queer; his boyfriend might have done it. Who knows?'

James helped himself from Michael's packet of cigarettes. 'So Paul's teacher was fond of a bit of bum was he? Uurgh! Them blokes make me shudder.'

'Me too. But how's all the others? Do they know?' Suds asked.

'Dunno. I ain't seen any of them. Suppose they must do. Paul's house was swarming with coppers and half the street was out watching when they took him off. So it ain't exactly a state secret.'

Suds ground out his cigarette in a saucer. 'When's the funeral? I take it we're all going?'

'How do I know? Anyway, I'm not sure I can face it. You lot can all go though.'

'Well we will, won't we Jimmie. It's only right, got to show your respects.'

Michael rested his elbows on the table, put his hands to the sides of his head, and groaned. 'What a shitty thing to happen. It should have been me. I should be the one who's dead, not him, poor little sod. He did it for me.'

'Do what! Paul killed himself for you! Why?' Suds cried out.

'I didn't mean that, I meant… oh, never mind what I meant. He's done it now, let's just leave it.' Michael lowered his head and banged it onto the table.

'Come on, Suds. Let's leave Mike alone. He looks like he's had more than enough.'

Suds ignored James and gently shook Michael. 'Come on, mate. Let's go for a burn up. Where's yer bike?'

Michael scratched his head. 'In the street somewhere, I'm not sure. To tell the truth, I don't even remember riding here.'

Footsteps on the stairs stopped the talking.

'Here you go, lads. Sorry they took so long. Do you want anything else?'

'Cheers, Ma. No thanks, we're just off. Come on Mike, we'll have a race. The mad mile, then the King's Arms. Last one there gets the first round!'

Michael shook off the cloak of lethargy threatening to engulf him. 'You're on. But fair's fair, you gotta let me find me bike first.'

Suds grinned. 'Yeah, and we get time to scoff these!'

The three motor cycles raced down the unofficial race track with James in the lead. But both Suds and Michael were gaining on him.

Other riders were approaching on the opposite side of the dual carriageway. As the two groups passed, one of the youths gave a two finger salute. A quick glance over his shoulder confirmed Michael's thoughts; insignia on the back of the leather jackets marked these riders as members of the 'Chieftains.'

Turning his head back, Michael was shocked to see a body sprawled out on the road ahead. Braking hard to miss it he fought to control the skid. The body got to its feet and reached out. Michael closed his eyes. It was Deiter!

Contact with the grass bank jolted Michael back from his horrors. Opening his eyes he swung his machine back onto the road and coasted to a stop. Sweating, despite the chill in the air, he sat with both feet on the road and breathed deeply. *Shit! That was close! I must be going nuts. That's the second time I've seen him, why don't he leave me alone?*

James and Suds, hearing the squeal of brakes behind them, both looked back in time to see Michael mount the bank. Reaching the roundabout the pair rode around it then back toward Michael.

'What's up, Mike. Got trouble with your bike?' Suds shouted across.

'No, I just lost it. Bit of shit on the road I think. I'm OK. - Hang on, I'll come over.'

Michael put the Road Rocket into first gear and bumped it across the central reservation to join his friends.

'Did you see that bloke give us the V sign? Looking for bother I reckon,' Suds lit a cigarette and passed the packet to James.

'Yeah. I had a run in with him at a party. Me and him have got a score to settle.'

'Oh, so you recognised him then? Don't tell me,' James smirked. 'I bet there was a bird involved. Right?'

'Got it in one. Come on; let's get a beer before Brian calls last orders.'

Chapter 48

Michael sat on his motor cycle and watched from a distance as the hearse turned into the church. He swallowed, trying to shift the lump in his throat. Glancing around, he wiped his eyes with a sleeve of his shirt. *Why did you do it, mate? It would have been alright; me and your mum are going to get married. At least, I hoped we were. That's all on the back burner now. She won't even speak to me.*

Four motor cycles, three with pillion passengers, followed slowly behind friends and relatives of Mrs Parker.

As the funeral procession disappeared from sight, Michael kicked his machine into life and raced away.

'How did it go today?' Michael asked.

'Well, it weren't a barrel of laughs, that's for sure. Paul's mum cried buckets.' Roy picked up his coffee cup.

'You can say that again,' Tony said. 'What with her, Christine and Elaine all grizzling, I thought it was never going to end.'

'What about Kay? She wasn't there, was she?'

'No. I asked her Nan, but she said Kay wasn't feeling too good.' Tony put his hands up behind his head and leant back. 'I thought you might have come, Mike. Why didn't you?'

'I was going to, but I changed me mind. First Deiter, now Paul. I couldn't face it.'

'Don't blame you really, mate. There ain't no future in all this dying lark. Let's forget about it. I'll put the jukebox on, cheer ourselves up a bit.'

Michael shrugged, 'Please yourself, I don't care. Beginning to wonder what it's all about. What's the point of it all?'

'Oh my god, you've really got the arse ache ain't you,' Roy exclaimed. 'Go on, Tony. Sort the music out, I want to talk to Mike. Take your drink and go and chat them birds up over there. You never know your luck.'

'But ...'

'No buts. Just *do it*, mate.'

Tony scowled at his friend's abruptness but sensed that something serious was in the air. He walked across to a group of young girls laughing and giggling near the jukebox. Plonking his cup down he smiled, 'Wotcha girls, mind if I join you? I'm just going to put some music on. Got any favourites?' He grasped the arm of a fair haired girl sporting a pony-tail that hung halfway down her back. 'Come on, darling. Help me choose.'

She looked around at her friends then got up and walked with Tony.

'Right, mate. Now what's up with you? I've never seen you like this. Tell me what's up.'

'Nothing.' Michael stirred his coffee, added more sugar and stirred it again.

'Bollocks. Look, we're all upset about Paul but there's nothing anyone can do. You going all moody isn't going to change anything.'

'It's not just Paul. It's every bloody thing. It's all getting on my tits,' Michael sighed. 'Give us a fag, mate.'

Roy passed a cigarette, struck a match and lit Michael's before his own.

'That's better. Cheers.'

'Now, spit it out. What's getting you down?'

'I don't know. I'm just pissed off. I can't see the point of anything. Nothing ever works out like you think.' Michael picked a piece of loose tobacco off the end of his tongue. 'I can't be bothered to get up in the mornings, then me boss chews me lug 'oles off about being late. Things go wrong at work and it's always *my* fault. Everyone seems to have it in for me.'

'Well that makes a change! Usually it's you having it in for everybody!' Roy laughed.

'Silly bugger. You know what I mean. It ain't funny. Sometimes I wish I was dead.'

Roy tapped the ash from his cigarette ash onto the floor. 'The way you push your luck on that bike of yours, you soon will be.'

'I don't care. Bollocks to the lot of it. Life's a crock of shit if you ask me. You can have my share, the sooner I'm out of it the better.'

'This ain't like you, Mike. You're the one we all copy. You're always up for it and two fingers to anyone who gets in our way. And you always stood up for Paul. Where would he have been without you?'

Alive for a start! Michael frowned. 'I don't know. Any prize for guessing?'

'You must admit, we've had some brilliant times ain't we.'

' Yeah. But when we was kids it was *all* fun, playing up the woods, building camps and things. And all them games we played in the street. Blimey, I remember playing by torchlight some evenings. They was the good times.'

'Yes, but we're still having fun, Mike. Birds, bikes and rock 'n' roll, what more do you want?'

Michael slumped on his chair. 'I want to get married.'

Roy sucked his breath in. 'Oh.'

'But it won't happen now, and don't try asking me why. It's my secret.' Michael tipped back his head and stared at the ceiling. 'Just leave me alone. I'm not in the mood for company. Piss off and join Tony. I'll see you later.' Getting to his feet, he ambled toward the door leaving Roy looking concerned.

'Come on, Roy! We've pulled. Where's Mike off to? There's three of them.'

'Forget it, mate. Elaine would have me guts for garters for a start.'

'Great! I get them all steamed up and you two leave me to it. Thanks a bundle!'

'You dive in then, give 'em one for me. I'm off. I'm going for a beer, Mike's giving me the heebie jeebies. If them birds blow you out, I'll see you down the King's Arms.'

Chapter 48

Christine took hold of Alfred's hand as the single decker bus pulled away. 'I'm looking forward to this! I love the circus. What a good idea of yours.'

Alfred tripped on the pavement and dropped his walking stick. He recovered swiftly and held the top of his leg.

'Are you OK?' Did you hurt your leg?'

'Yes, a little. It is of no importance.'

'How did your leg get injured in the first place? Mike said you were bombed in the war. Is that right?'

Alfred smiled and shook his head. 'No, that was my brother. I was damaged in Russia. My unit was attacked and my leg was almost lost. They sent me back to Germany, when I came out of hospital I was sent to France. British soldiers captured us. I was taken to England and put in a prison camp.'

'How horrible. What where you doing there? In France I mean.'

'We had Flak guns to protect us from enemy aircraft. We were the gun crew.'

'Oh Alfred, what a life you've had. And your brother …'

'Life is a trial, only the strong deserve to live.'

'What a strange thing to say.' She looked at him as if seeing him in a different light. 'Come on, let's get to the circus. You're making me shiver. You can buy me a candy floss to make up for it!'

Circus tents, caravans and animal cages sprawled across the park. Set apart to one side, brightly painted Indian tepees added an exotic flavour to the scene.

The accompanying funfair was in full swing with roundabouts, dodgem cars, and stalls offering all sorts of prizes. Shrieks of laughter from the helter-skelter tower proved its enduring appeal to children of all ages. Noisy generators, supplying the much needed electricity, added to the general hubbub.

Queuing for the big top, she snuggled up against Alfred. All around them the smell of canvas and sawdust filled the air. Strange scents of animals and wet straw permeated from nearby trailers. Snarls and grunts intermingled with the bellow of elephants. Strings of coloured bulbs cast pools of light. Fairyland and the jungle all mixed into one. Wide eyed children clung to adult hands. Lovers walked on air with their arms around each other.

The planked seating surrounded the circus ring in tiers. The front rows were full.

'Will you be alright up the steps, Alfred?'

'Yes. I climb ladders at my work place. And you?'

'I'm fine; you choose where you want to sit. Better hurry though; there were still a lot of people behind us, waiting to come in.'

Alfred sat on the end of a row. 'This will be OK, I think.'

'It's lovely,' she said, squeezing his arm. 'We can see everything from here.'

As she spoke four clowns ran into the ring. Two carried a tin bath full of water while another held up a rubber doll for everyone to see. The fourth clown paraded around the sawdust holding up a placard offering a reward of ten shillings for anyone who could bath the baby.

The bath was put down and a clown began to make a great show of washing the baby. A packet of soap suds was added to the water and thrashed about until bubbles ran over the side.

'Roll up, roll up! Let's have a volunteer. Ten shillings to wash the baby. Roll up, roll up.'

A young man, sitting in front of Christine, shook off the hand of the girl next to him and bounded down the steps.

'Give him a big hand! He's come to wash the baby!'

The volunteer rolled up his shirt sleeves and bent down. One of the clowns produced a black cloth, approaching from behind he tied a blindfold around the unsuspecting man's eyes.

'Anyone can do it with their eyes open. For ten shillings you need to wear this!' he shouted.

The man leant forward and put his hands in the water. From the entrance to the ring another clown appeared pushing a pram with a large red box balanced in it. He wheeled it around pointing to the black lettering: 10,000 Volts! Moving it close to the bath he took two leads and clipped them to it. Raising his arms in the air he counted. 'ONE, TWO, THREE!' On the count of three he pulled a huge switch. The man jumped to his feet shaking his hands as the doll flew into the air. There were gasps from the stunned audience.

Pulling the mask from his face the victim glared at the huge 'battery' that had supplied an electric shock. The clown with the placard came across and handed him a ten shilling note.

'Let's have a big round of applause for a good sport! I think he earned the money, don't you!'

'Yes!' The audience yelled, and, 'Give him the money!'

Alfred looked at Christine. 'Was that funny? The man could have been killed. Why are people laughing?'

'I think it was just a tiny battery in that box. But I still think it was a silly thing to do.'

Christine sat transfixed throughout the first half of the show. She held her breath as tight rope walkers performed high over head, marvelled at bare back riders hurtling around the ring, held Alfred's arm tighter as the lion tamer held the ferocious beasts at bay with only a kitchen chair and a whip. Alfred spent much of the time looking at Christine, enjoying the look of pleasure on her face, admiring her hair, breathing in her scent every time she moved closer.

Once the lion's iron cage had been taken down, the ring master entered and announced a spectacular show after the interval. Cowboys fighting off warlike Indians to protect the wagons, fire eaters, leopards and tigers, and for the finale, the opportunity to see the largest group of elephants performing in the circus ring anywhere.

'This is brilliant, Alfred! What do you think?'

'I think I am lucky.'

'Lucky? Why?'

'Because I have you as my girl.'

'Silly! I'm the lucky one. After Paul and I split up I was very - I don't know, - sad I suppose. I thought a lot of him really, but he was too young for me I think. Now I'm sad because he's gone.'

'I understand. I too was sad the day my brother died.'

'I'm sorry, Alfred. Of course you were. But we're together, that's all that matters.'

'I wish to ask you something. It is important. I need you to answer.'

'Well ask me. I can't answer unless you do. What is it?'

Alfred was interrupted by a car being driven by one of the clowns. Explosions, imitating an engine back firing, accompanied clouds of smoke. A bulbous horn being zealously sounded by the driver added to the cacophony of sound.

He took hold of her hand. 'Later. There is too much noise in here.'

The elephants left the ring, each clutching the tail of the one in front with its trunk. From the opposite side of the big top the rest of the performers streamed in, acrobats performing cart wheels, clowns juggling large skittles, girls in sparkling costumes smiling and waving at the audience. The cowboys entered to be greeted with cheers, the Indians with theatrical boos. Midgets followed stilt walkers; bare back riders stood astride two horses each, the lion tamer brandished his whip.

Christine drew a deep breath and sighed. 'That was wonderful, Alfred. I'm so glad we came.'

He smiled. 'It was very good.'

'What shall we do now? Can we go on the rides? Please!'

'If that is what you wish for. Let us see what is here.'

Christine hung onto Alfred's arm as they jostled through the crowds. 'Look! Over there! The Caterpillar, that looks like fun! Take me on it, please, Alfred.'

As they made their way toward the ride, a hand reached out and clutched Alfred's sleeve, pulling him off balance.

'Look who we've got here! The German geezer who hangs about with that bastard I want to see. Where is he, mate?'

'Let go of me. Who are you? What do you want?'

'Watch out, Alfred! There's five of them and I know who they are, they call themselves the Chieftains.'

'Tell the bitch to shut it! We're looking for that Mike bloke, I owe him some grief.'

'He is not with us. We came alone. Now, let go of my arm!'

'Or what, Adolph? Going to call your army? We don't like your kind, do we lads. Get him!'

Alfred tried using his stick to defend himself but the odds were against him. A blow to the stomach doubled him up in time for his face to meet a knee. He sank down to the grass and lay groaning in pain. Motor cycle boots crashed into his ribs time and time again.

Christine's screams were drowned by the tumult around them. Using her fists, she pounded the back of one of Alfred's attackers. The studs on the jacket cut her knuckles and she sucked at the blood.

'Finish him off boys!' Bad breath yelled.

'Oi! What's going on! Get off! You'll kill him!' A man in khaki uniform pulled one of the Chieftains away from the fight.

'Fuck off, mate. This ain't got nothing to do with you.'

'You're right. But let's even things up a bit shall we.' He put two fingers in his mouth and whistled. Next minute more soldiers appeared.

'What's up, Jack? Natives getting restless?'

'You could say that. Five against one, let's see how they like a taste of their own medicine.' He struck the nearest leather jacketed youth squarely on the chin. His victim stumbled, then turned and ran, followed swiftly by the others.

'Tell your mate we're going to get him!' one of them yelled back over his shoulder.

Bending down the soldier helped Alfred to his feet. 'Are you OK, mate?'

'Thank you, yes.' Alfred wiped at the blood on his face and put his arm around Christine's shoulders for support.

'Oh gawd, we've just saved a jerry from a hiding! If I'd known I'd have left them to it.'

Christine stood with hands on hips, glaring at the soldiers. 'You should be ashamed of yourselves. The war's over. Leave him alone, he's living in England now.'

'Come on lads. Leave him to Miss goody two shoes. Where's the beer tent?'

Christine spat on her handkerchief and did her best to clean Alfred's face. He winced as she dabbed at the swelling around one eye. Blood dribbled from his mouth.

'My chest hurts.'

'My poor darling, I did try to stop them. We were lucky those soldiers helped you.'

Alfred laughed, and then clutched at his ribs. 'How different it is. Not long ago they would have been the people trying to kill me. The world is a strange place.'

'I think you'd better go to hospital, it's about a mile or so. Do you think you could walk that far?'

'No. No hospital. Help me to the bus stop. Please.'

Christine looked at the pleading look in his eyes and nodded. 'Hang onto me, it's not far. But you must promise to see a doctor in the morning.'

'Yes. I will. I promise. Thank you.'

She shepherded Alfred through the throngs of people and smiled in return to their enquiring looks. At last they reached the bus shelter and she helped Alfred sit on the seat. 'Are you alright?' she asked, brushing strands of hair back from the wounds on his face.

'Mmmm, yes,' he murmured. 'It is not so bad. I have suffered more than this.'

She put her arm around him and rested her head on his shoulder. 'Alfred, what was it you wanted to ask me?'

'I will ask you when I am healed. This is not the time.'

Chapter 50

Michael knocked at the door and stood back apprehensively. *Will she speak to me or not?* While he waited, he used the reflection in the window to check his boot lace tie. The door opened.

'Yes, can I be helping you?' A man, who could use his stomach as a resting place for both arms, stared at Michael.

'I've called to see Pauline, er Mrs Parker. Is she in?'

'Mrs Parker, you say. There's no one going by that name here.' The man scratched himself through a hole in his string vest.

Michael glanced at the door number. 'But there must be. This is the right house.'

'Maybe so. But she don't live here now, that's for certain sure.'

'But I saw her two weeks ago, just after the funeral.'

'The funeral you say. Now you're making some sort of sense. You must be meaning the tenant we've done the exchange with. Excruciating circumstances or some such ting the council said. I don't recall her name though. The missus does all the paperwork don't you know.'

'Exchange! She can't do that! Where's she gone to?'

'Well there's a question. I tink she's staying with a sister of hers. Just while the council decorate our old house. Nottin wrong with the place if you was to ask me. But, as God's my witness, this one's better. '

'Do you know where her sister lives? Did she leave a forwarding address?'

The man stuck a finger in his ear, removed it and stared at the end. 'No and no. Now I'll bid you good day, young feller me lad. Me Guinness is getting cold, so it is.'

The door slammed shut before Michael could ask any more questions.

Now what? How the hell am I going to find her now? Bollocks!

'Wotcha, Mike. How's it going then?'

Michael dropped into a chair with all the elegance of a sack of potatoes. 'Don't bleedin' ask, Roy. Everything's gone tits up.'

Out on the dance floor the youth club regulars were doing their utmost to keep up with Jerry Lee Lewis pounding out, *Great Balls of Fire.*

'What about you? How you doing?'

'Not so bad, Pat's arranged for us to go up the smoke for an audition in a couple of weeks time. Could be the big break we've been waiting for.'

'Oh. Good.'

'Bugger me, is that it? Nice to hear you're so enthusiastic!'

'I can't help it. I'm brassed off. Paul killing himself like that. What a nutter.' *Still, at least he ain't got to worry about getting nicked for murder. Perhaps he had the right idea.*

'Yeah, I know what you mean. Gets to you, don't it.'

'Who else is here?' Michael asked, looking around, disinterestedly.

'No one yet. - Hang on, Tony's just come in with Kay. Mind you they both look pissed off. Must be something catching.'

Tony pulled a chair back from the table for Kay. 'Surprised you're here, Mike. Thought you'd be getting us all together to sort them out.'

'Sort who out?'

'The Chieftains of course! After what they done we ought to take 'em apart.'

'Whoa. Slow down, mate. Let your brain catch up with your gob. What have they done to ruffle your feathers?'

'Alfred. They beat him up something chronic. If some geezers hadn't waded in to help they could have bloody killed him.'

'What! When was this! How did you find out?'

'We met Chris. Alfred took her to the circus, you know, that one that comes every year. Well, they was minding their own business when the Chieftains started on Alfred. She tried to help him but there were too many of them.'

Kay looked across at Michael. 'It was *you* they were after, Chris said. But it seems any of the gang will do. What's it all about, Mike? We all ought to know.'

'I dunno. I know that bloke I had a fight with at the party that night has a grudge against me. It's got nothing to do with Alfred. Excuse my French, Kay, but that git's asking for it and it's between him and me, none of you lot are involved.'

'Yes we are, mate. We've always said; anyone who picks on any of us; picks on all of us. Right?' Roy glared at Michael. 'I know Alfred ain't really part of the gang, but Christine likes him and that's good enough for me.'

Tony joined in. 'You can count me in. And Suds and Jimmie, I bet they'll be up for it. We ain't had a decent bundle for ages. Be just like the old days, brilliant.'

Michael put a hand in his pocket and fondled his flick knife. 'That's that decided then! We just need to find the right place and time. Then he'll be sorry he ever saw us.'

Roy pulled a handful of change out of his jacket and passed it to Tony. 'There you go, mate. Get the drinks in, I'll have a coffee. Cheers!'

Tony began to protest but one sullen look from Michael changed his mind.

'Give us a hand, Kay.'

Roy placed a hand over her arm and held her back. 'You can manage, Tony, you big girl's blouse. Let Kay sit down for a while.'

Elaine left the dance floor and joined the gang at their table. 'That was great, Roy. You should have come out there with me. That girl I was dancing with is new here, she loves it.'

'Yeah, yeah, yeah. We got things to sort out. Plenty of time for dancing later.'

'What things? Now what's happened?'

'The Chieftains attacked Alfred. Beat him up while he was out with Christine. We're going to sort them out.'

'Poor old Alfred. Why did they have to pick on him? He wouldn't harm a fly. I don't blame you boys from wanting to settle things.'

Michael narrowed his eyes. 'We will, don't worry about that. But how to set it up bothers me. Don't want to wait until they show up, that could take ages. This needs doing now!'

'I could get a message to them,' Elaine said.

Roy looked surprised. '*You?* How?'

'I went on the bus to Woolwich with my mum on Saturday; she wanted to cash her Co-op dividend. Anyway, for a treat, she took me in a café and who should be one of the waitresses but that big busty girl who hangs about with them.'

'Did you speak to her?'

'No, but it was her. She can't have a double.'

'No, only a double helping,' Tony laughed.

'This ain't funny, mate.'

'Sorry, Mike.'

'Anyway, there's no need for you to go, Kay. I'll ride over on my bike and tell her to tell them that we're ready for a punch up. They can name the place and day. I'd prefer to get him to meet me alone, but I think he prefers to fight in numbers.'

After calling in at the café and finding that she didn't start work until eleven, Michael decided to wait. Carrying a chipped mug of coffee and two sausage rolls he made his way downstairs to the extra seating area. He was greeted by walls adorned with sea life. Vivid colours, bearing little resemblance to real life depicted giant squids pulling lost souls from the decks of ships. Well endowed mermaids sat on rocks combing their long tresses, admiring themselves in hand mirrors. Fish and crustaceans swam and crawled amongst vast forests of seaweed. Starfish littered the sandy bottom; sea horses hovered above them with tails entwined.

Bugger me! Someone likes painting! His thoughts turned to Paul, remembering how he loved to paint and draw and how the gang had labelled it a sissy thing to do. Michael's feelings changed. Despondency took the place of the testosterone filled urge to challenge the Chieftains.

Sinking deeper and deeper into black thoughts he chewed a sausage roll without enthusiasm. Taking his knife from his pocket he flicked the blade open and began trying to carve a heart and initials into the Formica table top. It resisted his efforts and did nothing to improve his temperament. Spitting a large piece of gristle at a pirate leering down at him, he sipped the hot liquid masquerading as coffee.

What the hell am I doing here? What's the point.

Voices from upstairs jolted him back from the abyss. 'That's *them!* Right, you bastards, let's be having you!' Michael jumped to his feet, sending a chair crashing to the floor.

'Oi! You! Yes, you, you piles of shit! You're the scum who pick on cripples. Takes all of you to beat up a guy with a gammy leg, does it? Well how about a fair fight? You lot against us?'

Bad breath spun around to face Michael and took a step toward him. 'It's you I want, not your mates. You're the one that shagged our bird, not them.'

'Good! Now suit yer?' Michael reached for his knife.

'Oh no you don't! Get out, you yobbos. I don't want any fighting in here. You can kill each other for all I care, but do it somewhere else!' The burly owner wiped his hands on his greasy apron and lifted the counter flap.

The Chieftains turned and left without arguing, one muttering about 'not wanting to cost her her job.' Michael followed them outside.

'Well, come on then. Let's settle it,' Michael scowled.

'Hang on, what about us? Don't we get a say in this? She's ours as well don't forget. We ought to take him *and* his mates, teach 'em not to mess with us.'

Bad breath looked at Michael, then at his gang. 'OK. If that's how you lot want it.' He bared blackened teeth. 'Saved by the bell, mate, as they say. Where do want to do it, and when?'

The stench had Michael feeling the sausage rolls were preparing for an encore. Swallowing, he answered quickly. 'Woolwich common, Saturday, around three in the afternoon. That do yer?'

'We'll be there. And if you bunch of no hopers don't show we'll come over and winkle you out. Understood?'

'I can't wait! We owe you for Alfred.' Michael picked more gristle from between his teeth and spat it onto the pavement, narrowly missing one of the Chieftains.

'I'll make sure I see you Saturday!' the pimply youth growled as he leant toward Michael.

'You ain't got the balls, mate. Why don't you stay at home and play with your toys. Mummy wouldn't want diddums getting hurt, would she.'

'Why you …'

'Leave it! Wait till Saturday. Then we'll carve 'em all up together.' Bad breath walked back toward their motor cycles, the others meekly followed. Once astride his machine, the dot to dot faced youth raised two fingers and rode off.

Michael sat on his bed, head in hands, listening to his records. *Poor Little Fool, Who's sorry now* and *Someday you'll want me to want you,* doing nothing to lift his spirits. He got up and opened the window as the pile of cigarette ends in a saucer on the bedroom floor grew larger.

You'd think someone would know where Pauline is. I've asked in the butchers and all the local shops. Nothing. It's like the Invisible Man, but with tits. I gotta find her; I can't face not ever seeing her again. Sometimes I think I might as well top myself and be done with it.

The stack of records finished and Michael switched off the record player. 'I'm going out, get a beer. I'm going stir crazy sitting here thinking about all this. It don't change a bloody thing,' he said out loud as he punched the wall.

Alfred sat holding Christine's hand in a darkened corner at the King's Head. 'This light is good to my eye,' he said, gingerly touching the blue black swelling.

'Does it hurt much, darling?'

'Not as bad as my ribs. The bandages are of help but sleep is hard.'

'Oh, you poor thing. Alfred, you still haven't asked me that question. You know; the one you were going to ask at the circus. Ask me now. Go on, please.'

Alfred cleared his throat, picked up his glass and swallowed the last of his beer.

'I wish to… I wish to ask you…'

'Yes! What Alfred? What is it?'

'I wish to ask you to engage me. I want you for my wife.' The words came rapidly as if the speaker was afraid his courage would fail him before he could finish.

Christine put her arms around him and smothered him with kisses. 'Oh yes, darling! Yes, I'd love to become engaged to you.' She released him and her face beamed. 'But in England, when a boy asks a girl to marry him, he does it on one knee.' Before she realized the implications of her words Alfred dropped to the floor and took her hand.

'Like this?' he winced as pain surged through his body.

'Oh, darling, I'm so sorry. I didn't think. Please get up.'

The door opened and a familiar voice called out. 'What's up, mate. You stuck or something?'

'Oh, Mike. It's you. Help Alfred, please. It's all my fault. He got down and now he can't get back up.'

'I can see that! Come on, give us your arm. Ready? Right, up you come.'

Alfred sank onto the chair and smiled. 'Thank you, Michael. Let me buy you a beer.'

'Why not. But give us the money; sounds like you've been in the wars lately from what I hear. Oh, sorry Didn't mean it to come out like that. But what were you doing down on the floor, or shouldn't I ask.'

'Alfred has just asked me to marry him!'

'Congratulations,' Michael said without emotion. Taking the pound note he went to the bar. 'What do you want, Chris?' he asked while Brian pulled the pints.

'Babycham please, Mike. Ought to be champagne really, but the bubbles get up my nose.'

'What means affray?' Alfred asked.

'Affray? What made you ask that, darling?'

'Some one has forgotten to take their newspaper, look. It states that teenagers are to face a charge of causing an affray.' Alfred passed her the paper.

'Well, it means that they were in a fight or something. Wait a minute, I'll read the article. See if there's any more details.'

Michael set the pints down carefully while balancing Christine's drink.

'What's that you're reading Chris? Catford dog track results?'

'No, Mike. It says a gang of youths from Charlton have been charged with affray after a disturbance in Woolwich docks. They are accused of attacking three lascar seamen. The case is to be heard at Woolwich magistrates' court on Friday.'

'Wonder if they're the same bunch that the Chieftains had a fight with a while back. Could be I suppose. Anyway, why are you interested?''

'I'm not. It's just that Alfred asked me what affray meant.'

'Oh, that's easy. A punch up, a bit of bother, doing some geezer over.'

'I think Alfred has got the point.'

'OK, Chris, keep yer hair on. Anyway Alfred, don't worry, we're going to sort those idiots out for you. It's all arranged for the middle of Saturday afternoon, a fight between them and us three. There's bad blood between us and it's time we spilt some of it.'

'Three? Who is the three?' Alfred looked concerned.

'Me, Roy and Tony, who else? And well, perhaps Jimmie and Suds, who knows?'

'I will join also.'

'No disrespect, mate, but you're having a laugh. These are tough bastards, opps, sorry Chris. What I mean is, they don't fight by any rules. They'll be tooled up, razors, coshes, chains, you name it, they'll have it. And they won't be scared to use them.'

'But I fought in the war. I was …'

'Yes, but that's when you were wounded, remember? Now, how the hell you going to run if the coppers turn up?' Michael looked for support from Christine.

'Mike's right,' she said taking her cue. 'But why he's agreed to fight them at all I don't know. There's five of them against three.'

'But it was me they attacked. I should be there. I want to be with you.'

'Leave it out, Alfred. I'm not being funny but you'd just be in the way. We'd have to protect you and that would cramp our style. Just let it alone, we'll show 'em who the top dogs are round here.'

'Please, darling. Do as Mike says. He knows you're not afraid of them, but you can't help.'

'That may be true. But it may not.' Alfred lit a cigarette and sat lost in thought.

Michael frowned. 'Cheers, mate. It's OK. I'll smoke my own thanks.'

Alfred nodded absentmindedly.

Chapter 51

'What do you think, Suds?' James slashed the air with a knife.

'I'm glad you're on my side, them commandos certainly had some great weapons. Who'd have thought of making a knife handle into a knuckle duster. Two for the price of one, brilliant!' Suds released the buckle of his belt and lashed out at the garden fence. The heavy brass buckle, aided by the weight of studs punched through the leather, split the timber panel. 'Handsome! Wait till they feel that!'

James stared at the damage. 'What else you got? Not just a belt, surely?'

'Piss off, course not. I've had me belt snatched away before. Me back up is a cut throat razor and a sock full of pennies. The last bloke I hit with that, I broke his jaw. What about you? What else you taking?'

'Got a chain with a large ring so I can get me thumb through it. It fits under me collar a treat and pulls free easily,' James smiled. 'This should be a good bundle, how many of them will be there do you reckon?'

'Enough to go round. Five against five I think.'

'Sounds good to me!' James punched the air with the knuckle duster part of the knife before lunging at an imaginary foe.

'Come on then, let's get going. Don't want to keep Mike and the others waiting.'

Roy passed the bottle of cider to Tony. 'There you go, mate. Have a swig of that. Not too much though, don't want you stabbing the wrong blokes.'

Tony took the cigarette from his lips and tipped the bottle back. 'Good drop of gear that,' he said, wiping his mouth with the back of his hand. 'Watch it! Here's Mike coming. Don't want him seeing us drinking.' Tony tossed the bottle over a privet hedge into a garden. It shattered on a rockery constructed from broken concrete pieces, the remnants of an Anderson shelter.

'Ready you two?'

'Right behind you, mate. Let's go get 'em!' Roy answered getting onto the Triumph. Tony nodded in agreement and climbed on behind him.

Michael patted his pockets and asked. 'You got all you need? This ain't going to be no walkover.'

'Are we waiting for Suds?'

Before Michael could answer, James and Suds roared up the road. Two dogs began barking and chased the bikes down the street.

'Bugger off!' Suds yelled, lashing out at one of the mongrels with his boot.

Roy laughed. 'He's eager, look, he's started already!'

Michael signalled for the newcomers to keep going and swung his bike out to join them. Tony and Roy swiftly followed. Michael moved into position, taking the lead. The vee shaped formation swept through the suburbs heading for the common, the arranged meeting place for the two rival gangs to fight.

'Leave the bikes here where we can see them,' Michael said gazing across to another road bisecting the common.

'That looks like them coming now,' Tony said. 'This is it, them against us. Let's go and get stuck in!'

'Lead on mate, it's what we came for,' Suds grinned.

The afternoon sun cast long shadows across the common, two or three times larger than life size, stretching out across the grass in front of them.

'Look at that!' Roy exclaimed. 'Our shadows make us look like cowboys in the final shootout scene at the pictures.'

Five leather jacketed youths parked their motorcycles and began walking toward Michael's gang. Even from a distance it was easy to see that they carried baseball bats and pick axe handles. They were not here for a picnic.

The opposing sides stopped in lines facing each other, yards apart.

'Look at this bunch of tossers,' Bad Breath said, clearing his throat and spitting. 'Like a load of pansies, seems a shame to mess 'em up.'

'Hark who's talking,' Michael taunted. 'We ain't all on walking sticks, you sure you can fight blokes what ain't cripples?'

'You'll be more than cripples in a minute. Lucky for you the hospital's only just down the road.' Bad Breath raised a baseball bat and moved toward Michael.

'Get 'em lads!' Michael yelled and lunged out with his knife.

Suds yelled a warning. 'Watch yerself, Jimmie. There's more of them over there on that other road. We're outnumbered!'

'Oh, shit!'

Bad Breath and Michael had briefly lost contact with each other in the melee but were vigorously fighting other opponents. Above the noise of shouting and swearing Michael heard a sharp crack behind him. Looking around he saw James standing with a broken arm hanging by his side. James clutched it and dropped to the ground, leaving his assailant to join forces with Bad Breath.

Michael stepped back as a bicycle chain was aimed at his head.

'You're right Suds!' he yelled, catching a quick look at other youths parking their motorcycles and coming toward them. 'Christ! There must be dozens of the buggers!'

Bad Breath looked surprised and turned to look in the direction that Michael was pointing.

'The Charlton boys! Fuck! Where did *they* come from!' He dropped his bat and pulled a knife from his pocket. 'You! This is our fight. Come on; let's finish it here and now.' He thrust the knife forward and Michael ducked to one side.

'Not good enough! That your best shot?'

'Get him Mike, get him quick, before all that lot get here.' Roy wrestled one of the Chieftains to the ground and rained blows to his head.

Again Bad Breath thrust his flick knife at Michael. This time Michael moved toward his attacker, dropping his own knife and wrapping his arms around him. Bad Breath felt the blade scraping bone as it entered Michael's body.

Michael groaned and slid to the grass, holding the weapon stuck fast in his chest. Blood oozed through his fingers. Bad Breath looked down at Michael, panicked and ran off. The newcomers cut off his escape and he disappeared beneath a crowd of bodies. His friends were fighting desperately to escape the whirlwind that had enveloped them. The Charlton gang had a score to settle with the Chieftains.

Back over at the edge of the common a bus pulled up. Alfred and Christine alighted and hurried toward the disturbance.

'It did not go to plan,' Alfred said, shaking his head. 'They should have been here before.'

'What plan, Alfred? Who should have been here?'

'I attended the court yesterday and waited for the men in the news paper. I told them the Chieftains would be here because I knew there was trouble between them. It was my attempt to help Michael.'

'Oh, you clever thing, my darling. I'm sure you *did* help. Look at them running.'

'Some are not.'

'Alfred!' She grasped his arm. 'That looks like Michael and James on the ground! They must be hurt! Hurry!'

'He's in a bad way, Chris. Stabbed. Look at all the blood he's losing. Suds has gone to find a 'phone box, to call an ambulance.'

Christine covered her mouth with her hand. 'He looks so grey, Roy,' she whispered. 'Is he still alive?'

'Only just, I reckon. And Jimmie over there keeps fainting; I think his arm's busted. We need to get them both to hospital, and quick. Suds has gone to find a phone box.'

'Yes, you said that. Which way did he go?' Alfred asked.

Roy pointed.

'Then I will go the other.' Despite Christine's protestations Alfred began to return back the way they had come.

Roy scratched his forehead. 'I saw it happen, Chris. The strange thing is it looked to me like Mike deliberately threw himself onto that bloke's knife.'

'That's stupid! Why on earth would he do a thing like that? Mike would never let anyone get the better of him.'

'Beats me. But that's how it seemed.' He looked puzzled. 'It was almost as if he wanted to die.'

Christine dropped to her knees and cradled Michael's head. She wiped sweat from his brow and lowered her face nearer to his.

'Come on, Mike. Don't let the Chieftains win. There's help on its way, just hold on.' She brushed at the tears running down her cheeks. 'We've all got our lives in front of us, and there's so much to live for. Bikes, birds and rock 'n roll, remember? That's what you always said.'

Michael struggled to open his eyes. His only answer a feeble groan.